AS BEAUTIFUL—AND AS DANGEROUS—AS THE RED RIVER ITSELF

Seth gave Eli a glance. "There's two of 'em, Cap'n. Tell me we ain't gonna keep 'em. Hell, there ain't hardly room in that lean-to now with that wounded boy an' all. Promise me you ain't gonna let them women stay. They's only gonna get in our way."

Eli didn't answer him. The Indians rode their ponies into the near-freezing water and started across. He paid closest attention to Senatey when her pony struggled through river-bottom mud until it was belly-deep in water.

"It's her, all right," he said when he could see her face underneath the hood of her robe.

Seth let the muzzle of his rifle tip downward. "I got this feelin' we's gonna have us some female company this winter. But you remember, I said it was a big mistake."

Rivers West
Ask your bookseller for the books you have missed.

RIVERS
WEST

THE RED RIVER

Frederic Bean

BANTAM BOOKS
NEW YORK · TORONTO · LONDON · SYDNEY · AUCKLAND

THE RED RIVER

A Bantam Book / December 1997

ISBN 0-553-56800-0

Published simultaneously in the United States and Canada

Bantam Books are published by Bantam Books, a division of
Bantam Doubleday Dell Publishing Group, Inc. Its trademark,
consisting of the words "Bantam Books" and the portrayal of a
rooster, is Registered in U.S. Patent and Trademark Office and in
other countries. Marca Registrada. Bantam Books, 1540 Broadway,
New York, New York 10036.

PRINTED IN THE UNITED STATES OF AMERICA

OPM   10 9 8 7 6 5 4 3 2

To Jory & Charlotte Sherman

Introduction

It begins in eastern New Mexico as a tiny spring trickling toward Texas. In Deaf Smith County it is joined by tributaries carving out the spectacular Palo Duro Canyon of the High Plains farther east, before it leaves the vast Cap Rock Escarpment. Where it crosses the 100th meridian it becomes the boundary between Texas and Oklahoma, and is soon joined by the Salt Fork to form its main channel. Early explorers knew it by a number of names; *Rivière Rouge* in French, *Rio Rojo* in Spanish, or the *Red River* in English, by which it became most widely known in the early 1800s.

It takes its name from its distinctive color, provided by drainage from clay and clay loam soils colored a deep ruby red. Some have likened it to the color of blood, a fitting way to denote the river's more troubling menaces. The Red presented early travelers with some of the most treacherous quicksand beds west of the Mississippi, and its highly variable currents drowned animals at such an alarming rate that cattlemen often waited on its banks for weeks until floodwaters subsided.

The Red River flows 440 miles before it sweeps into Arkansas and then across Louisiana, where it joins

the Mississippi and on to the Gulf of Mexico. Its history
is as varied as the lands through which it passes. Early
western exploration of the Red was by canoe and flatboat, since it is too unpredictable to be navigable by
larger craft, at times low, at others a raging red torrent.
It flows through what was once the domain of several
bloodthirsty Plains Indian tribes, notably the fierce Comanche bands controlling the upper reaches, or the sim-
ilarly warlike Kiowa farther east. Osage, Arapaho, and
Southern Cheyenne raided along the Red, often fighting
each other over buffalo herds or wild horses. A tribe
ruled as much territory as it could defend, with few alli-
ances between neighboring bands.

Into this long-standing system of territorial dispute
between native Indian tribes in the late 1600s came
French explorers such as René-Robert Cavelier, Sieur
de La Salle; Spanish adventurers Francisco de Coro-
nado and Hernando de Soto, Cabeza de Vaca, Catholic
missionaries sent forth by the Spanish viceroy in Mexico
City to establish missions for converting Indians to Ca-
tholicism; white explorers, trappers, and later, settlers,
bringing diseases and firearms and plows and woodcut-
ter's axes to build permanent homes in Indian territo-
ries. It is small wonder these Indians resented the
intrusion. Settlements and farms drove away the Indian's food supply—roving buffalo and antelope herds.
Along the Red River, no one fought any harder to halt
this incursion than the Comanche and Kiowa.

But in the beginning, as explorers first made con-
tact with a few Kiowa and Comanche bands, there was
usually only curiosity between races. Indians met outsiders peacefully for a number of years, even offering them
hospitality. This changed almost as soon as the explorers' intentions became known. Early adventurers found
lands rich with furs and fertile soil, and the lure was too
great to be ignored in crowded cities.

Before that time there was a brief period of inno-
cence when two peoples discovered each other, neither
one seeking control of what the other had. It was a

tragically short moment in American history. America began to pursue a relocation policy that made no sense to Indian tribes who had never been confined to one geographic area unless they did so by choice. And when they rebelled, the American military concentrated their efforts on total annihilation of the Indian problem, as evidenced by General William Tecumseh Sherman's order to General Canby's troops during the Modoc War of 1872 when he wrote, "You will be fully justified in their utter extermination."

Sherman's prediction was not long in coming to pass where the Red River flows. Yet there was a time when explorers entered a pristine river valley four hundred miles long where nature and man lived in particular harmony.

Early white adventurers and Spanish missionaries from Mexico City wrote about the Red, the only record we have of what someone might experience paddling a canoe along quiet shores lined with bulrushes through the land of the Kiowa. . . .

Part One

Chapter One

Elias McBee dipped his paddle into the smooth crimson water without taking his eyes from the shoreline. He was sure he saw movement somewhere in a stand of slender oak trees on a ridge to the north. Their bullhide canoe swished through the Red's quiet waters like a knife through warm butter, despite its wide beam. Seth Booker sat in the prow, muscular arms paddling easily as if he experienced no fatigue from previous weeks of travel against strong, steady currents. His sable skin bore a sheen of sweat catching late-day sunlight and gave the giant mulatto an aura not unlike the dark oiled barrel of the Whitney rifle lying near his feet.

"I'd nearly swear I saw something up yonder," Eli said.

"This sun can play tricks on a man's eyes," Seth warned as he studied the same wooded ridge. "I ain't seen nothin' move. Maybe it's the light."

It was true, the way a setting sun sometimes brought changes to even the most familiar shapes. It had been a dry fall and the sun was gauzy, dropping toward the earth through a haze of dust on the horizon, splashing colored light on bare ground, painting an oc-

casional tree trunk with ocher hues, turning fall oak and
maple leaves into sizzling displays of bright reds and
dazzling yellows as though they were ablaze. The beauty
of a western sunset never ceased to enthrall Eli, particu-
larly in this land of flaming reds and softer pastels. Even
the land itself was blood colored, as they traveled farther west. Where the land turned red, they were warned
to be on the lookout for savages. Red land meant red
men along this river, according to Moses Walker. Mose
had traveled this river once before with the crazy
Frenchman, Girreaux. Mose warned them that Indian
savages riding wiry little horses watched every foot of
the way when you entered their territory.

Eli paddled slowly, examining the ridge. Once, he
glanced down to the Colt Paterson revolver lying atop a
bundle of traps, its frame mottled by time and weather.
The pistol wasn't accurate for any distance, but at close
range a properly charged .36 caliber ball made a hell of
a hole. For long-distance shooting a Whitney .54, like
the ones they carried, could center a raven's eye on the
wing, in the right pair of hands.

He watched the trees backgrounded by the soft colors of the sky, trees glazed gold from the sun with leaves
of crimson, orange, burnt umber, and lightly freckled
browns. Blue shadows forming below leafy limbs that
turned to slate where no sunlight penetrated, a soft gray
spot here and there, where he thought he saw something move earlier. He couldn't be sure.

The gentle gurgle of Seth's paddle passing through
sluggish current distracted Eli from a closer look at a
shadow beneath a sinewy branch. Then he saw another
movement and a splash of blue as a jay flitted from limb
to limb, stirring the stillness with the flutter of its snow-
edged wings. An oak leaf twisted on a breath of wind
and fell from a branch, dancing, trembling as it swirled
toward orange-red earth below.

"I'm seein' things, I reckon," he told Seth in a voice
tinged with relief. They weren't looking for a confronta-
tion with Indians. In one of the packs they had glass

trading beads and cheaply made iron knives, some colorful ribbon, items Mose told them to carry. Indians liked bright colors and they had few iron weapons. Arrows and spears were tipped with flint, according to Mose, and they seemed fascinated by iron knives and glass beads, cheap trinkets requiring little in the way of an investment.

"Maybe," Seth remarked softly, squinting in the sun's hard glare, crow's-feet webbing around his heavy-lidded eyes while he let his gaze wander upstream.

The burble of water forking around the canoe's prow had a voice all its own, and there were times when Eli didn't hear it, growing accustomed to its gentle music after so long paddling in silent surroundings up a quiet river. For almost two weeks they moved steadily west with the sun at their backs each morning. A grizzled boatman poling a raft of logs told them five days ago they'd seen the last of civilization at Bell's Hill a day before, a small settlement on the southern bank where Texas-bound travelers bought supplies for the journey into the new Republic. Eli and Seth heard stories of the war there, of a fight with Mexico promising to be long, full of hardship for Texans, not the sort of thing two veterans of fights with flatboat pirates had even the slightest interest in. For years the upper Mississippi had been like a series of private wars between flatboat captains and pirates. Eli had seen all the blood he wanted to see during those difficult times. Heading west into uncharted wilderness to trap furs held the promise of peace, if relations could be established with Indians.

Again, he saw something move in the forest and it was not a bird this time . . . he was certain of it. "There," he said, pointing to a cluster of oak atop a knob where a feeder stream entered the river. "Look yonder in those trees, Seth. It sure as hell looked like somebody's hidin' in those oaks."

Sunlight streamed through a profusion of tree trunks and branches where Eli was pointing, making it difficult to separate real objects from shadows.

"I don't see a damn thing 'cept trees, Eli."

"Maybe it was nothin'."

Seth's paddle dipped into dark water, making ripples across the glassy surface. Cattails along the bank bent slightly when a whisper of air moved among them. Eli watched the oaks steadily, unwilling to entirely dismiss what he'd seen, even though he had no idea what it was.

"Time we started lookin' for a place to camp," Seth said, turning his broad face toward the south bank. "Maybe we oughta look on that side, seein' as you're so sure there's somethin' on this side to worry 'bout."

"I ain't worried. Bein' careful, is all."

"It'll be plumb dark in another hour. I'll fry up this big catfish for supper."

"I'm gettin' tired of fish. Truth is, I've been sick of the taste of fish for years. If I never saw another fish in my whole life, it'd suit the hell outa me."

"Too many years on that damn Mississip', Eli. We both spent way too many years on that bitch of a river. I can boil up some beans, only it's a shame to waste all this catfish meat." After a sweep of his paddle, Seth lifted a piece of thick line from the water to inspect a squirming yellow cat trailing along beside the canoe on cord threaded through the catfish's gills. "Turtles will get him tonight, 'less we eat him. Turtles, or one of them big ol' coons. Biggest coons I ever saw in my life livin' along this river. Weigh maybe forty pounds."

Eli was only half listening. Something had moved again high on the ridge. He shaded his eyes with a freckled hand. One tree in particular seemed highlighted by the sun's radiance, a huge leafy torch standing alone among others in the forest. Behind it, behind the dark outline of its trunk, stood what looked like the silhouette of a man.

"See that biggest tree yonder," he said, pointing again to the ridge. "There's a man standin' behind it. I'd nearly swear an oath it's somebody watchin' us."

Seth returned his fish to the river. He stared at the

ridge for a time. "I see it now," he said, speaking so softly Eli had trouble hearing him. "I reckon it could be a man. Mose said to use sign language when we saw 'em from a distance, so they'd know we come here friendly."

Eli rested his paddle across his lap and gave the sign for peace. Their canoe slowed against the current when neither man was rowing. He judged the distance at three hundred yards to the tree, maybe less. He signed again when nothing moved.

"Maybe it's only a tree," Seth suggested. "Hard to tell in this light." He picked up his paddle and continued rowing with slow, deliberate strokes.

"It's an Indian," Eli said. "He's standin' real still so we can't be sure. I figure he's a lookout. He'll go back and tell the others about us. We could have visitors tonight."

Seth wasn't quite ready to agree yet. Paddling steadily, he kept glancing to the ridge between strokes. "Mose said we'd know if they was Osages by their shaved heads. Kiowas have long hair braided in a single strand down their backs. Comanches got two braids, only they'll be farther upriver, he said."

Eli recalled almost every detail Mose and the Frenchman gave them about traveling this river. Back in Natchez Under The Hill it all sounded so perfect, an empty land in need of exploring by men who weren't afraid of the elements or primitive Indians who didn't own guns. For a couple of seasoned flatboat pilots with experience battling gangs of river thieves and the most brutal weather imaginable in winter, this trek up the Red held few real challenges, or so it seemed then, hearing about it from old Mose and Frenchy Girreaux. Eli wondered if he'd been too quick to judge the ease of it. "Whatever breed he is, he ain't movin' at all, just standin' there behind that tree like he was a part of it." He resumed paddling in concert with Seth as the canoe came abreast of the ridge, gliding silently toward a setting ball of orange-red sun hovering above the river, flaming over the landscape. Changing the angle from which he watched the tree made no visible change in the silhouette beside it.

"Leastways he ain't shootin' arrows at us," Seth said under his breath, "if it is an Injun."

"I suppose we oughta be grateful for that," Eli agreed, as they slipped past the ridge unmolested. When he looked up at the tree again, the silhouette was gone. Now he was certain it had been someone watching them. "He's gone, Seth. The shadow ain't there no more."

"Light changed, is what it was. Don't go gettin' so jumpy on me." Seth's head turned quickly to the north as soon as the words left his mouth. He stiffened, halting the motion of his paddle abruptly. "Look yonder, Eli," he said, suddenly sounding grave. "You was right, only there's five of 'em. They's ridin' scrawny little ponies . . ."

As the canoe drifted past a deep ravine leading down to the river, Eli saw what Seth had seen. Five bronze-skinned men on small, multicolored horses watched the canoe from a canebrake at the bottom of the wash. Two carried lances with feathers tied to painted shafts. The others had bows slung over their shoulders or resting across the withers of their ponies.

"Sweet Jesus," Eli whispered as his heart started to pound. He sat there, frozen like he was trapped in a block of ice for several seconds, holding his breath until he heard Seth speak.

"Give 'em the peace sign, Eli."

He opened his palm and held it forward, fingers together as Mose had showed him, with his thumb extended. The Indians seemed to ignore him, sitting passively on the backs of their ponies as he continued to give the sign. Straight rays of sunlight made them appear as red as the river, somewhat copper colored perhaps, after a closer examination.

"They don't act like they know what it means," he said, as they drifted slowly past the mouth of the ravine in full view of the Indians. He continued to hold his hand in the same manner. Stalks of cane teetered in a current of air around the riders, swaying gently behind five lean, bare-chested men. Eli had seen a few Indians before, "tame" red men in Natchez and New Orleans, so-called civilized Indians from the Seminole tribe, Delawares, a Cherokee or two dressed in buckskins serving as scouts for groups of wagons headed west from river ports like Vicksburg and Cairo and as far north as Saint Louis. He'd only heard stories about more savage tribes roaming the West, never having seen them in the flesh. As he gazed upon western Indians for the first time, he understood why they inspired so many tales of terror. These men were quite clearly part of a far more primitive race than Cherokees or Seminoles. He had the feeling he was seeing something truly wild, like antelope or deer. They looked like ordinary, smallish men at first glance, from a distance, until he got a closer look at them. In some hard-to-define way they were unlike any human beings he had ever seen. They stared at him and he stared back at them. It was only a feeling, a vague uneasiness he felt when they looked at him, that they viewed him and Seth as prey.

"They ain't Osages," Seth said quietly, sitting motionless as the canoe continued to glide past the ravine. "They's got a whole headful of hair . . . black as crow feathers."

Current tugged at the canoe, slowing it to a crawl. Eli lowered his hand and whispered, "Keep paddlin'. They don't act like they'll harm us. If we keep paddlin' maybe they'll see we don't mean them no harm either." He gripped his paddle in two gnarled fists and forced the blade to take a deep bite out of the river.

One Indian on a blue roan pony turned his head and spoke to the others, making some sort of gesture with his hand just as the canoe carried them out of sight. Eli's mouth felt dry, cottony, as they continued westward toward a glowing sunset, watching the riverbank for evidence they were being followed. Now light and shadow became so intermingled in trees lining the river he found it impossible to distinguish shapes or movement. With his heart hammering he paddled harder while guiding the canoe farther from the north bank, just in case the air filled with speeding arrows or feathered lances. Seth's powerful strokes helped carry them toward the middle of the broad river quickly.

A blazing sun dipped toward the distant Pacific Ocean half a continent beyond them, dropping below a hilly horizon lined with trees where a watery highway stretched endlessly to touch a fiery sky. Eli worried about the colors, so many reds, like a veil of blood over the land.

Chapter Two

Crickets chirped from tall grasses near the fire. Fireflies danced in black forests around them, winking just beyond a circle of light from crackling flames. A drooping willow near the water cast a dark shadow over the river where their canoe was tied to a low limb. Eli sat with his back to the trees gazing north across the river while Seth turned pieces of frying catfish in a cast-iron skillet.

"They'll see our fire," Eli said. "They'll know we're here."

Seth's face appeared more deeply etched by angry lines with the fire below him. He was past forty, almost bald, yet still as fit as any man Eli had ever known. He stood six and a half feet tall in boots and possessed incredible strength. His mother had been Creole, he said, speaking French and a few words of broken English. His father was Negro, a slave brought over from Africa. Both his parents died during a cholera epidemic in New Orleans. He was eleven years old, homeless, starving when he went to work on a flatboat poling the Mississippi.

"They already know we're here, Eli. They seen us plain as day."

He'd been edgy ever since their first look at the Indians. "They didn't act like they were all that glad to see us," he muttered, staring across silver water, eyes roaming up and down the bank like he expected to see more of them in the dark.

"Maybe they never saw no bald Nigras or red-haired Scotsmen before. We ain't exactly no ordinary pair, you an' me. One's got hair long as a woman. Other ain't got no hair an' he's near dark as pitch. Leastways they wasn't shootin' no arrows at us. You got to learn to thank the Almighty for small things. We ain't dead yet. . . ." He turned a catfish strip and frowned when he saw how black it was. "This fish is ready."

"I'm not all that hungry. Eat what you want an' I'll eat some later."

Seth grinned a little. "You got a bad case of the nerves, Cap'n." He still called Eli "Cap'n" from time to time, a habit from years on river barges. Flatboat crews rarely numbered more than four men, depending on the size of a craft, but the man in charge was still referred to as captain.

"I'll admit I'm a mite jumpy after layin' eyes on 'em up close like that. They didn't look like men, exactly. I'd call 'em something in between an animal and a man. I know that don't make a hell of a lot of sense, but that's the feelin' I got when I saw them, that they weren't anything like regular men."

"Can't be no worse'n river pirates," Seth said, bringing a strip of catfish steak to his mouth with the tip of his knife, testing it for heat with his tongue. He chewed thoughtfully. "Remember that bunch jumped us south of Tiptonville in thirty-one? Those boys hailed from Kentucky. They was all kin, three brothers an' the rest was cousins. Jumped us from that island when we poled by. I still got scars from that one, where that ball like to have took off my leg. Indians can't be no worse'n them. They was damn sure plenty hard to kill . . . like a wild pig that's wounded, chargin' straight at us like they wasn't afraid of dyin'. Too dumb, or too crazy to know they was gonna get killed, I reckon."

Eli remembered. Seven pirates tried for their cargo of rum below Tiptonville that time, shooting from a wooded island in the middle of the Mississippi, some rushing their flatboat in a smaller craft under the cover of night. A musket ball caught Seth in his thigh during the first volley, leaving Eli and old man Bridger to fight them off. When three tried to board them from a rowboat in the dark on the starboard side, Seth managed to hobble over with his machete and a pistol, killing one instantly with a ball fired into his mouth, hacking off the arm of another as he tried for the deck. But it was the third pirate Seth killed that Eli would remember longest, cutting off his head with a single swipe of the blade, leaving a stump and a portion of his lower jaw with blood pumping from a sodden mass of flesh between his shoulders. Only someone with unusual strength could have sliced through bone and muscle as easily as Seth did that time. Eli still dreamed about it now and then, seeing that headless corpse kicking and bleeding all over the deck until it finally lay quiet.

"If we can, we're gonna deal with these Indians peacefully," Eli said, watching the river. "We'll get rich bringin' furs to New Orleans in the spring. The only way they'll let us trap in this country is we convince them we're peaceful. Offer beads an' iron knives for the right to stay here."

Seth ate more fish. "The part 'bout gettin' rich sounds real good. I've been poor so long I ain't sure I'll know how to act."

"Stayin' alive long enough to sell our furs will be the only trick. If we find as much beaver as Mose promised we would, it won't be long 'til we're rich men. Three or four winters, maybe five. We can live like kings the rest of our days. Drive fancy carriages, wear the best clothes, even buy a house. Beaver pelts are bringin' a half-dollar down there. Mose an' Frenchy struck it rich, remember? If Mose hadn't gotten sick they'd have come back every year."

Seth seemed to be contemplating something. "When more folks hear 'bout all this fur-trappin' country, they'll be comin' too, like us. If we was to open ourselves a tradin' post up this Red aways, we could sell 'em supplies. Maybe even buy their furs at a fair price an' boat 'em down to New Orleans ourselves. Flatboat can work this river, what we've seen of it. We could get us some flatboats an' hire honest crews."

"I've been thinkin' the same thing, Seth. Only problem's gonna be those Indians. I wasn't expectin' them to look so wild. I can't figure how we'll explain what we aim to do to a bunch of savages. When I showed that sign for peace, they didn't understand."

"Could be they was waitin' to see what else you was gonna say."

Eli listened to the river. "It didn't appear they cared all that much what we were sayin'. All they did was watch us like we wasn't supposed to be here."

"You worry too much, Eli." Seth glanced around them at the trees, nibbling fish from his knifetip. "If they wanted to stop us they'd have fired arrows at the canoe, at us. All they done was sit there, watchin' us float by like we was driftwood. Time to worry is when they start shootin' at us. 'Til then I'm gonna rest easy. You could see they ain't got any rifles. If it's a fight they're after, we'll oblige 'em, only I don't think they know what to do 'bout us. We're a curiosity."

Eli wasn't so sure. Remembering the way they looked, he was less inclined to call their attention curiosity. "I reckon we'll know in a few days, if they let us pass. Mose said to paddle up to where that river joins the Red. That's where we'll find most of the beaver dams, up that river comin' from those mountains way to the north. Frenchy called them the Wichitas, after some tribe of Indians."

Seth stirred around in the skillet with his knife until he found the right piece of fish. "That's where he said we'd find mostly Kiowas, where them rivers join." An owl hooted across the river as he spoke.

"I remember. I figure those were Kiowas we saw today, only I didn't get a look at how they wore their hair."

"They had hair," Seth agreed. "So far, we've still got ours connected to our skulls. Mose told me I didn't have as much to worry 'bout as you." He chuckled softly. "Maybe it's a help not havin' none to start with."

Somewhere to the south a nighthawk screeched, as though it had been disturbed. When Eli turned that way he found Seth was looking too. They both recognized a nighthawk's cry.

"Likely only huntin' rabbits," Seth remarked, casting a look at the sky. "They scream like that when they're huntin', sometimes."

Eli watched the river again. He felt restless, more so than usual tonight. "I keep thinkin' about what those Indians looked like up close. They reminded me of somethin' I've seen before, I think, only I can't recall just what it was."

When Seth didn't answer him, he glanced over his shoulder. Seth was still staring into the darkness south of camp as though he'd heard or seen something out of place. "What is it?" he asked.

"Can't say for sure," Seth replied, lowering his voice. He reached for his rifle, resting it on his knees. "Could be you've got me jumpy. Somethin' moved out there just now. Maybe it's only a wild pig feedin' at night. I thought I heard somethin'."

Eli grabbed his Whitney, checking the percussion cap with his thumb. "Which direction? Point to it."

Seth aimed his knife. "Yonder, I think. Couldn't be sure of it. Only heard it once. . . ."

They sat in silence, craning their necks to listen to forest sounds.

"Crickets stopped chirpin'," Eli said, suddenly aware of how quiet it was. A bullfrog was singing somewhere upriver.

"Somethin' out there disturbed 'em," Seth replied, coming to a low crouch with his rifle. "Let's move away from this fire." Sheathing his knife, he reached for his pistol and tucked it in his belt.

Eli grabbed his Whitney and took his pistol from one of the packs, hunkering down as he crept away from the firelight toward a tree trunk. "I can't see a damn thing movin' out there besides fireflies," he whispered, moving over to the tree on the balls of his feet. "Maybe we oughta douse those flames. . . ." He stuck the Paterson inside his pants.

"Too late for that," Seth answered softly from a nearby tree trunk, peering south into the night. "They already seen it, if we've got company. Maybe it's nothin', only it sure as hell got quiet just now."

Eli listened. No crickets were chirping. Behind him, the river burbled quietly as the current drifted by their camp. Off in the distance the same bullfrog croaked endlessly, sounding like a huge fireplace bellows with a hole in it. "It's too damn quiet," Eli agreed.

They remained hidden in the forest for several minutes. Eli began to sweat until his hands felt clammy around his rifle stock while tiny beads of perspiration formed on his face and neck and arms. The silence lingered, deepening when the bullfrog suddenly stopped croaking upstream. "I can't see anything," he whispered. Their fire cast wavering shadows among the trees, creating the illusion of movement.

"Me neither," Seth said a moment later, leaning around the trunk of an oak when a breath of night wind stirred dry leaves on branches around them, "only I sure as hell don't hear no crickets makin' music. Even that grandaddy bullfrog shut his mouth. . . ."

That was the disturbing part, Eli decided, the absolute quiet. Even creatures of the night sensed something out of place in the forest, some danger that kept them silent. "Maybe we oughta break camp an' move upriver. I don't like this, Seth. It ain't natural for things to be so still."

Seth didn't offer an opinion right away. He continued to sit quietly behind the tree with his rifle ready, looking around at the dark. "Ain't no wild pig," he said later, "or we'd hear him rootin'. Maybe it's a big cat, a cougar."

Eli blinked when he thought he saw a large shape between two trees. "There, Seth. Look right there between those big oaks to your left. It looked just like a horse. I'd nearly swear I saw a horse walk between 'em."

Seth examined the trees carefully. "You're seein' things, Eli. Ain't no horse over yonder. Besides, we'd have heard it if it was somethin' big as a—" He stopped abruptly when a shadow stirred, taking shape before their eyes. Then more shadows began moving to the left and right, inky forms advancing closer to the firelight.

"Indians," Eli gasped, keeping his voice low. "They're all around us." He swung his rifle to his shoulder and thumbed back the hammer. His hands were trembling.

"Don't shoot," Seth warned. "Maybe they didn't come after our hair. Let's see what they want before we start shootin' at 'em. Could be they're friendly."

Now Eli could see men, bare-chested Indians on the backs of willowy ponies. "It's them," he told Seth gravely, "the same ones we saw before. They must have crossed the river to get at us, only there's a hell of a lot more of 'em this time." He counted more than a dozen Indians in forest shadows around the fire. When firelight showed their faces Eli saw a curious thing that was different tonight. Streaks of white paint adorned their cheeks below their eyes. "They got painted up for some reason. Their faces weren't like that before," he added in a hoarse whisper, trying to control shaking in his arms that would ruin his aim if the Indians attacked. "They sure as hell don't look friendly."

"Wait an' see. Don't shoot or make no sudden moves 'til we know what they're after." Seth didn't sound all that convinced they were peaceful.

When the Indians were a little more than fifty yards

away they stopped almost in unison, as though there was some prearranged distance they meant to keep. They had bows, and some held feathered spears like the ones Eli saw at the river before dark.

"Give 'em the peace sign, Eli," Seth urged, straightening up behind the oak. "Let 'em know we ain't lookin' for trouble."

Eli lowered his rifle, wondering if showing himself might be a mistake. He stood up slowly and held out one hand, making the sign for peace just the way Mose showed them.

Not one Indian moved or returned the sign. They sat on their ponies quietly, staring at Seth and Eli. Eli kept his palm open, waiting for some show of recognition. "They don't understand it at all. All they're doin' is starin' at me." Fear knotted in his belly and his knees were shaking, although he tried not to show he was afraid.

"Maybe they never saw a white man before. Just hold your ground an' keep givin' 'em the sign." Seth still held his rifle to his shoulder, but with the muzzle aimed down. "We want 'em to know we're friendly."

"How the hell are we gonna tell them? They don't act like they know what sign language is."

"Could be it's these guns. If we put down our guns maybe it would convince 'em."

Before Eli could offer a word of protest against Seth's fool idea, an Indian wheeled his pony and rode back into the forest shadows. The others turned and disappeared as silently as they had come.

When the last Indian was out of sight, Eli lowered his palm and let out the breath he was holding. "Wonder what that was all about?" he asked Seth, bewildered by their sudden departure.

"Maybe they was just testin' us," Seth replied, sounding as relieved as Eli felt when they found themselves alone again.

Chapter
Three

H e was still shaken long after the Indians departed, and he'd been unable to sleep. As dawn came he allowed himself to relax somewhat, although he still found himself examining the forest closely, half expecting to see early-morning skies fill with a swarm of speeding arrows.

Seth crawled out of his bedroll at first light, stretching, yawning before he took their coffeepot to fill it at the river. He gave Eli a sideways glance. "You don't look so good this mornin', Cap'n."

"I couldn't sleep. Didn't appear those Indians bothered you any, all that snorin' you did."

He sauntered back to the fire and put a handful of coffee beans in the pot before nestling it in a bed of glowing coals. "If they wanted to scalp us they'd have tried it. They showed themselves instead. All in all, they acted peaceful as any man could ask for. You're headed for an early grave with all that worryin'."

Eli watched the sun rise slowly, not yet visible above the horizon. "It's hard to figure why they came. They let us get a good look at them, but that's all. No sense to it. Why didn't they try to find out what we're up to? Why we're here?"

"Maybe they could guess we was trappers. Maybe they was only curious 'bout us, seein' what we looked like up close."

"They had their faces painted. Somebody told us that means they're lookin' for a fight. I think Frenchy said that, about how they got all painted up for war. Remember?"

"Can't say as I recall Frenchy sayin' it, but I've heard it said before 'bout Injuns. This bunch didn't act like they wanted a war with us. They just rode off mindin' their own business."

Eli got up, feeling stiff from sitting with his back to a tree all night. "Sure don't make any sense to me, that all they wanted was to get a look at us." He walked down to the river and knelt to splash water on his face, paying only scant notice to his reflection on the surface. A tangled mane of dark red hair fell below his shoulders, and his beard needed a trim. He'd lost so much weight since they started up the Red his broadcloth pants fit too loosely, requiring another notch in his belt, and he judged he weighed less than his usual 170 pounds. He thought of himself as fit for a man his age, forty this spring. Twenty years poling flatboats hardened his muscles to iron. When he saw dark circles under his eyes, he shook his head and chuckled. Maybe Seth was right, that he was worrying himself into an early grave over a few Indians.

He rinsed out his mouth and washed his face, gazing across the river absently. It would be a while before he forgot about their visitors last night, how close they came. They looked even more like wild creatures up close, with slashes of white paint on their cheeks. At times like this he had vague doubts about their chances of success at making any sort of arrangement with Indians here, no matter what Frenchy and Mose said. How could someone expect to make a deal with people when they didn't speak the same language?

Eli inspected their canoe carefully before wandering back to the fire, smelling coffee. "Let's hit the river early," he said, squatting near the flames. "I'd just as soon put some distance behind us today." Scanning the forest, he couldn't quite shake the feeling that they were being watched.

It was a most unexpected sight. A two-wheel cart drawn by a shaggy brown donkey was bogged in shallow water near the river's edge. A man dressed in priest's garb stood belly deep in water, trying to free his stranded animal, pulling on its bridle for all he was worth. A noonday sun shone down on the priest's floundering efforts as Seth and Eli paddled around a bend in the river.

"Can't believe my own two eyes," Seth exclaimed, swinging the prow toward the south bank where the donkey was bogged. "I never figured we'd see another soul up this river besides wild Injuns."

Eli watched the robed cleric with the same amazement. "Hard to figure what he's doin' way out here. He's dressed up like a priest. Why would a priest be so far from any kind of church?"

"Maybe he's lost. He's sure as hell stuck. That's liable to be quicksand, Eli." Seth hurried his paddle strokes, taking deeper bites out of the river.

Eli quickened his paddling. Their canoe sliced through red water soundlessly, but its movement caught the priest's attention. He looked up from his efforts to dislodge the donkey and cart. For a moment he stood motionless in the river, staring at the canoe like he couldn't quite trust his eyes. Then began to wave frantically, yelling, "Over here, my friends! Over here!"

Eli noted the priest's darker skin. "We're coming! Don't fight the sand! We'll pull you out!"

The canoe moved swiftly toward the bank. Now Eli could see the priest's face clearly. He was Spanish or Mexican, judging by his skin color, and looked frail, thin to the point of starvation. A bald spot on the top of his head shone brightly in light from the sun, although he appeared to be young, in his middle thirties or perhaps even younger.

They paddled closer to shore. Eli noticed how the priest's arms were shaking with fatigue.

"My mule is sinking deeper!" he cried. "He can't move and I can't lift his hooves!"

"We'll help you!" Seth shouted, aiming for an open spot near a willow tree shading the bank. "You're in quicksand. We've got ropes."

They reached land and stepped out in murky shallows. Eli took a length of rope from one of the packs. "Just hold on until we get there, Father," he said, feeling sucking sand tug at his feet. Moving through quicksand required know-how, something any seasoned riverboatman learned early if he meant to stay alive.

Seth reached the donkey cart first, as Eli was coming with the rope.

"I'm so thankful," the priest said, smiling weakly, his face beaded with sweat and river water. "This is surely an act of God that the two of you came through this wilderness now. My mule would have drowned . . . he can't free himself and I am not strong enough to help him."

Eli struggled over to the donkey's head, slipping a noose around its neck. He nodded to the priest. "We were surprised to find anyone else so far from civilization, Father. All we've seen so far are Indians." He tossed the end of the rope over to Seth and said, "I'll lift its feet while you pull him around. I can tell he ain't buried all that deep."

Seth wound the rope around his waist and leaned against it as Eli grabbed the donkey's right foreleg. So near shore, the water was not fully waist deep.

Seth's pulling freed the donkey almost at once. It made a lunge to free its rear legs as Seth swung the animal around to lead it from the river. The wooden cart made a cracking noise, wheels groaning in protest as it came out of the mud and sand. Seth led the donkey up the bank while Eli and the priest pushed the cart from behind.

Once on dry land, the priest sleeved sweat from his brow and turned to Eli. "I'm so very, very grateful to you both. My name is Father Bolivar." He offered his hand to Eli, then to Seth. "I have been lost for weeks now, with almost nothing to eat and no map to guide me. I managed to snare a few rabbits to keep me alive. By the grace of God, you came along just when things were at their worst. I was trying to cross this river, hoping to find an outpost, some form of civilization. I was told there was a place called Bell's Hill along the river, a trading post. I've been traveling down this bank for days now and there had been no sign of habitation."

Eli grinned. "You missed it by many miles, Father. It's east of here, maybe by a hundred miles or more. I'm Eli McBee and this is Seth Booker. We're headed upriver to trap furs this winter. We passed Bell's Hill five or six days ago."

"Dear God," Bolivar whispered, leaning against the side of his cart for support, shaking his head. "It would appear I have no sense of direction. I used the sun as my guide. For days I went with nothing to eat and I grew so weak I was dizzy. I must have wandered off course." He took a deep breath, and there was sorrow in his voice when he spoke again. "Quite clearly, I'm not suited for this inhospitable land. I don't belong here. If you hadn't come along my mule would have drowned. I was too weak to pull it out without your assistance."

"We'll fix you something to eat, Father," Eli promised. "As soon as we get a fire goin' we'll cook some bacon and coffee. If you want, lie down and rest for a spell. You look like you're a little bit unsteady on your feet. I'll unharness your donkey for you while Seth gets the fire started. Then you can tell us what it was that brought you, what you're doin' way out here."

He nodded his thanks, adjusting a piece of rope girding his robe around his stomach. "I'm in your debt, Mr. McBee, yours and Mr. Booker's. If you had not

come along when you did I would be without my mule.
God has been merciful, sending you to me in my hour of
need. I can help with the harness. The offer of food is
greatly appreciated, kind sirs. As you must be able to
tell I'm not adaptable to this wilderness. My superior,
Father Tomas, gave me a map to Mission San Miguel,
where I was to help with our efforts to teach the Indians
Christianity. As you can see, I've gotten lost."

Eli began unfastening harness straps while the
priest was talking. "Never heard of no mission named
San Miguel, Father. Wherever it is, it sure ain't so far up
this river. As to bein' where you can help teach religion
to Indians, there's plenty of them around, only I
wouldn't count on them bein' interested in learnin'
about bein' a Christian. The ones we saw looked mighty
uncivilized. I'd hate to be the first man to try to preach
to 'em." He peered through the cart's slatted sides, finding canvas packs and a large wooden crucifix almost
four feet long wrapped in a piece of burlap.

"San Miguel was to be a new mission to the Indians. Father Augustine and a party of five workmen traveled here last fall to build a church. They sent a
messenger to San Antonio asking for more supplies,
describing the hardships. Father Tomas directed me and
a young priest, Father Esteban, to bring what was
needed to Father Augustine. We had our carts full of
sugar and corn and a variety of seeds to prepare a garden, and two soldiers from the garrison to protect us.
But quite unexpectedly, war was declared by the Texans
against General Ramirez y Sesma's garrison and the two
soldiers escorting us northward revolted, robbing me of
my purse and all our supplies, leaving only a few sacred
ornaments for the church. Father Esteban was killed. I
felt I could not turn back. Alas, it would seem I should
have done so. I have failed Father Augustine and his
workers quite miserably. Even if I am able to find them,
they will starve. Most of my seeds were taken when they
stole our food. I still have a few seeds, but what will it

matter if I'm unable to locate Father Augustine and the mission? I'm utterly lost without my map. . . ."

Seth struck flint to a handful of tinder. "Sounds to me like you're lucky to be alive, Father Bolivar. Those soldiers could just as easy have killed you."

Hearing this, Bolivar bowed his head as though in shame. "I'm afraid I ran away into the woods, leaving poor Father Esteban to his fate. I hid from them until they left with our supplies." He said it softly, keeping his face to the ground. "I was never a brave man. I vowed to give my life to the Order, helping the poor, devoting my life to the Church. If I had known Father Tomas meant to send me into a wilderness full of hostiles, I might have chosen otherwise. This experience has sorely tested my faith, I fear. My prayers have asked God to be patient with me."

Eli lowered the donkey's shafts and led it over to a tree, tying it to a low limb. "I wouldn't exactly call this the best place to build a church, Father." He watched Seth blowing gently on a few sparks in the tinder, begging flames to life. "We've got a real crude map of this river. If you can remember anythin' at all about where that mission is supposed to be, maybe we can show you which way to go."

Bolivar walked unsteadily to a tree trunk near Seth's fire and sat down against it, removing his muddy sandals. For a time he rested his head against the tree, breathing deeply. "It was to be built north of a place where two rivers joined. We were instructed to follow the smaller river to a mountain range where a tribe of nomads live. They call themselves Ki-was."

"Kiowas," Eli said, squatting down to watch Seth add sticks to his fire, thinking out loud. "Sounds like we're headed to the same place, nearly. We intend to trap along the Washita River, which runs right through Kiowa country. The Washita joins this river west of here someplace, only we ain't exactly sure where it is ourselves. We know there's plenty of Kiowas, an' they can be mean as hell."

Bolivar frowned a little. "Father Augustine wrote that he made peace with them. They left him alone; however, they did not appear to be interested in learning the word of God. It was his plan to win them over with gifts and kindness. With a garden and an orchard, gifts of fruit and vegetables would clearly show our friendliness. Sadly, I have very few seeds left, some peach and pear seeds, and almost no vegetables. By Father Augustine's writings, these Ki-was are predominantly meat eaters. They worship things in nature, such as the moon and sun, the earth itself which they call Earth Mother. I spent months in preparation for this journey, learning some of their language, as much as I could from the journal Father Augustine sent to Father Tomas in San Antonio. Now, all is lost. I have failed Father Tomas miserably, and perhaps because of my failure, Father Augustine and his five young Franciscans will also fail."

"You learned some of their language?" Eli asked, glancing over to Seth briefly.

"A few words and simple phrases."

Eli saw a plan unfolding, one that would help him and Seth establish relations with the Indians. "If we took you along with us to that river you're lookin' for, you could explain to those Kiowas what we wanted, that we wanted to trap furs in exchange for some trinkets we brought with us."

Bolivar seemed puzzled. "But you said you were not sure of the mission's location . . ."

"That's true, but we have a map showin' where a river comes down from some mountains to join this one, an' that sounds like the river you're lookin' for, don't it?"

"I suppose it could be," he agreed thoughtfully.

Seth got up, looking west, "You could follow along in your cart until we got there, Father. We've got food, and me an' Eli would enjoy the company." He ambled down toward the river to get a frying pan and coffeepot without waiting for Bolivar's reply.

"We don't speak any Kiowa," Eli said. "Looks like we'd be helpin' each other, you doin' some talkin' for us when we find more Indians, and we'd make sure you got to the place where you say this Father Augustine is buildin' his church. Sounds like a good trade for both of us."

The priest sat quietly for a moment, then he nodded. "It is clearly God's will that you found me, Mr. McBee. Let us travel together. I will speak for you with the Ki-was, and if you wish I can teach you some of their language as well. I gladly accept your proposition. We shall travel together, wherever the will of the Lord takes us."

Eli offered no opinion as to what forces would take them to good beaver country. Privately, he was convinced a keen eye and a steady hand on a rifle stood the best chance of getting them where they wanted to go.

Chapter

Four

Eli glanced back, watching the donkey cart's slow progress along the south bank of the river while he and Seth paddled upstream. Without a trail to follow, Father Bolivar could only travel at a snail's pace, picking his way around stands of oak and elm where his cart was too wide to make it through. Keeping the priest in sight required that they paddle slowly, although the potential benefits of having someone who spoke a few words of the Indians' tongue far outweighed any slight delays Father Bolivar might cause them.

"He'll be able to help us make a deal with those Indians up yonder," Eli said. "At least they'll be able to understand what we want from 'em. Besides, we'll enjoy havin' his company for a spell and I don't figure he'll be any trouble. Sharin' our food with him won't amount to much. Come sundown we'll see if we can hunt up a wild turkey roost or maybe a deer, so we can have some meat. He won't be a bother. We was aimin' to go hunting in a day or two anyhow."

Seth nodded. "He seems likable enough, but he sure as hell don't have no gift for travelin' through this country. He's near starved down to skin an' bones."

"I'll agree he don't seem to belong out here. It's

odd that Mose or the Frenchman never made no mention of a mission up this way. Looks like they'd have known if there was one. . . ."

"Could be the Kiowas scalped 'em before they got it built," Seth surmised. "Or maybe Mose an' Frenchy never went far enough up that Washita River the priest talked about. Sounds like the same river they told us to trap this winter. It looks like Mose an' Frenchy woulda known 'bout a church bein' built up there someplace. . . ."

Eli wondered about it too.

They'd been paddling slowly for almost two hours when they heard a commotion upriver, like the rumble of thunder, only the sky was clear, not a cloud in sight.

"What the hell could that be?" Seth asked, scanning the northwestern horizon as the sounds grew steadily louder.

An answer appeared suddenly around a bend in the river. A herd of buffalo numbering in the hundreds galloped along the river's edge, crashing through trees and brush, snapping off limbs in a blind rush eastward as though something was chasing them. Then Eli saw what was causing the stampede, when a few mounted Indians rode around the bend at the back of the herd, firing arrows into animals lagging behind. A cloud of dust arose from the pounding of so many hooves, drifting north on gentle breezes as more buffalo were struck with arrows and spears, staggering when their wounds weakened them, until some finally crashed to the ground or tumbled sideways into the river where they floundered to regain their feet, thrashing wildly in the shallows while murky red water turned to foam.

"A buffalo hunt!" Seth cried, shouting to be heard above the noise.

Indians galloped their ponies back and forth across the rear of the buffalo stampede, sending more arrows into wounded animals before they dropped to their knees or collapsed on their sides, legs kicking, making a

plaintive bellowing sound. As the runaway herd charged
toward Eli and Seth, several Indians halted their ponies
to stare at the canoe. Some were pointing, while others
simply watched, holding prancing horses in check while
they gazed at the boat gliding through quiet waters close
to the south bank of the river.

"They see us now," Eli warned, reaching for his
Whitney and a pouch of percussion caps. "Let's hope
they don't stop killin' buffalo to start shootin' at us."

Seth rested his paddle across his lap. "The range is
too far for an arrow, Eli, unless one of 'em gets lucky.
Just sit still an' we'll see what they aim to do about us."

None of the hunters made any attempt to fire an
arrow across the river. They watched the canoe, allowing most of the buffalo to escape downstream in an
all-out charge.

"They can't figure us out," Seth said. "They ain't
quite sure what to make of us or who we are, or what
we're doin' here. This is their land, I reckon, so we're
trespassers. Try givin' 'em the peace sign again."

"Can't say for sure it's the same bunch," Eli replied
as he raised his right hand, palm open.

"Don't suppose it matters, if they're friendly," Seth
said.

Eli was comforted by the feel of a rifle in his hands.
"We could just keep paddlin', mindin' our own business.
Maybe that's enough to let 'em know we don't mean no
harm." He glanced over his shoulder to see Father Bolivar driving his donkey between a stand of oaks half a
mile behind. "We oughta wait for the priest to catch up,
I 'spose."

"Let's tie off to a limb over yonder an' wait for
him," Seth said. He swung the canoe toward a cottonwood tree where branches grew over the river.

After only a few paddle strokes they were in shallow water on the south side of the river, secured to a low
limb. They sat for a time, watching some of the
mounted Indians continue their hunt, chasing the re-

maining buffalo as a handful waited among the fallen animals with their attention turned toward the canoe.

"They can't decide what to do about us," Seth said. "It's real plain they don't understand that peace sign Mose showed us. Maybe they's another breed of Injun who don't speak the same kind of sign language." His eyes drifted up and down the riverbank. "All that matters is they ain't shootin' at us. If we keep on up this river, maybe they'll leave us alone."

Eli glanced back to Father Bolivar again. "As soon as that priest catches up, we'll move on."

An Indian swung his pony around and rode over to a fallen buffalo, dropping to the ground beside it. He was bare-chested, like the others, and when sunlight struck him, his muscles rippled underneath his coppery skin. He took a knife from a belt around his waist and knelt down, tearing open the buffalo's belly with a sawing motion. Several more Indians appeared to lose interest in the canoe and rode over to the buffalo carcass, jumping down to help carve open the creature's furry underbelly. They seemed to be ignoring Eli and Seth now, going about gutting and skinning the animal as though no one else was watching.

Eli watched one Indian pull a handful of bloody meat from somewhere inside the buffalo's ribcage. He stood up and took a bite of it. "He's eatin' that buffalo raw," Eli said softly, outright astonishment in his voice. "They don't cook their meat, Seth. Can you believe it? They eat it plumb raw."

"It's the liver," Seth replied. "I can't hardly stand the taste of it when it's cooked. Frenchy an' Mose were damn sure right when they called these Injuns savages."

"They're a lot closer to bein' wild animals than men, if you was to ask me. I never saw nobody eat raw liver before. . . ."

"It sure ain't natural," Seth agreed. "Regular folks cook whatever meat they eat, if they's civilized."

Eli felt his uneasiness over their fur-trapping enterprise growing as he watched a wounded buffalo struggle

to its feet in the river shallows. "It's gonna be mighty
damn hard to make a deal with a bunch who don't even
know about cookin' their food. Maybe trappin' beaver
in these parts ain't such a good idea."

"We've come this far, Eli. May as well keep goin'
until we find that river where it feeds in. We've come
too far to turn back just because a few Injuns like the
taste of raw liver." Seth glanced over his shoulder.
"Wish the hell he'd hurry that jackass, before those Injuns decide to swim their horses across to get a better
look at us. That priest is slowin' us down."

"Havin' someone who can talk to 'em for us is
worth some extra time. We shouldn't be all that far from
where the Washita feeds into the Red. Besides that, we
can't just go off an' leave Father Bolivar on his own.
He'd have starved to death in another week if we hadn't
found him."

Seth nodded. "He sure do seem mighty helpless."

Eli looked across at the Indians again and at a lone
wounded buffalo standing in the river with its furry head
lowered, slowly bleeding to death from arrow wounds in
its side. Far to the east dust from the main herd rose
skyward, spiraling in lazy currents of air. He noticed
that some of the Indians were riding back to help with
the skinning. "Appears they all have a taste for raw liver
meat, I reckon. The rest of 'em are headed back this
way."

Seth made a face. "I'd just as soon not watch no
more of it, if it's all the same to you. Let's keep paddlin'
upstream. The priest ain't far behind now."

"I've seen enough myself, watchin' a man eat raw
meat comin' right out of the belly of an animal while
blood's runnin' down his chin. In my book it makes 'em
hardly more'n animals themselves, to eat it raw like
that. Untie that rope an' we'll move upstream a mile or
so. Just make sure we keep the priest where we can see
him."

As Seth was loosening the rope, Eli noticed Father
Bolivar waving both arms over his head. "Hold on a

minute, Seth. That priest is behavin' like something's wrong back there. See him yonder? The way he's wavin' his arms?"

"He sure do act excited. Wonder what's got him so all-fired agitated?"

The donkey cart rolled slowly through a line of oaks while Father Bolivar continued to wave his arms in the air. For a moment he was hidden by trees and shadows. When his cart came out of the forest to cross a meadow running beside the river, he cupped his hands around his mouth and yelled, "Don't shoot! Hold your fire!"

Eli glanced down at the rifle he was holding. "He figured we was gonna start shootin' at those Indians. He saw my rifle."

Seth wagged his head. "He's none too smart, to figure we're lookin' for a fight with 'em. Maybe some of his troubles are that he just can't count . . . there's at least twenty Injuns over yonder an' only the two of us. He must think we're plumb crazy."

Now some of the Indians began pointing across the river at Father Bolivar, and their curiosity quickly spread to the others. They ignored the canoe to watch the donkey cart. Eli rested his Whitney beside his right leg, fascinated by the way the Indians appeared to be puzzled by the priest's arrival . . . or was it the cart and donkey they were so curious about? "Maybe they never saw a wagon before, or a man wearin' a funny-lookin' robe like that."

"Hard to say," Seth muttered quietly, his gaze fixed on the Indians too. "Folks who don't know 'bout cookin' meat ain't all that likely to know much of nothin'."

Eli could hear the rattle of cart wheels moving closer. "I can't help but wonder why they rode up in the dark just to get a look at us the way they done last night. Seems like they'd have tried to talk to us, find out what we were doin' here instead of just ridin' off like that." He glanced up at a lowering sun to the west. "Maybe they'll come back tonight. Then the priest can tell 'em what we aim to do, an' tell 'em we're friendly."

Seth frowned a little. "If they'd wanted to try an' scalp us, they woulda done it already. They's just curious. So long as we don't cause no trouble, I don't figure they'll bother us if we keep movin'. The trouble's gonna come when we find that river where we plan to stay. Those are the Injuns who ain't so likely to be happy to see us, if they know what a beaver pelt is worth in New Orleans. Mose claimed they didn't have no use for beaver pelts. Ain't none of them over yonder wearin' hats."

"I 'spect hat makin' is too complicated for Indians. Either way we're gonna offer them a trade for what we want. That oughta be what makes our deal, if they like glass beads an' knives as much as Frenchy said they did."

Father Bolivar arrived in his donkey cart and reined to a halt. "I'm so relieved you didn't shoot at them," he said as he climbed down. "When I saw you reaching for your rifles I feared you might think they meant to harm you." He walked to the edge of the river, looking across as more buffalo carcasses were being skinned and gutted. "From what Father Augustine wrote, this is a hunting party, and by the way they wear their hair they appear to be Ki-was . . . Kiowas, as you have called them. These are the first of their tribe I have seen so far." He shaded his eyes from the sun, watching Indians butcher their buffalo. "I'm quite certain they won't behave in a hostile manner if we show them no signs of hostility. On my way north I encountered a small band of Tonka-was and they were very mild-mannered people. These, however, do appear to be Ki-was. Father Augustine mentioned that they seem to have very aggressive natures when provoked. They are often in conflict with other tribes in disputes over buffalo."

Eli had a thought. "If those are Kiowas, maybe you could talk to them for us now. Tell 'em all we want is to trade beads an' knives for the right to trap beaver this winter. . . ."

The priest looked askance. "I confess my knowledge of their language is severely limited, Mr. McBee. Father Augustine wrote a list of common words which Father Esteban and I were to learn before we arrived." He crossed himself after mentioning Father Esteban. "Perhaps it would be best if I refreshed my memory from the list of words before I attempted any negotiations with them in your behalf."

Eli was a bit surprised at the priest's admission. He had hoped Father Bolivar could explain what they wanted to a Kiowa chief without any difficulty. "I reckon it can wait," he said, wondering now if Father Bolivar was as incapable of speaking the Kiowa language as he was at crossing the Texas wilderness without almost starving to death. "Let's keep movin' west until it gets dark. We ain't covered much distance today."

Father Bolivar's embarrassment showed. "I'm sorry to be slowing you down, kind sirs. My mule is traveling as fast as it can, I'm afraid."

Seth untied the rope again. "No real hurry," he said in a gentle voice. "We got 'til winter to set our traps."

They paddled away from shore as Father Bolivar climbed back in his cart. Eli took a last look at the Kiowa hunting party as the canoe moved into stronger currents. The Indians were still watching the donkey cart like they'd never seen such a contraption before. Or was it a robed priest they hadn't seen until now?

The river lay before them, a glassy highway of smooth water stretching to the horizon. The soft sounds of their paddles and the gurgle of water passing on either side of the prow accompanied their slow but steady progress toward a ball of setting sun.

Chapter
Five

Father Bolivar seemed in high spirits as they prepared their evening meal at dusk. Seth managed to land another big yellowcat with a hook and grubworm, panfrying slices of fish while a pot of beans bubbled softly over the fire. Evening shadows deepened beneath oak limbs around their camp as the priest talked excitedly about the Kiowa buffalo hunt they had seen, rummaging through his packs until he found a tattered leather-bound book.

"I do believe Father Augustine mentioned that they ate parts of some animals raw," he said, untying a piece of discolored blue ribbon holding the pages closed, his sunburned face twisted into lines of concentration.

"It was the liver," Seth told him, shaking his head in a way that clearly conveyed his disgust for the practice. "Several of 'em took the liver right out of the carcass before them buffalo was plumb dead . . . legs was still kickin'. I seen what they did plain as day."

Eli merely listened, watching the river as Father Bolivar spoke again.

"I'll admit it does seem a rather revolting practice, but you must remember these people know very little about civilized living, according to Father Augustine."

He began turning pages carefully. "I'm quite sure he mentioned that, and several other practices, like the removal of a lock of hair from the heads of their enemies."

"It ain't just hair," Seth remarked, turning strips of fish in his frying pan. "They cut off the skin attached to the skull along with it. Mose an' Frenchy told us about it."

The priest's color paled somewhat. "One cannot expect them to understand heathen practices until they have been taught the word of God, Mr. Booker. This is why we have been sent to them, in order to teach them how to live a God-fearing, civilized way of life. Franciscans take an oath to devote their lives to spreading the word of God among those who do not know of God's existence. Under the leadership of Father Augustine we shall build a mission among them and show them the pathway to eternal life."

Seth grunted. "You may find out this Father Augustine an' his followers never got the chance to teach 'em nothin'. If it didn't go the way they planned buildin' that church, they could wind up bein' dead."

Father Bolivar looked across the flames at Seth. "We were prepared to give our lives, as did my companion, Father Esteban. If God has chosen us to make this sacrifice, then it is His will and we accept it." He returned to his book, turning pages one at a time. "Before we assume Father Augustine has failed, we must find this river he mentions coming from the northwest. It joins the river we travel now, *El Rio Rojo*."

"We're lookin' for that very same river comin' down from the Washita Mountains," Eli said thoughtfully, watching eddies swirl around hidden sandbars as sunlight bathed the river's sluggish waters with shades of pink. "First off, we've gotta find the chief of those Kiowas so we can explain why we're here. While you're talkin' to 'em, you can ask about Father Augustine and if they know where he built his church."

The priest was frowning over a particular page.

"There are many Ki-wa words with several different meanings. Apparently it can be difficult to know how to use them properly. We studied as many as we could, Father Esteban and I, on our way north from San Antonio. Alas, Father Esteban had a gift for mastering language which I do not, it would seem. If I am to teach them Christianity I must broaden my vocabulary considerably. I've had little spirit for mastering the Ki-wa tongue alone." He gave both Seth and Eli a look. "Traveling alone in this empty wilderness has been disheartening, to say the least, with no one to talk to."

"You're welcome to stay with us," Eli said. "Somewhere up this river we'll start lookin' for a crossing so you can get the donkey an' cart on the other side. We'll float the wagon on a couple of big logs an' hope the donkey can swim to the far side on his own. Stayin' clear of quicksand is gonna be the biggest problem. This river's got more quicksand than any I ever saw."

The priest nodded vigorously. "I was on the verge of losing my mule and cart to those treacherous sands when you came along to rescue me. It was surely an act of God when you appeared around that bend in the river. . . ."

"Lady Luck," Eli offered. "We happened to be at the right place at the right time, I 'spose."

Father Bolivar smiled. "Lady Luck, as you call her, has a name. The Holy Virgin watches over us. We offer prayers to her every single day, asking for her blessings in our daily lives. I will gladly teach you those prayers, gentlemen, so that Mary will also watch over you and keep you from harm."

"Didn't appear this Holy Virgin was doin' much to watch over you back yonder in that quicksand," Seth said, by the tone of his voice showing his lack of interest in learning any of Father Bolivar's prayers. "I'd just as soon not get preached to, if it's all the same to you. Never was much on churchgoin'."

"But you see," the priest explained quickly, "the

Holy Mother was watching over me. She brought you to that bend in the river at just the right time."

"I'd say it was luck," Seth replied, stirring fish to keep it from burning. "But if you believe your Holy Mother is gonna keep us safe, maybe you oughta pray real hard that them Kiowas don't decide to lift our scalps when we get where we're goin'."

"I will pray for us all," he said, pausing when his gaze came to something on one of the pages. "The Ki-was have names for different seasons, as we do. They call winter *Pai Aganti,* a time of cold weather coming soon, according to Father Augustine. They have several chiefs, or leaders, depending upon what sort of decision must be made. Before important decisions are made they smoke a mixture of leaves and bark which they call *kinnikinick,* and they have holy men who see visions telling them what to do. These holy men also keep a sacred idol, called the *taime,* which is a vital part of their sun-dance ceremony. Ki-was worship the sun, moon, and the earth as representatives of their gods. In his diary, Father Augustine believes it will be very difficult to explain Christianity to them because of their limited vocabulary and belief in pagan rituals. Their horse herds serve the same purpose as money. Horses are given, it says here, for all things, including the most desirable women. Powerful men in the tribe have several wives, a practice they show little inclination to abandon. As you can see, our work promises to be long and most difficult, bringing God's teachings to a race who worship pagan idols and practice butchery upon their enemies. Both the Ki-was and their allies, the Comanches, are widely feared by other more peaceful tribes due to their savagery. Both tribes lack written language. They keep a record of their history by drawing scenes on pieces of deerskin. Thus our only means of communication will be with words they understand when spoken correctly. I have been able to learn some of them. Tonight, and in the days to come, I shall do my best to learn as many as I can."

Eli stood up as dusk became dark across hills surrounding the river valley. "All we're hopin' you can do is help us tell them we aim to trade beads an' knives for the right to trap our beaver here this winter. If you can figure out how to get that said, we'll be obliged."

"You have my promise I'll do the best I can. And should I fail to explain things properly, I'm sure Father Augustine will be able to speak for you . . . as soon as we can find him."

"Fish's ready," Seth announced. "Beans near 'bout tender enough, too." He placed pieces of fish on a tin plate and gave it to Father Bolivar.

"How can I ever repay your kindnesses?" he said, taking a few spoonfuls of beans before he began eating hungrily, stuffing his cheeks with food.

"If you can figure a way to explain to those Injuns what we want, that'll be payment enough, Father," Seth said, taking his own plate to the trunk of a tree where he rested his back to eat slowly, watching the last rays of light fade in the west. "But if I was you, I wouldn't count on bein' able to find that other priest an' his workers. The men who told us 'bout this place was here last year an' they didn't make no mention of seein' a church bein' built or nothin' of the kind. Only thing they said was, to be real careful when we got to Kiowa country, on account of they was real mean to tangle with if things don't go just right."

Father Bolivar looked down at his plate. "I have been forced to consider the possibilty that Father Augustine and the mission is lost . . . that they met with some ill fate. These things are in the hands of God, my friends."

"Maybe," Seth replied, chewing. "I reckon you could say it's in the hands of God an' a bunch of Injuns who eat raw liver an' take scalps."

Eli said nothing, although from what he'd seen so far it was unlikely much of anything would persuade the Kiowas to let anyone get what they wanted from this territory without offering them something in exchange.

He hoped Mose and Frenchy were right, that glass beads and poorly made knives would be enough.

At sunrise the sky was clear. Eli had slept soundly during the night without dreams. As they broke camp after coffee and fried bread for breakfast, he inspected the canoe for leaks and tied their gear down while Seth helped Father Bolivar with harnessing his donkey. Dry fall leaves rustled in early gusts of wind passing through limbs above them when they were ready to depart. The priest climbed into his cart and waved before he urged the donkey westward.

Eli took his place at the back of the canoe as Seth settled in the prow, pushing them away from shore. As they paddled out into the current, Seth spoke over his shoulder.

"That priest believes God is gonna save him from them arrows an' spears. I never was much on religion . . . didn't learn it when I was young, like most folks. But if I was a gamblin' man I'd bet he don't make it far, once we leave him to go on his own. Some men just ain't got no business bein' out here."

Eli steered the canoe toward the middle of the river. "I've had a dose or two of Bible teachin', not all that much, really. But I'm of the same mind as you when it comes to Father Bolivar. He don't strike me as the type to know how to survive. Unless he can find that Father Augustine up the Washita, I figure he's as good as dead before spring. He can't feed himself, an' I never did know anybody who could stay alive doin' nothin' but prayin' for things to get better. . . ."

Chapter
Six

It was the narrowest spot in the river they'd come to since morning, and when Eli tested its shallows, he found no quicksand beds that would bog the donkey. They went about gathering dead trees with which to buoy the priest's small cart—it weighed very little, and within an hour they had logs lashed to the underbelly and rolled it down to the river to float it across. Seth ferried Father Bolivar over in the canoe while Eli readied the cart and mule for the crossing. Upon Seth's return, they led the donkey out in the river with a rope tied to its neck. Eli paddled while the donkey reluctantly began to swim with Seth holding onto the rope to keep it from turning back. The little brown animal swam easily and with very little assistance once it struck deep water, and they soon came to shallows on the north side of the river where the donkey could stand.

"Blessed is the name of the Lord!" Bolivar cried, taking the rope while the donkey shook water from its coat.

Seth grinned. "You might oughta bless that donkey's nature because it was willin' to swim without no trouble. Ain't many of the jackass breed takes to water without persuasion."

Eli backpaddled their canoe away from shore. "We'll tow the cart across," he said, looking up and down the riverbank. "Keep one eye on the trees, just in case some of those Kiowas show up before we get back across."

They were able to pull the cart to the north bank without mishap, although the work was tiring under a blistering noonday sun. It required only a few minutes to harness the donkey, and in slightly less than two hours after beginning the crossing, they were under way again.

The north bank of the Red offered fewer obstacles for the cart, fewer thickets to navigate, and gentler terrain in most places. For another pair of hours they continued west at a good pace. They saw no sign of Indians, and with the passage of time, Eli found himself relaxing. Ahead lay more miles of quiet river winding gently through a shallow, forested valley, sprinkled here and there with vast, open meadows deep in drying fall grasses. Now and then, they saw small groups of antelope, but no more of the huge buffalo they'd seen the day before. The serenity of their surroundings lulled Eli into a sleepy daze as they paddled slowly along sloping banks lined with cattails and bulrushes. As the sun lowered, fall colors again dazzled his eye with their brilliance. Red and yellow leaves seemed ablaze in trees growing close to the river. Occasional willows spread drooping branches over the water. Towering cottonwoods with fans of bright yellow leaves rose above the rest of the forest near the water's edge. Gusts of soft wind took leaves from many of the branches, sending them twirling off in downward spirals to the forest floor. Eli reveled in the raw beauty of the scenery as they paddled westward through the river's gentle currents. He had all but forgotten about yesterday's encounter with the Kiowa buffalo hunters, listening to the quiet gurgle of paddles and a softer sound made by the prow knifing through slow-moving water.

Not far behind, the priest made relatively good

progress on the riverbank, occasionally crossing shallow
feeder streams that slowed him down where banks were
steep. As the afternoon wore on, some of Eli's appre-
hensions over making a trading agreement with the Kiowas lessened. The silence of the empty river valley
made him forget everything else for the present. Passing
time, he was soon dreaming of a bountiful trapping season when their beaver pelts would earn them a small
fortune in New Orleans.

As it had for days, the sun turned gauzy as it lowered into a thin haze hovering above the earth before
sunset, and with it came a subtle change in the colors
around them. Again, the river turned blood red, shim-
mering in slanted sunlight as though some endless crimson ribbon had been laid across the land. As darkness
approached they saw more and more wild animals coming to the river to drink . . . a small herd of doe with a
wary buck standing back in the forest, until the sounds
of Bolivar's cart sent them bounding away into the trees.

Seth pointed to a small clearing at the water's edge.
"If we made camp there, we'd have a view on all sides,
Cap'n. Looks like there's plenty of grass for the jackass,
too."

Eli looked upriver a moment. "Can't see anything
looks no better up yonder. Let's head for shore an' wait
for the priest to catch up. Everything considered, after
the crossin' we made, I figure we made pretty good time
today. No sense gettin' a big hurry."

They swung their canoe for shore. Off to the east,
Father Bolivar's cart rattled over a section of rough
ground little more than a quarter mile away. As the
canoe edged to a halt in soft mud beside the riverbank,
Eli felt thankful for an uneventful day without encoun-
tering any more Indians. He wondered if the priest had
anything to do with it, praying to his Holy Mother for
their safe journey. It was possible, he supposed, that
someone other than Father Bolivar himself had been
looking out for him. There was no better explanation

for the fact that he was still alive, as ill equipped as he seemed for surviving in this wilderness.

Seated around their campfire, Bolivar read from the diary as crickets and bullfrogs sang their songs to the night. "The Kiowa word for trade is *nodemah*. In order to ask, how are you, friend? it must be pronounced, *hi, hites*. It would appear from Father Augustine's writings that to correctly say you wish to trade with them, you would first say, *Hi, hites. Coon-ah nodemah*."

Eli said it to himself. "How do we tell 'em we want to give beads an' knives for furs?"

"It may be difficult," the priest replied, scowling down a page. "The word for knife is *we-iti*. I am unable to find a word for beads or jewelry. As to explaining that you want beaver fur in exchange for those items, it may best be accomplished showing them what you want. Alas, there is no word listed for beaver or pelts of any kind. There is one notation here . . . a white man is called *tosi*." He glanced up at Seth. "A Negro is called *to-oh tivo*. Being Spanish and a priest, they will call me *powva*. I am afraid there isn't much else we can use here to tell them what you want. However, when we do find Father Augustine I'm quite sure he'll be able to explain it."

"That's if you find him," Seth said. "If they ain't killed him by now."

Bolivar closed the diary and looked down at his worn sandals for a moment. "I believe God has seen to their safety and the building of the mission. Father Augustine lived among the Ki-was for some time before he wrote this account for the bishop. If they meant to harm him, it would seem they would have done so as soon as he arrived."

Seth sipped coffee from a tin cup. "We didn't hear about no mission called San Miguel up this river, nor no other kind of a church, when Mose an' Frenchy told us about this place. If I was you I wouldn't count on findin' nobody up there."

Bolivar gave him a thin smile. "As Franciscans, we have faith in what we are doing, and faith that God will provide for our needs and see to our success spreading His word."

Seth wagged his head. "Faith wasn't enough to keep your friend, Father Esteban, alive. Now, I ain't sayin' I've got no belief in the Almighty." He gazed up at the stars. "I figure there's somebody up there, most likely, only whoever He is, He ain't gonna keep a man from gettin' hisself killed if that man ain't real careful. If this Father Augustine is alive, it's because he's learned to be real careful 'round Injuns."

Bolivar put the diary in his lap. "Honesty in dealings with their fellow man, even if they are Godless nomads, and faith in the Lord will keep them safe. By dealing with the Ki-was fairly, Father Augustine was able to establish relations with them and learn some of their language. I believe he is there, building our mission. Sadly, he will be sorely disappointed to learn that I have failed him."

"You ain't no fightin' man, Father," Seth said, softening his expression. "You ain't got a gun, so there wasn't no way you could have saved those seeds or the life of your partner from a couple of soldiers. Sounds to me like you done about the only thing you could, an' you told us you've still got a few of them seeds."

Bolivar stared into the fire. "I failed when I ran away, Mr. Booker. I should have stayed with Father Esteban and our cart. My faith was tested and I chose to hide, rather than face danger. All I can do is ask for forgiveness from God and Father Augustine."

Seth grunted, showing how plainly he disagreed. "You showed good sense, Father. Ain't no other way to say it. Time comes when a man has to choose between dyin' and runnin', runnin' makes a hell of a lot more sense."

Eli turned his attention to the river. An unknown distance to the west lay beaver country, and judging by the way the Kiowas watched them enter their territory, a time might come when he and Seth had to choose between running away or fighting to the death. There was something about the appearance of those wild men on their horses that made him doubt they could accomplish their fur trapping this winter without difficulty. Somehow, Mose and the Frenchman had done it. So why was he having so many doubts about it now?

They were paddling near the mouth of a creek feeding into the river when Seth abruptly stopped rowing, looking upstream. Early-morning shadows still lay like murky puddles below trees lining the banks of the creek as the sun rose slowly behind them. In the wake of their canoe, tiny whirlpools flattened as current swept them away toward a golden sunrise reflecting warm yellow light off the river as though it were a piece of glass.

"I heard somethin'," Seth warned quietly, "like voices. I know I didn't imagine it. Sounded like somebody was laughin'."

Eli craned his neck to see upstream around a bend where the creek narrowed. "I don't hear anything," he said.

Water burbled past the canoe's prow. All was quiet until a blue jay cried and flew from a willow branch near the bank.

"There it is again," Seth whispered, "comin' from that creek yonder, only it's way off. I just barely heard it that time."

In the distance Eli thought he could hear water splashing, a waterfall's sound. "I can't hear nothin' besides this river an' maybe a waterfall up the creek aways. I sure never heard nobody laughin'."

They floated closer to the small creek's mouth. The stream was scarcely a dozen yards wide and shallow, looking to be no more than a couple of feet deep in the middle with gently sloped banks lined with slender red oak and cottonwood. They could see upstream only a short distance before a bend obscured the creek's course from view. Eli doubted the priest would have any difficulty crossing it in his cart.

"I don't hear a thing, Seth. Let's keep paddling. Father Bolivar can cross it without us. . . ." As he spoke, he wondered if he might have heard a noise, and he let his voice trail off so he could listen closely. "I did hear somethin' then, an' it could have been somebody laughin', maybe." Then he heard it again and this time it was distinct, the sound of laughter, a woman's voice.

"It's a woman," Seth said, cocking an ear, confirming what Eli thought he heard. "Sounds like a girl. Maybe more'n one of 'em."

It did sound like a girlish giggle coming from around the bend, a distance Eli couldn't judge, closer than he first imagined. "It is a young-soundin' voice, ain't it?" he added.

Another burst of laughter came from the bend, and the voice was different, slightly higher than the first.

"More'n one, like I said," Seth remarked. "Figures to be Injun girls. Can't hardly be nobody else."

Eli's curiosity continued to mount. "Row over to the bank real quiet. We'll slip through those trees an' have ourselves a look."

"Might not be such a good idea, Cap'n. Where there's Injun women there's liable to be Injun men."

"We'll go careful . . . won't get too close." Eli swung the aft of the canoe around and started paddling into the stream before Seth could voice any more objections. Girlish laughter continued to echo among trees lining the creek bank.

They paddled slowly toward a stand of cattails, listening to more laughter somewhere to the north. Eli pointed to the cattails and whispered, "We'll hide the canoe in there. Be sure you bring your rifle, just in case we run into more than we bargain for."

The bullhide boat slid quietly among the cattails and came to a halt in mud and sand. Eli stepped out, feeling his boots fill with water where the lasts had pulled away from the stitching.

Cradling their Whitneys, they beached the canoe among tall reedlike leaves with their fuzzy brown flower spikes and waded ashore.

"This way," Seth said quietly, hunkering down to creep among scrub bushes and undergrowth beside the water, carefully placing each foot so it made as little sound as possible.

Eli fell in behind, listening to the voices ahead. Several girls were laughing, and now he could hear water splashing back and forth as if they were playing while bathing in the stream.

They moved quietly to the spot where the creek made its turn westward. Seth crouched even lower as he shouldered through a tangle of tall grass and branches to the base of a cottonwood on a little knoll above the creek bank.

As Seth was peering around the cottonwood trunk, all noises coming from the stream stopped suddenly . . . there were no more of the splashing sounds, and the laughter abruptly ended. Before Eli could get a look himself, Seth quickly drew back behind the tree and held a finger to his lips.

"They saw me," he whispered, "and they's runnin' into them woods yonder. Be best if we clear out of here before they bring back some of their menfolk."

Eli started inching backward. "Who were they? Did you get a look at them?"

Seth gave what might pass for a grin. "Injun girls, naked as the day they was borned. Five or six of 'em. Wasn't enough time to get a count." He moved quickly away from the tree as Eli hurried back toward their canoe in a crouch. "They didn't have a stitch of clothes on, Cap'n, and damned if they wasn't a pretty sight, bathin' in that pool."

Hearing about naked Indian maidens bathing in a pool brought Eli a rich cloud of memories. He'd been without a woman for many months. For most of his adult life, beginning at age fourteen, he had sought the

company of women in drinking parlors and seedy broth-
els, wherever he could find them.

Eli reached the canoe first and pushed it into
deeper water before he climbed in, placing his rifle near
his feet as he took the paddle. Seth swung easily into the
boat while Eli rowed them backward away from the cattails.

"Were they pretty?" he asked, taking deep bites
with his oar until they were well away from shore.

"Pretty as a picture," Seth replied, swinging the
prow with powerful strokes, and soon they were gliding
into the main course of the river. "One was sittin' on a
rock watchin' over the rest of 'em. She saw me, or heard
me, an' she clapped her hands just once. They all took
off runnin' into them trees like they wasn't ever gonna
stop. Before you could blink twice, they was gone."

Eli conjured up a vision of what naked Indian girls
looked like bathing in a stream. "Sure wish I coulda
seen 'em," he said as they turned the canoe sharply to
the west.

Seth chuckled softly. "You'd be like me if you'd laid
eyes on 'em, willin' to trade every string of beads an'
ribbon we got for just one."

Faint stirrings in Eli's groin made him wonder if
Seth was closer to the truth than he knew. It seemed
such a long time ago when he was with Marybeth . . .
when he was happy, content, before a case of wander-
lust drove them apart. . . .

Chapter Seven

They'd talked about women most of the morning, a result of sighting the Indian girls bathing after sunup. Seth recalled a Creole girl he knew in New Orleans named Bessie, twenty years his junior, who worked the cribs on backstreets near the wharfs for a modest living. He'd become a regular caller of Bessie's, and as time passed they became better acquainted, then friends. Bessie became his lover and they even spoke of marriage, until a trip up the Mississippi took Seth away for nine weeks. When he returned there was no sign of Bessie Thibedeaux, nor any word of where she might have gone.

"She couldn't leave me a note because she never learned how to write," Seth remembered, finishing his story with a touch of sadness in his mellow voice. "I truly had a fondness for that young gal. She had the most beautiful body you ever saw, Eli, and her cookin' was near 'bout the best I ever tasted. I reckon I'll always wonder what come of her. Her dresses an' such was gone from the wardrobe. Maybe it was only that I was away too long. That bitch of a river takes a while to pole. I've told myself a thousand times it was the Mississip' that took Bessie from me. I blamed the river, only it was me that was gone for so long."

"Women don't take to a man who ain't home real regular. I know it for a fact. That was what come between me an' Marybeth over the years. Every time I came back she told me she couldn't stand the loneliness no more, that she'd take up with another man if I didn't stay home. Back then, I believed a river gets in a man's blood, like poison. You get this itch to be back on a damn flatboat, seein' the country. Stayin' in one place too long was never my nature, an' I reckon that's what cost me Marybeth. She wanted a man who stayed put."

"How come you never did marry her, Cap'n?"

He had to think about his answer. "We talked about it a few times, but she told me she wouldn't marry a man who was married to a riverboat. She was a good woman, only she never did understand what it was that made me take to the river. To tell the truth, I ain't rightly sure what it is inside of me that makes me want a river to travel. I reckon I was just born that way."

Seth saw an eagle land in the highest branches of an elm overlooking the water. It folded its wings to watch the canoe pass. "There's things about a man's mind most women won't ever understand. I never did understand Bessie's way of thinkin' at all. She talked crazy, sometimes, 'bout havin' land of her own an' fields full of cotton. A big house with servants. She never did understand how those things cost a pile of money, more money than she'd make in a lifetime, workin' the cribs."

Marybeth had wanted a farm, Eli remembered. The little room they rented near the wharfs was cramped and musty, cold during the winter, sweltering hot in summer, and the docks always stank of rotting fish. He was about to mention Marybeth's wishes for owning farmland when he thought he smelled smoke coming from the west.

Suddenly, the eagle shrieked and took off, flying low over the river as though something frightened it, beating its powerful wings until it flew out of sight above the treetops.

"Wonder what spooked that bird?" Seth asked, searching the forest near the tree where the eagle had perched.

For a few moments there was silence, until a distant scream came from the west, a human voice. Eli froze. It was a woman's scream, and immediately a chorus of screams arose from the same direction. The cries were clearly those of fear, and now there were so many screams they became like a single noise.

"What the hell . . . ?" Seth scanned the forest ahead and saw nothing moving. "Maybe it's those Injun girls. Wonder what the hell is happenin' to 'em?"

Eli couldn't guess. "Let's see what it is. Head for shore an' we'll take a look."

"May not be such a good idea, Cap'n, to stick our noses in where they don't belong."

"We won't do nothin' but look. Somethin's damn sure happening to those women or they wouldn't yell like that." Eli swung the canoe for shore and paddled as hard as he could. "Be sure to bring your pistol an' rifle," he added, hearing the screams grow louder, more frenzied. "Somebody could be after those girls we saw at the creek. Won't do no harm to see what it is."

They reached the riverbank and jumped out with their rifles and pistols in hand. Eli took off in a run through a canebrake and then a thicket of oak while Seth was securing the canoe to a limb. Dodging back and forth in the forest, he heard one of the women yelling words he couldn't understand and then scream, her voice trailing off into a series of gasping moans.

He reached an opening a quarter mile deeper in the woods and stumbled to a halt when he saw a sight that brought him up short. In a clearing just beyond the trees, dozens of strange, cone-shaped tents sat in the sunlight. Several mounted Indians galloped among the tents on spotted ponies, while Indian women and children ran in every direction, screaming as the horse-

back men chased them into the woods or in circles
around the tents. Smoldering campfires burned across
the Indian camp, making it harder to see what the
mounted Indians were doing to the women and children
fleeing on foot. For a few seconds Eli simply stood beside a tree trunk and watched, until an Indian on a
black-and-white pony galloped up behind a running girl
wearing some sort of animal-skin dress. A club in the
Indian's right hand swung downward, striking the girl on
her head. She groaned and collapsed on her stomach as
the mounted Indian galloped his pony past her. More
screams came from all across the camp as women and
children raced back and forth to escape swinging clubs.
Eli was horrified. Why were these men attacking defenseless women and children?

As one Indian rode his pony around a tent, Eli
noticed something peculiar about his head—his skull
had been shaved.

"Osages," he said aloud, remembering a descrip-
tion Mose gave them of Indians who meticulously
shaved off their hair.

He heard Seth running up behind him as he tucked
the Paterson into his belt to shoulder his rifle. "Osages
all over the place usin' clubs on women!" he cried,
swinging his sights to a mounted Indian. "We got no
choice but to take a side with those women an' kids!
Shoot the sons of bitches without any hair!" As he
spoke he thumbed back the hammer. Peering through
the V-notch rear sight, he gripped the black walnut
stock and gently squeezed the trigger.

His .54 caliber muzzleloader belched flame, slam-
ming into Eli's shoulder with a mighty roar. The Osage
jerked when a ball of lead passed through his side, and
in the same instant, all the shouting and screaming
stopped. The Osage flew from his pony's withers, driven
sideways by the ball's impact. His pony lunged and
bounded away, snorting, turning its head toward the unfamiliar sound of gunfire. The Indian tumbled to the
ground with a fountain of blood squirting from a hole in

his back. And now every eye in the camp was on Eli and
Seth—the Osages halted their ponies and the women
stopped running away from them.

Seth drew a bead on an Osage aboard a prancing
white pony and fired. The explosion seemed to rock the
trees around them as smoke and fire erupted from the
muzzle of Seth's Whitney. The Indian was torn from
the back of his horse as though he'd met a mighty gust
of wind, spinning him off the pony's rump with his arms
and legs flailing, until he landed on his back beside one
of the cone-shaped tents and lay still. As Seth fired, Eli
hurried to reload, forcing a ball and wadding down the
muzzle of his rifle with the ramrod's brass tip.

The echo of a second gunshot faded. Every Indian
in the clearing was staring at the trees where Seth and
Eli stood. An eerie silence spread over the camp, and
for a few moments, as Eli fitted a percussion cap on the
nipple, not one Indian moved or made a sound. Two
loose ponies trotted off into the woods, one with blood
covering its rump and flanks.

"Don't shoot no more, Eli," Seth whispered. "Look
what's happenin' . . ."

Mounted Osages turned their ponies, pointing at
the trees as they began shouting unrecognizable words
to each other. Three of them took off in a gallop as hard
as they could ride away from the tents, heading north,
disappearing into thick oak and elm at the edge of the
clearing. The others followed, drumming heels into
their ponies' ribs, and in less than half a minute every
one of the Osages had ridden away, leaving their dead
behind.

Eli took a deep breath. "Whatever was goin' on, I
couldn't just let 'em club those women an' children.
These women are most likely Kiowas, an' it appeared
they was bein' raided by Osages, maybe while their
menfolk were off huntin' buffalo, the ones we saw
huntin' downstream. I couldn't just sit an' watch it, Seth.
I had to take a side with these women."

Seth was looking at the women. The ones who

hadn't hidden in the forest merely stood in plain sight, watching Eli and Seth in silence. "Maybe you got it figured right, only it seems like they's afraid of us. No way to make 'em understand why we came to help. They don't understand us an' we sure as hell don't know how to understand what they're sayin'."

"I figure none of 'em ever heard a gun go off before. It's the noise that's got 'em scared."

Seth relaxed his grip on his rifle. "It didn't hurt none that we shot two of the bastards who was botherin' 'em. Maybe that'll count for somethin'."

"I've got an idea," Eli said, resting his rifle against his leg. "If we leave a few of our beads an' some ribbon, maybe it will prove we're friendly. We could just put some beads an' a piece of ribbon out in plain sight an' then get back on the river like we aimed to mind our own business. That oughta show 'em we don't mean no harm."

One of the women, wearing a badly stained deerskin dress, crept cautiously over to the woman who had fallen from a blow to the head by an Osage. She knelt, still keeping a wary eye on the two strangers, to touch the downed woman's shoulder. Slowly, a few at a time, more women came from the trees and tents to stare at Eli and Seth. Somewhere behind one of the tents, a child began to cry. Smoke from the fires drifted across the clearing, making it harder to see any of the Indian women on the far side who were still close to the woods.

"No reason for us to stay any longer," Seth said. "Let's fetch 'em some beads an' ribbon so's we can clear out of here before the Kiowa menfolk show up. It don't appear none of them Osages want any more of our guns."

"I'll keep an eye on things here while you bring back a string or two of beads an' some ribbon," Eli offered, "just in case."

Seth nodded and turned for the river. Eli watched the women stare at him, wishing there was something he could say to them to let them know they wouldn't be harmed. Almost as an afterthought he took a few short steps out in the sunlight and held up the sign for peace, keeping his rifle beside his leg.

His movements caused alarm among some of the women, who backed away when he stepped from the trees. But when Eli stopped and gave the sign, one young woman standing near a tent said a few words to another girl beside her. The girl looked at Eli and gave him a slow smile, then held up her own hand, returning the sign for peace.

"She understands," he whispered to himself, taking note of how pretty she was. Long black hair fell below her shoulders. Her eyes were a dark chocolate color, and her high cheekbones were covered by pale bronze skin so smooth it appeared flawless. Her short dress of wrinkled deerskin bore designs that had been drawn or painted on the hide . . . a running horse, a drawing of the sun, other symbols he couldn't identify at this distance. He returned her smile, still holding his palm open, and for a few moments they simply stared at each other.

One older woman walked cautiously to the body of the Osage Seth shot, peering down at it. Then she did a strange thing for which Eli was totally unprepared—she spat upon the corpse and kicked it savagely, saying something under her breath.

Eli stood rock still, not wanting to cause fear among the women until Seth returned. He gazed around the camp, taking note of clay pottery here and there, and the curious conical shape of the tents, but several times his eyes returned to the pretty girl, and when he saw her again, he smiled. She watched him, but now she no longer held up the peace sign, merely standing where she was without taking a step in any direction. Several minutes passed and the silence grew uncomfortable.

Seth came up behind him. "Here's two strings of beads an' a length of red ribbon," he said quietly. "Maybe if I hang 'em on a limb of this tree, they'll see

we aim to leave presents if we walk away an' get back on
the river."

Eli agreed, nodding. "They keep starin' at us like
they don't quite know what to make of us."

"It was the guns, Eli. They's scared of the noise an'
they seen what happened to them two Osages. It's
plumb natural they'd be scared of a loud noise that
killed somebody." Seth placed the beads and ribbon on
the end of a low branch where sunlight made the glass
beads sparkle. "Let's pull out before anythin' can go
wrong. We did what we came here to do. Maybe they'll
tell their menfolk what we did an' show 'em our
presents. That'll help us make a friendly start with this
particular bunch, anyways."

Eli backed toward the trees, smiling at the pretty
young girl one final time before he lowered his hand
and followed Seth back through the forest. There was
something about the girl's face that lingered in his memory. "One of 'em was damn sure a pretty girl," he said
quietly as they walked through the forest and then down
to the edge of the river where the canoe was tied.

Seth chuckled, although he continued to glance
over his shoulder until they pushed the canoe away from
shore. "You always did have an eye for a pretty gal,
Cap'n, only I wouldn't count none too strong on gettin'
a chance to know her. She's an Injun, in case you forgot,
an' she's liable to have a man who'd cut your throat in
order to keep her."

They climbed in and paddled away from the bank,
moving due west toward a thickly forested section of
river valley where the river broadened in the distance.

"All the same," Eli said, "she sure as hell was a
beauty, an' she understood when I gave her the peace
sign. She gave it back to me, an' that's when she smiled
a little." He looked back when he remembered the
priest. "I hope Father Bolivar stays clear of their camp
when he smells smoke. Maybe we oughta double back
an' warn him about what's ahead so he'll stay wide of
that Indian village."

Seth turned the prow in a slow circle to the east. "Likely he heard the gunshots anyway. We'd better tell him to stay close so he don't have a run-in with them Osages himself. One thing's for sure . . . he's liable to get in trouble if we leave him all by his lonesome. For the life of me I can't figure why anybody'd send a man like him out in the middle of nowhere. He can't hardly harness that jackass without some help."

They paddled back downstream looking for Father Bolivar, riding easily with the flow of the current.

Chapter Eight

Seth was preparing a feast over their supper fire, roasting a young turkey hen he shot while hunting along the river as the sun went down. Eli and Father Bolivar sat around the flames at dusk while Seth attended to the turkey, turning it on a roasting stick above the fire. Eli was telling the priest what happened at the Indian village, filling in details they hadn't given him when they found him beside the river earlier in the day.

"The girl understood sign language," Eli continued, recalling her slight smile. "She nearly grinned when she gave it back to me, like she knew we wanted to be friendly."

Bolivar watched the hen drip juices into the flames, giving off wonderful smells. "It was indeed a wise move to leave them gifts as you departed. They can have no doubts as to your good intentions." He frowned a little. "How odd it is that Osage men would attack women and children. Father Augustine speaks of all Indian men as warriors, yet it hardly seems fitting for a man who sees himself as a warrior to make war on women. The Kiowa word for warrior is *vi-ses,* and they apparently take great pride in their fighting skill and bravery. It would seem that Osage men are not as concerned about showing bravery, using clubs on female Kiowas the way you described."

"I couldn't stand by an' watch it happen," Eli remembered. "Even though it wasn't our fight, I wasn't gonna let those girls get clubbed down when they were defenseless like that. It goes against my grain when a man beats a woman, don't matter what the reason."

Bolivar looked off at darkening hills to the north. "It may have serious consequences, my friends, although I feel I understand why you took action. The Osage warriors may return to seek revenge for their killed brethren."

"Let 'em come," Seth said evenly, looking across the flames from hooded eyelids, his deeply lined face taking on a savage countenance as he tested the turkey with the tip of his footlong skinning knife. "If they's lookin' for another fight I've got just the remedy for it. The ones we don't shoot I'll split open like ripe melons." His expression relaxed some. "I don't figure they'll come after us, not after they seen what a Whitney rifle did to their friends. The others ran like scared rabbits when they saw what happened. If they'd wanted a fight, we was right there to oblige 'em. But if they do come back I'll spill their guts all over this red ground, so's the dirt's got an excuse for bein' red."

Bolivar's face mirrored surprise, even a trace of fear as he listened to Seth. "At first meeting, you seem like such a gentle fellow in spite of your tremendous size, Mr. Booker. Hearing you now, I see you have another side, a violent side, yet you are so gentle with my mule and you've shown me nothing but kindness."

Eli grinned when Seth said nothing. "He's gentle, unless he gets riled. If I were you I wouldn't get in his way when he gets on a mad, 'cause he don't know his own strength an' he sure don't take well to somebody pushin' him. There's a few river pirates down at the bottom of the Mississippi feedin' turtles who wished they'd never tangled with ol' Seth Booker."

Bolivar swallowed, glancing from Eli to Seth. "Then you've killed men before?" he asked softly.

Seth gave the priest a chilly stare. "Some, them that had it comin'. Can't recall ever killin' nobody who didn't need killin'."

Bolivar seemed reluctant to pursue the subject further, but he added one more quiet observation. "You should ask God for His forgiveness, Mr. Booker. If you wish, I'll hear your confession and offer prayers for your eternal salvation. I feel sure you believe there were circumstances requiring you to take the lives of other men."

Seth's irritation was beginning to show. "There damn sure was circumstances, Father, like when some son of a bitch comes at me with a knife or a gun. I don't reckon I need none of your prayers. If the Almighty asks me why I done it, I'll remind Him of those . . . circumstances you was talkin' about. But until there comes a judgment day, if there is such a thing, I'm gonna keep on killin' the rotten bastards who need it. Like them bald Injun cowards who beat up on those women today. I figure the Almighty was real glad to see us come along when we did."

A bullfrog began croaking somewhere downriver. Bolivar turned his attention to Eli. "In Father Augustine's diary he warns of a Kiowa's hostile nature. Perhaps an Indian war between the Kiowas and Osages will begin over today's encounter. Our lives could be in danger if we are caught between warring Indian tribes."

Eli listened to the frog a moment. "Not much we can do if that happens, besides stay out of the way. There's a war goin' on in Texas with the Mexican army. It's been my experience that it's mighty hard to find a place on earth where men ain't tryin' to kill each other. One reason me an' Seth came up this river is we got tired of fightin' river pirates. This country seemed real peaceful, 'til today. I reckon it don't matter where a man looks for peace, there's always somebody else lookin' for trouble. If they'll allow it, we aim to trap beaver in this neck of the woods without givin' those Kiowas no reason to start a fight. We're offerin' an honest trade with 'em, if somebody can make 'em understand."

"Father Augustine will know how," Bolivar assured him as he edged closer to the fire.

Eli left his doubts unsaid. Mose and Frenchy would have known about it if anyone else was in Kiowa country. For now his worries centered around the return of an Osage raiding party looking for vengeance against the men who interfered with their raid on a Kiowa camp. He looked across the flames and spoke to Seth. "We shouldn't be too far from the Washita by now. I'll take a look at that map later on. There's hardly any landmarks to speak of."

Seth shrugged. "I don't figure the map's done us a bit of good. Damn near every mile of this river looks the same. Back yonder aways I did see what looked like a low mountain way off to the northwest. Maybe we ain't far from the Washita Mountains Mose told us about. If we don't run into no more trouble with Injuns, maybe we'll see that river's mouth in a few days."

"I'll take the first watch tonight, just to be on the safe side. Let me know soon as that turkey's done. I'm hungry enough to eat the stick runnin' through it." He got up and gathered his ammunition pouch and rifle, looking both ways along the river for a piece of high ground.

"You are expecting trouble from the Osages, aren't you?" Bolivar asked in a tight voice.

"Just bein' careful, Father. A man learns to stay alive by seein' trouble before it comes." He walked softly into the dark toward a line of trees running east and west on a rise above the river, cradling the Whitney in the crook of his arm.

He tread lightly across fallen leaves and twigs until he found the spot he wanted with a view of the river and hilly land along the north bank. Settling down with his back to a tree, he let his eyes grow accustomed to the darkness. Down below, their fire twinkled in the night, flickering when slow night breezes swept gently across the river. He listened to crickets chirp and an owl's haunting call for several minutes. More bullfrogs up and down the bank croaked endlessly.

He rested his head against the tree trunk, remembering the pretty Kiowa girl and her tentative show of friendliness when she returned the peace sign. "Maybe things'll work out after all," he muttered softly. Gazing across the river now, he found he was enjoying the night's tranquility, its peace. Scenes like this had floated through his mind ever since Frenchy and Mose told him about Red River country. He let his imagination wander, to the possibility he might find an Indian girl like the one he saw at the village. How nice it would be, he thought, to have a pretty woman like her to share his life out here in the wilderness. He knew he would be happy, content.

Off in the night a coyote barked, then it howled, and the sound was so mournful and lonely it made him feel a touch of sadness. He decided, after a bit, that this land was a place created for solitary men like him, those who sought empty spaces unspoiled by civilization. Parts of the Mississippi had been like that in the beginning, until westward expansion brought towns and farms to more and more miles of its shores. He recalled feeling a trace of sadness then, when there were fewer empty regions for his flatboat to travel. He understood even then he was built differently, seeking solitude rather than the company of others. Perhaps this was why Marybeth left him so long ago . . . she never understood his need to be away on a river where the crush of city life made him so restless.

He looked down at the rifle resting on his lap when he grew tired of thinking about Marybeth. In light from the stars its brass mountings and patchbox appeared dull, neglected, and he resolved to give the Whitney a good cleaning and oiling tomorrow morning. The gun had killed an Osage Indian today with a suresightedness he'd come to trust. He wondered if his rifle would kill again before they found the peace he and Seth were looking for. He'd never kept a tally of the men he killed, not after the very first one. Someone . . . he couldn't remember who, told him a man always remembered the first life he took. Eli had been just shy of nineteen when an argument with a sailor turned ugly, mean. The Portuguese was big, scarred from previous fights and tattooed on both cheeks, he recalled. He had pulled an old flintlock from inside a moth-eaten seaman's coat, waving it back and forth while he cursed Eli for tripping over his shoe in a smoky barroom in the New Orleans wharf district. Eli grabbed for the gun, twisting it free of the sailor's grasp just as it went off with the muzzle underneath the sailor's chin. The Portuguese's head came apart in bloodly fragments, flying all over the bar and ceiling and Eli's arms in sodden chunks of bone and flesh and hair. He still dreamed about it now and then, awakening in a cold sweat.

Since then there had been others, faces he scarcely remembered from encounters he couldn't recall without difficulty. He had never wanted to kill another human being . . . events had given him no choice over the years. Life on a flatboat was always full of danger, from the river itself and a rough breed of men who plied it for a living. He'd grown to manhood among them, these river people, and survived somehow. A few Indians with flint weapons could hardly be any worse than the types he'd known.

Listening to the Red River's gentle sounds, he knew why he had come here. It wasn't to escape pirates or dangers along the Mississippi. He was looking for a new start, a new life away from his past, a place where he could begin again and live in peace among beautiful, unspoiled surroundings.

"Just a few more days," he whispered, briefly closing his eyes to think about what lay in store.

Chapter

Nine

The land changed slowly as they continued west, broken by deep gullies twisting through thickly forested hills. More creeks fed into the river now, and along some of the streams they saw beaver sign— gnawed stumps where the animals felled trees to make their dams.

"We're close," Seth said from his vantage point in the prow as they paddled steadily into strengthening currents where creeks added flow to the river. "I can feel it in my bones, Cap'n."

"This is damn sure beaver country. If we wanted, we could set traplines right here this winter. No tellin' how many dams are up those feeder creeks."

"Frenchy claimed the best trappin' was off that Washita," Seth remembered. "I've got a feelin' it ain't far to the mouth of it."

Eli had been examining the surrounding hills for signs they were being watched by Indians. "If you're right, this figures to be the heart of the Kiowa range." He let his gaze wander from one hilltop to the next, pausing where a shadow didn't seem natural. "Sure hadn't seen no trace of an Indian since we left that Kiowa village. Kinda strange, that they don't seem to be watchin' us like they did."

"Frenchy said they hunted buffalo real hard in the fall so's they'd have meat for the winter. Maybe that explains why none of 'em are around just now . . . they's off followin' buffalo herds like the one we saw that day."

"Makes sense, I reckon." Eli glanced back to see how far the priest had fallen behind. "Father Bolivar ain't makin' very good time through all these trees." He noted the angle of the sun. "It's nearly noon an' we've already lost sight of him back yonder. Let's find a place to pull out of the water where we can wait for him . . . maybe up the next creek we find with beaver sign. We can walk upstream an' see how big their dams are, maybe get a guess as to how many make up a colony in these parts."

Seth's expression said he wasn't too happy over the delay. "We'd have been there by now if it wasn't for him, only I don't s'pose we coulda just left him where we found him." Squinting in the glare off the river, he pointed west. "Yonder's a creek feedin' the channel. We can tie off an' walk it out . . . see if there's a dam somewheres."

They rowed steadily into the current for half a mile before they came to the stream. Farther up the creek's banks they saw a number of gnawed stumps. Seth aimed the prow for a low spot where marsh grasses grew among scattered cattails and reeds.

The canoe edged into still waters. A fish darted away from the sound of paddles, leaving a telltale swirl near a clump of marsh grass. Seth stepped out and towed the boat ashore before Eli left his seat carrying his rifle.

"Bring your guns just in case," Eli said, casting a look up and down the riverbank. "Just because we ain't seen any Indians don't mean they aren't close by." He tucked the Paterson into his belt and hefted the rifle.

They walked along the steam, pausing where bea-

ver had chewed down smaller oak and elm. Narrow beaver trails ran back and forth through thickets on either
side of the creek. Moving slow and cautious, they went
several hundred yards beside a shallow ribbon of water
glistening over rocks where sunlight beamed down
through thick branches.

"This creek's mighty small," Seth observed. "Damn
near down to a trickle. Those beaver must have built
one hell of a dam up yonder someplace."

Eli was paying more attetion to the forest. A feeling down the back of his neck had begun to worry him.
"Maybe we hadn't oughta go no farther, Seth. Somethin' don't feel quite right around here."

Seth scanned the wooded slopes carefully. "Don't
see no reason to worry," he said quietly, balancing the
Whitney in his palm, "but if you've taken a notion to go
back, it suits me." He took a few more steps toward a
bend in the stream. "Look at that big dam, Eli! It's just
around the bend. Big, an' as wide as a paddle wheeler.
We come this far. Let's have a look."

Still feeling uneasy, he nodded agreement and
trudged along behind Seth, keeping an eye on the forest. But when they rounded the bend and saw a massive
logjam daming the creek, he forgot all his concerns and
grinned. "Let's see how many beaver domes we can
count. I see half a dozen from here. . . ." He started
off in a hurried walk toward the dam, when suddenly,
slapping noises came from all sides of a pond created by
the logjam. Several beaver had begun to slap their
broad, flat tails on the surface of the pool as a warning
to the others that danger was near.

"Look at 'em run!" Seth exclaimed, pointing to
furry brown animals racing out of thickets near the water, scurrying low to the ground until they splashed into
the pool. "Damn! Ain't that a pretty sight?"

Eli counted eight or nine beaver swimming across
the pond toward domes made of mud and sticks floating
on the surface. "It is a mighty pretty sight," he agreed,
stopping beside an oak tree to continue making his

count. "There's better'n two dozen we can see, an' no tellin' how many we missed. We're gonna be rich as kings, Seth, come springtime." All at once he forgot about weeks of monotonous river travel, confronted by a scene he'd dreamt about almost every night since he and Seth made up their minds to go up the Red.

Seth was grinning. " 'Stead of countin' beaver it's the same as countin' money. Hardly no need to cure coon pelts at two bits apiece when there's so many beaver. Coon's only gonna get in the way, bein' as they's half the price. We'll have to build us a log raft big as a house to get all them furs back to New Orleans. It'll be so heavy our biggest worry's gonna be sinkin', furs an all. Frenchy an' Mose was right . . . this is sure enough the best beaver country in the world."

Eli examined a wide clearing around the pool where beaver had taken down virtually every tree. "This dam's been here for a long time," he said. "Nobody came along to disturb 'em while they built it. Trappin' here is gonna be easy, like pickin' corn at harvest time on the Mississipp'."

Beaver swam toward their domes, cutting tiny wakes across the smooth surface of the pond until they disappeared underwater to hide in their floating nests. Eli was satisfied. "Let's head back to the canoe. I'll grind up an' boil some of those coffee beans you fried this mornin' until the priest catches up. We're in beaver country, so there ain't no reason to hurry." He gave the pond a final look and sauntered away from the beaver dam with high expectations. With pelts bringing half a dollar next spring he and Seth would amass a small fortune by the time ice melted.

They could hear cart wheels creaking and the rattle of chain to the east. It had taken Father Bolivar almost three hours to catch up through a dense forest. Eli savored his last mouthful of coffee . . . they had precious few beans to last them until spring, and whenever possible they boiled the last drop of flavor out of every parched handful.

Seth was standing beside the river with a baited hook trying to catch a catfish for supper, having little success. A warm wind blew from the west, rippling otherwise calm waters across a broad expanse of river where they built their fire on a high bank so the priest could see their smoke.

"Don't look like we'll be havin' fish tonight," Seth said, moving his line to a deeper spot when he wheeled around, crouching down, pointing to something. "Get your gun, Eli!" he cried, tossing his fishing line down before he ran to the canoe to pick up his pistol and rifle.

Eli scrambled for his Whitney—his Paterson was in his belt. "What is it?" he asked, hunkering down behind the cottonwood he'd been leaning against earlier.

"Injuns. Lots of 'em. See yonder?" Seth hid behind a tree, peering around it.

Movement in the forest quickly caught Eli's attention. He saw several horses walking among shadows beneath limbs thick with colorful fall leaves. "Damn," he whispered. "Can you tell if their heads are shaved?"

"Can't see from here. Most likely them Osages, come back to square things for the men we shot." Seth cocked an ear. "I can still hear that priest's wagon. Wonder why they ain't already took his hair?"

Bolivar's wagon rattled closer, banging iron-rimmed wheels over hard ground and rocks. "I can't figure it," Eli replied, as the shapes of mounted Indians appeared to be moving down a tree-studded slope toward them. "They're headed straight for us, it looks like." Slowly, he lifted his rifle to his shoulder.

Crossing a patch of sunlight, one Indian, Eli noticed, had a flowing mane of hair. "They ain't Osages," he called over to Seth. "They've got long hair, whoever they are."

Eight or nine Indians came through the forest, winding around trees, spread out in an uneven line. Mottled sun and shade made their ponies look dappled.

"They's got us with our backs to the river, Eli. We got no place to run when they rush us."

"Use your pistol when they get real close. Won't be time to load our rifles but once or twice."

One Indian rode into an opening in the forest where the sun struck his face. Eli noticed his hair, how gray it was, almost silver. The old man halted his bay pony and sat perfectly still in the sunlight, watching Seth and Eli. He carried no weapons Eli could see, no bow and arrows or a spear. The other Indians stopped their ponies now, and for a moment the only sound was the rattle of Father Bolivar's cart.

"It don't appear they're armed," Eli said quietly.

Seth was looking east. "Here comes that damn fool priest, ridin' right into the middle of 'em like he didn't know they was there. They'll kill him for sure. . . ."

The cart came bouncing over the crest of a wooded hill with Father Bolivar slumped on the seat.

"May not be anything we can do to save him," Eli observed as the cart rolled over the hilltop, moving almost directly into the midst of the Indians. He turned his attention back to the old man on the bay pony, wondering why none of the Kiowas seemed to be paying any notice to the priest's arrival. "I can't figure why they ain't carrin' any weapons . . . at least the old man up yonder don't have any."

Bolivar saw Eli and Seth and he immediately cupped his hands around his mouth. "Don't shoot at them! They've come peacefully! They've been following me for leagues!"

"Wonder what this is all about?" Seth muttered. "Wonder how come they didn't kill him?"

"I 'spect we'll find out soon enough."

The cart creaked and bumped down to the fire, where Bolivar stopped his donkey and jumped from the cart. He hurried over to Eli, pointing uphill at the Indians. "It's a party of women, led by the older man you can see. I believe they are making it quite clear they wish to speak with us. They took no hostile action at all when they first saw me."

As the priest was speaking the old Indian urged his pony to a walk, riding closer, while the other Indians moved their ponies alongside his downslope toward the river. When they came to the edge of the forest, again the old man stopped his pony.

"They's all womenfolk, 'cept for the old one," Seth said.

Eli recognized a face among the women. "It's the girl who gave us the peace sign back at that Kiowa village . . . she's with them, third one from the left." He lowered his rifle and took a step away from the cottonwood, lifting his right hand, palm open.

The girl raised her hand, returning his sign, as did the old Indian a second later. For a few moments they sat their horses holding open palms.

"Try an' talk to 'em for us," Eli told Bolivar. "Tell 'em we come as friends, that we don't want no trouble."

Bolivar's face flushed. "I'm not sure I can say all of those things, Mr. McBee, however I shall do my best to let them know we have only peaceful intentions." He turned to the slope and strode forward, showing more courage than Eli guessed he might.

"Hi hites. Hein ein mah-su-ite."

Eli doubted the Kiowas understood. Bolivar's words sounded more like grunts than recognizable things.

The old man lowered his palm. *"Hi hites, Powva. To-quet. Hah-ich-ka sooe ein conic?"*

Bolivar looked over his shoulder. "He returned my greeting and he says it is good. I believe he is asking where we live, or where we come from. I don't know how to answer him."

"Try an' tell him we came to trade for furs," Eli suggested. "Try to explain why we're here."

The priest turned back to the hillside. *"Nodemah. Nodemah. Hites. Hites."* Saying this, he spoke to Eli again. "Show him a few of your beads, or a knife. I don't know the words in Kiowa language. I've forgotten the word for knife."

Eli leaned his rifle against the tree and walked over to the canoe, opening a pack while keeping his eyes on the Kiowas, in particular the pretty girl he remembered. He took out a string of beads and a knife. All of the Indians were watching him very carefully, yet none had moved.

He walked back to Bolivar, standing beside him, holding out the knife and beads. "Tell them these are for him, for the old man. I figure he's some kind of chief."

Bolivar pointed to the old man. *"Ein mah-heep-cut."* Then he took the knife and beads and began walking slowly uphill to the spot where the Indian sat his horse.

Eli watched closely as Bolivar handed the Kiowa a string of blue beads and the knife. The old man said something, and when the priest wagged his head, trying to show he didn't understand, the Kiowa repeated what he said.

The girl was looking directly at Eli, apparently ignoring what was going on between the priest and the old man. She did not smile this time, yet he was sure there was a friendliness behind her stare.

Bolivar backed away a few steps. The Indian examined the knife closely, feeling its edge, with the beads dangling from his wrist. He spoke again, and again Bolivar could only wag his head and shrug.

"I don't know what he's telling me," the priest cried over his shoulder.

Unexpectedly, the girl spoke. "Chocufpe say is good. You kill Nah-taih. Is good."

"She speaks English!" Bolivar cried, pointing to the girl as though no one else heard what she said. He looked at her in amazement. "I must ask you where you learned English," he went on quickly.

She looked to the old Indian, as if for approval before she spoke. "Know some. *Powva* show me."

"Powva? That's your word for priest, isn't it?" he asked.

Their conversation ended abruptly when the old man spat out a string of words. Two Indian women rode their ponies a few feet closer where they tossed big bundles to the ground. Before Eli had a chance to see the bundles clearly, the Kiowas wheeled their horses and struck a trot back up the hillside, departing without a word of explanation for the bundles they left behind.

"They's animal skins," Seth said. "Looks like big buffalo hides from here."

Before Eli could reply, Bolivar's excited voice interrupted him. "Did you hear what she said, Mr. McBee? A priest taught her English. This is proof Father Augustine and his workers are here! And they're alive!"

"I heard," he answered, watching the Indians ride out of sight among the trees. "I wonder why they wouldn't wait long enough for us to explain to the girl what we wanted. The old Indian was in a big hurry to clear out for some reason."

Bolivar knelt beside one of the bundles. "These buffalo skins are gifts, for saving them from the Osage attack when you found their village. I'm quite sure that's what he was saying."

Eli saw the last Kiowa disappear into forest shadows. "At least we know we can make 'em understand what we want. The girl can translate for us, only I can't figure why they left so sudden just now, before we had a chance to tell 'em what we're after. Don't make much sense they'd ride off like that . . . unless they figured we were up to somethin'."

Seth edged away from the tree, keeping an eye on the hills where the Kiowas had ridden. "Maybe they don't trust us just yet, Cap'n. Could be it'll take time before they let their guard down."

Eli wasn't listening. He was thinking about the girl.

Chapter
Ten

"*We-iti.*" Bolivar said the word over and over again as they sat by the fire. "*We-iti.* I must remember their word for knife. I was never good with languages." He frowned at the pages of the diary.

"You speak right good English for a Spaniard, Father," Seth observed.

"I was educated in English and Spanish. It was the bishop's order that we become fluent in both languages when we were small boys, to prepare us for work in the New World. I was young then, and learning came naturally. As you can see, I have no facility for learning languages now. I have difficulty with my memory."

"How old are you, Father?" Eli asked, stirring soup made from the last of their turkey meat.

"I am thirty-one this year. I grew up in a monastery in a Mexican village named Saltillo, where young Franciscans prepare for missionary work. Father Esteban and I were schooled together there, which has only worsened my sorrow, having known him most of my life. The Franciscan Order is a way of life for those who take the vows. We were as close as brothers . . .

the Order teaches that we are like brothers, committed to God's work. I have lost a brother, a dear friend, but I shall continue our work as though he were at my side. I'm quite sure the Ki-wa girl was telling us that Father Augustine is alive and well, teaching English and Christianity to her people here. I only wish she could have remained long enough for us to ask her where to find Mission San Miguel. She said *powva* taught her the words, and *powva* is the Ki-wa word for father, according to Father Augustine's diary."

Eli added a pinch of salt to the soup. "That's about the only explanation makes any sense. There sure as hell ain't no English bein' spoken out here otherwise. I hardly recognize the sounds they make. Don't sound like words at all."

Seth chuckled softly. "I tried to learn French from Bessie one time, a little bit, only my mouth wasn't shaped right to get it said. I remember my mama spoke real bad English. She used to scold me in French when she got mad, only I never understood what she was sayin'. My pappy never would allow her to speak French 'round the house, on account of he said we had to know English if we aimed to live in this country."

Bolivar turned a page in his book. "Father Augustine writes that Mission San Miguel is being built up a river coming from the mountains. Twenty leagues from where this river joins the Rio Rojo there is a small mountain overlooking the river valley and it is there where I will find them."

"That's about sixty mile, Father," Seth said. "I 'spect you go most of that distance alone. Me an' the Cap'n are gonna start lookin' for beaver streams off that Washita, ain't we, Eli?"

Eli thought about it. "We hadn't planned on goin' twenty leagues upriver, only maybe if we do find this Father Augustine, he'll know more about the country . . . the lay of things where we'd find the best trappin'. Maybe we could go that far up, seein' as it's so early in the fall. Beaver won't start puttin' on thick hair for a month or two, most likely."

"I'd be very grateful if you accompanied me," Bolivar said, "and I'm certain Father Augustine will know where beaver are the most plentiful."

Seth aimed a thumb over his shoulder, in the direction from which they had come. "Can't hardly be no better'n what we saw up that creek today. Beaver was all over the place, an' that creek was hardly more'n a wet spot."

"Accordin' to Mose, it gets even better after we find the Washita," Eli said. "Maybe we'll go up aways, just to see what the river's like. Let's wait an' see how deep it runs."

"I got the feelin' it ain't far," Seth offered, watching his fishing line as the last rays of sunshine beamed into a rose-colored sky. "We saw a few beaver before, but never so many as today. This is beaver country."

Bolivar returned to his diary. "*Po-ke* is the word for horse in Ki-wa," he said, tipping the book so more firelight struck the pages.

Eli couldn't get his mind off the girl. "She had one of the prettiest faces I ever saw. When she was lookin' at me, it made me feel a little loose in the knees an' my belly did this twitch inside me."

Seth laughed again. "Damn if you ain't got moon-eyed over a woman before you even knowed her name, Eli. That gal's all you been talkin' about since they gave us them buffalo hides. If I didn't know you better I'd nearly swear you was fallin' in love. Must be somethin' else, 'cause you ain't never stayed in love with the same woman more'n one night after you an' Marybeth went different ways."

"I wouldn't call it love, exactly. She's just so pretty I couldn't take my eyes off her."

"*We-iti,*" Bolivar mumbled, making it perfectly clear he had no interest in discussing women with them.

*   *   *

The mouth of the river was wide, running deep as though rain had fallen upsteam recently, increasing the Red's flow, which they felt rushing against the canoe for almost an hour before rounding a turn where they found what Eli believed was the Washita.

"Yonder she is, Cap'n," Seth announced. Far off to the west and north a range of low mountains purpled with haze.

"They shoulda named it the Beaver River," Eli said, paddling harder to make a swing into the river's mouth against an onrush of muddy water where the rivers joined. Eddies formed in slower backwaters, making for easier rowing when they finally got the canoe turned. "Never saw so much beaver sign in all my days. I gave up countin' stumps a long time ago. There could be more'n a million of 'em here."

Seth's muscular arms glistened with sweat from faster rowing, and his sleeveless shirt clung to his back like a second skin in midday heat. "This river's plenty wide enough for a log raft to haul down our pelts. Plenty of tall trees to make one, too. All we gotta do is make them Injuns understand what we want so's they don't give us no trouble this winter."

Eli had been watching the riverbank for Indians. "No sign of 'em now. Maybe they understood what Father Bolivar was tryin' to say." He scanned the trees again carefully, making sure. "It don't appear they're watchin' us like they did at first. Givin' the old man that knife an' those beads must have done the trick."

Paddling steadily for another quarter hour, they rounded a sharp bend and stopped rowing in unison, when, above treetops in the distance, they saw smoke billowing into a clear sky.

"Sweet Jesus," Eli muttered. "There must be a hundred fires up yonder." Smoke rose in dozens of swirling columns from a wide area beyond the forest. "We couldn't see 'em before because the trees along this river are so tall an' wind's carryin' the smoke smell away from us."

"It has to be an Injun village, Eli," Seth said, resting his paddle across his lap. "A big one. Sure as hell hope they ain't Osages."

"Me too," Eli added quietly, feeling a knot of fear form in his gut. "Whoever they are, there's a bunch of 'em. Fires all over the place. When we paddle 'round that next bend, they'll see us sure. An' this river ain't hardly wide enough for us to stay out of range of an arrow." He studied the forest carefully for a moment. Once, he thought he saw a shadow move from one tree trunk to the next. "I think they already know we're here, Seth. Somethin' moved over yonder near that big red maple tree just now."

"It'd be natural for 'em to post lookouts close to their village so nobody'd slip up on 'em unannounced. If they's Osages we could be in for one hell of a fight. The ones we didn't shoot will remember us. . . ."

The current began carrying the canoe backward when its slow drift upriver ended. Eli watched the woods with the glare of sun off water almost blinding him, paying particular attention to the maple tree where he felt sure he saw movement before. The quiet hiss of water against the canoe was the only sound he heard for several minutes. Smoke rose above treetops in thickening spirals beyond the next turn. He felt his heartbeat quickening.

"We can't hardly stop now. This here's the spot we've been headed for ever since we left New Orleans," Seth said. "Only way we're gonna find out what's up yonder is to paddle that direction 'til we come to it. I say we keep our rifles handy."

When nothing stirred in the forest, Eli said, "I've got this feelin' we could be makin' a big mistake, but let's keep goin', only paddle real slow." He picked up his rifle and laid it over his knees before he put the paddle back in the water.

Seth resumed paddling. They could see the river narrowing as it made its swing eastward.

"We're damn sure gonna be in range of arrows," Seth said as he dipped his paddle deeper with each stroke. "If any trouble starts, turn this boat around an' paddle hard as you can, Cap'n. I ain't lookin' for a way to get any more holes in this ol' body than I already got."

Keeping to the far side of the river, they paddled slowly in steady currents past thick brush growing along both banks, places where Indians could hide. Nearing the bend, Eli was sure he saw shadows moving in the forest now, more than one or two, following their progress upriver.

Long before they began the river's turn, he caught glimpses of fires burning beyond trees lining the bank. And they got a first look at the village moments later as they rounded a sandy shoal.

Across a broad, flat meadow, dozens of animal-skin tents sat in the sunlight . . . Eli guessed there could be fifty or more. All across the meadow hundreds of Indians, both men and women, tended to fires below curious wooden racks. Smoldering green wood gave off so much smoke it was hard to see the entire village. But it was easy to see the Indian men waiting for the canoe along the eastern shore of the Washita. Several dozen men, Kiowas by the way they wore their hair braided, stood by the edge of the river with bows and arrows and spears, watching Seth and Eli paddle into view.

Seth stopped rowing. "They don't look friendly, Cap'n. All of 'em has got weapons, an' they's lookin' at us like they just seen a couple of polecats. We'd best not go no closer."

Eli's heart was racing and his breathing was shallow. This was a moment he'd been dreading, finding a huge Kiowa village at the spot where they hoped to run traplines. "These are the ones we have to convince," he said quietly, paddle frozen in his hands as the canoe slowed to a crawl. "I hope it's the same bunch that girl came from, only there's no way to see her amongst so many of 'em spread out like they are. No sign of that old man, either."

"May not be the same tribe," Seth said. "Frenchy said there was five or six bunches, all with different chiefs. I say it's time to turn back, before we get in range of them arrows."

Now the canoe began to drift backward with the current. Eli had all his attention on men lining the riverbank, and he hardly noticed their slow change in direction. None of the Kiowas were fitting arrows to bowstrings for the present, although he knew things could change suddenly, without warning.

"I wish that priest was here so he could talk for us," Eli muttered.

"It'll be hours before he catches up," Seth said, keeping his voice down. "I remember a couple of words, Cap'n. He said *hi hites* meant, hello my friends, an' that *nodemah* was their word for makin' a trade. It'll be risky as hell, gettin' close enough so we can talk to 'em. That close, they could fill us full of arrows before we can sneeze, there's so many of 'em."

Eli was thinking out loud. "We can hold up a couple of our knives an' some beads while we paddle to shore. If we gave 'em the peace sign an' you said those words, maybe they wouldn't be so quick to shoot."

"If we're wrong, we're dead men," Seth warned. "It's takin' one hell of a big chance."

"We took a hell of a big chance comin' here in the first place. We knew all along this was the part that could be dangerous, makin' our deal with wild savages if we could. Mose and the Frenchman did it. . . ."

Seth turned back to look at Eli. His oversized, hairless skull glistened with sweat and his face was a mask, without a trace of readable expression. His countenance only changed when he was angry. "We ain't no less men than Frenchy an' Mose," he said quietly. "Take out some of them beads an' a knife or two while I row us toward shore. Hold 'em up so's they can see what we got. I'll try an' say them words real loud, if they let us get close enough."

Eli opened a drawstring pack and took out strings of red and yellow beads, and a knife. "Start paddlin'," he said, wondering if he'd just given Seth an order that was about to get them both killed.

Chapter
Eleven

Seventy-five yards from the riverbank, they rowed toward a group of thirty or forty Kiowa men gathering to watch the canoe approach. Eli could hear a few guttural words being spoken among them, senseless strings of noises he doubted that he would ever understand. The men wore a strip of animal skin covering their genitals, or leather leggings. Most were barechested, while some wore a type of deerskin vest. He searched faces of the women he could see working near the odd-shaped wood racks, and although he failed to find the girl, he discovered what the racks were used for. Strips of raw meat lay over a contraption made of small limbs above the flames. Smoke from green firewood surrounded the racks and meat, preserving it, he supposed, for use this winter. But no matter where he looked he found no trace of the pretty Kiowa girl who spoke a few words of English, and he concluded Seth was right when he suggested this group could be another tribe.

The conical tents across the village bore crudely painted designs and symbols similar to the artwork he'd seen on the Kiowa girl's dress, drawings of running horses and deer, buffalo, a sunrise. There was no obvious arrangement to the tents, scattered here and there over the clearing as if by happenstance.

Eli held up the beads and knife to allow as much sunlight as possible to strike them. With the other hand he gave the peace sign, when the distance closed to less than fifty yards. The Kiowa men showed no recognition and appeared to be paying little attention to the trade items. Seth paddled a few more strokes before he cried, *"Hi hites. Hi hites. Nodemah!"* He pulled off his shirt because of the heat and continued rowing.

A stirring occurred among the closest Kiowas. They spoke to each other, gesturing toward the canoe. They seemed confused, hearing a man of another race speak their language. Or was it that they didn't understand him at all?

Twenty-five yards from shore some of the men stepped back, while others simply stood there, holding bows without fitting an arrow to the bowstring, showing no signs of aggression.

"Hi hites! Nodemah!" Seth cried again.

Eli turned the knife and beads to show them clearly what he was carrying, still holding his palm open. They were in potentially deadly range of arrows now . . . at the very least, their bullhide canoe would sink quickly from arrow holes near the waterline.

Some Kiowas turned when a man emerged from one of the tents. He was slightly taller than the others, more muscular, and his face appeared flatter, more menacing, if Eli could judge by his expression. He strode toward the water, saying something to one or two of the other men before he reached the riverbank.

Seth shouted, *"Hi hites! Nodemah!"*

To emphasize what they wanted to trade, Eli held the items higher. "The big one's some sort of chief," he told Seth, never taking his eyes from the men with bows and spears. "If he gives the order to kill us, we'll be sittin' ducks, bein' this close."

The smell of smoke drifted across the water when winds made a slight change in direction. The canoe came closer and now Eli could see the Kiowas' faces clearly. They had steeply angled noses, bent down as though they'd been broken, with hard black eyes that never seemed to blink or waver. They watched the men in the canoe warily, but made no show of hostility.

Seth braked the canoe to a halt with his paddle, letting it sit still for a moment. *"Hi hites. Nodemah."*

The tall Kiowa came to the edge of the river, staring into Seth's eyes, then Eli's. He said something, only a few clipped sounds coming from the back of his throat, making a sweeping motion with his right hand.

"There ain't no way to tell him we don't understand," Seth said over his shoulder.

In the following silence Eli noticed a distant sound coming from the center of the village . . . it could have been women crying or wailing. "About all we can do is get close enough so I can give 'em these beads an' the knife," he said. "Looks like, if they aimed to kill us, they'd have started fillin' us with arrows by now. Let's paddle up to the bank. I'll get out an' hand the tall one what we're offerin'. Keep your rifle real handy, only don't shoot unless somethin' goes wrong."

Seth paddled a few more strokes, sending the canoe straight for shore. More Indians approached the riverbank, coming from all over the village to stare at the new arrivals. Most of them were staring at Seth, pointing to him.

Where water was barely a foot deep, Eli swung a leg over the side of the canoe and stepped out, extending his gift in an outstretched hand while trying to get his balance in river mud and sand. He walked toward the Kiowa leader, whispering to himself until he stood on dry land.

"Hi hites. Nodemah."

The Kiowa looked at Eli's beads. He made a grunting noise and reached for the knife, snatching it from Eli's palm as if he feared it might be taken away. He examined the blade carefully, touching the edge with his fingers, then the tip. His gaze went to Seth immediately thereafter as though he was curious about the color of Seth's skin.

Eli turned to a younger Indian standing beside him. He held out a string of yellow beads. The Kiowa seemed uncertain, after a sideways glance at his leader, then he reached for the beads very slowly and accepted them, saying nothing.

Eli offered the red beads to another Kiowa. *"Nodemah,"* he said. The Indian took them cautiously, keeping his eyes on Eli.

The leader spoke to Eli then, and no single word was distinguishable from any other. His obsidian eyes were fixed on Eli's face, and Eli felt sure he was awaiting some sort of answer to a question. Again, his eyes flickered to Seth, where they remained for several seconds.

"We don't speak your language," Eli said, noticing a sweet smell coming from the Indians' hair and skin, something akin to a flower's scent. "I don't know what you're askin' me. The only words we know in Kiowa are, *hi hites* an' *nodemah*. We can't say nothin' else in your tongue." As he spoke, he noticed several of the men standing around him had tiny red bumps on their faces and upper bodies. Some had become open sores oozing pus. He took a second, closer look at one of the young men covered by sores and he knew at once what it was.

Eli spoke to Seth without turning around. "Looks like some of 'em have got smallpox. Take a look at the red bumps on their faces." He and Seth had both survived smallpox epidemics sweeping through New Orleans back in the late twenties.

Seth answered very softly. "That do appear to be what it is they's got, Cap'n."

The tall Kiowa spoke once more, and as before, Eli could not recognize a word. The Indian was looking at Seth when he talked.

"We don't understand," Eli explained, certain now that the Indian had no idea what he was saying. He pointed to the river behind him, indicating that he and

Seth meant to travel upstream. "We may be able to find somebody who can speak your language for us in a few days. Meantime, we'll just be on our way."

As Eli was turning for the canoe, the Kiowa spoke sharply to an Indian standing behind him. The younger boy took off at a run into the heart of the village, causing Eli to stop and ponder why he'd been sent away.

Seth was wondering too. "Maybe they's got somebody who can talk English, Cap'n. Could be that's why one of 'em ran off just now. Let's wait an' see if he comes back. Maybe it's that girl you been daydreamin' about."

Eli noticed the Kiowa spokesman examining his knife again with a slight frown on his face, turning it over in his hands, letting sunlight reflect off its surface as though he'd never seen a metal object before.

A commotion in the village caused Eli to glance that way as voices ended a moment of silence. Then he saw a sight that made him take a deep breath . . . every muscle in his body tensed. A man was being led toward the river by a rope tied to a collar around his neck, pulled by two young Kiowa men. The man wearing the rope was starved beyond belief, completely naked other than the leather collar around his neck, little more than a skeleton with sun-darkened skin stretched over his bones. He staggered as the rope was being pulled and almost fell, struggling to remain on his feet while answering the pull on the rope with bony fingers holding his collar away from his throat to keep from strangling. Even from a distance it was easy to see he was not an Indian, and it was clear he was a prisoner here. His features were so badly sunken it was hard to tell what his face might have looked like otherwise.

The Kiowas pulled their starved prisoner down to the river, and when they arrived, the others stood aside. Eli gave Seth a quick backward glance, then he turned to the prisoner, looking for some sort of explanation.

The man's dark green eyes looked dull. He stared at Eli for a moment, swaying drunkenly to stay on his

feet, touching his bony ribcage with trembling fingers.
He had dark purple bruises over most of his body and
several old cuts that had begun to heal over with scabs.
"Are you Englishmen?" a thin, weak voice asked, looking past Eli to the canoe and Seth.

"We're from New Orleans," Eli replied softly,
barely able to speak after a closer examination of the
prisoner's tragic physical condition. "Why have they got
that rope around your neck?"

Tears brimmed in his eyelids now. "They made me
a slave of sorts. There was a misunderstanding. They
believe my followers and I brought a curse to their people. Many of them are dying from smallpox and they
believe we are the cause of it, that their gods have
turned against them because they listened to us."

"Your followers?" Eli asked without thinking.
"Who are you? And what are you doin' here in the first
place?"

"My name," he began, "is Augustine Huerta. I am
Franciscan, a Catholic priest. We came here last year to
build a mission in the wilderness to teach Christian principles to these people, the Ki-wa tribe. We began building our church. My stonemasons did splendid work and
we established peaceful relations with the Ki-was. Until
the terrible sickness began. Some of them died last fall.
During the winter it only grew worse. The disease has
spread to neighboring tribes, the Comonses and Osage.
They seem to have no natural ability to survive smallpox
and now they are dying at an alarming rate. This spring,
Chief White Mountain came with a hundred warriors.
They killed my Franciscan brothers in the most brutal
fashion imaginable, taking me prisoner, making me a
slave. They starved me, as you can see, and unless the
epidemic ends soon, they will kill me. They believe we
brought some evil spirit among their people. More are
dying every day. . . ."

"You're Father Augustine," Eli said. "One of your
priests, a fellow by the name of Father Bolivar, is behind
us, lookin' for you and a mission called San Miguel. He

was sent here from San Antonio to bring you seeds and supplies, only he got robbed by a couple of soldiers when war with Mexico broke out down in Texas. The priest who was with him was killed. Father Bolivar is only a few hours from here, travelin' by donkey cart, headed this way."

"They will kill him when they see his cleric's robes. They believe we are something evil. They are keeping me alive so they can torture me, believing it may appease their gods."

Seth spoke quietly from the canoe's prow. "Only way to stop smallpox is separate them that's got it from them that ain't, an' to burn their clothes an' bedding. How come you ain't told 'em that?"

"They no longer listen to anything I say, believing I am an evil spirit."

Suddenly, the Kiowa chief spoke, pointing to the canoe, at Seth. *"To-oh tivo. Tuh-yah po-haw-cut."*

Eli looked to Father Augustine for an explanation.

"Chief White Mountain asks if the Negro is a medicine man from some unknown tribe. In Kiowa religion they speak of black medicine men who returned from the dead in olden days. The chief is not sure if they should be afraid of him, of his spiritual medicine. He asks if the Negro can be a messenger god from the spirit world below ground. These are very superstitious people. They act like they are somewhat afraid of him, of the color of his skin and his tremendous size."

Eli was about to ask the priest to explain, when Seth spoke softly behind him.

"Let 'em think whatever they want, Cap'n so long as they don't start shootin' arrows at us."

All eyes were on Seth as he talked, and Eli wondered if the deep sound of his voice added to the Indians' fear of him. "Get out of the canoe, Seth, so they can see you're a man. Don't do anything to frighten 'em . . . just walk up here beside me so they can see you're made of flesh an' bone."

Seth stepped slowly out of the canoe with his rifle

in his hands. "I ain't comin' without these guns, Cap'n, no matter what you say. Don't none of 'em look all that friendly."

When Seth stood his full height, several Kiowa men backed away from the river's edge. Chief White Mountain remained where he was as Seth walked out of the river. But when Seth stopped alongside Eli, the chief looked up at Seth, being as he was a full head taller than the Indian, and for the first time Eli noticed a subtle change in the chief's flat expression. He looked at the rifle Seth carried, then he spoke to Father Augustine.

"To-oh tivo tuh-yah po-haw-cut te-bit-se." he said. *"Pe-ie ein mah-ri eh ah-hit-to."*

"Chief White Mountain says this black giant is surely the medicine man who comes back from the dead," Augustine explained. "He asks about the gun. He calls it a medicine rod or stick, and he has heard from other tribes of a medicine rod that makes a big noise and kills its enemies. He also says to tell the giant they want peace with him. They have never seen a Negro before, nor a man his size. To them, he is a medicine man sent from the spirit world and I'm afraid almost nothing will change their minds."

"Suits the hell outa me," Seth muttered. "They won't be as likely to try an' kill us."

Eli noticed Chief White Mountain was still glancing warily at Seth's rifle. "In that case, we'll make the best of it," he said. He spoke to Father Augustine. "Tell them Seth is like a medicine man, a doctor, an' if they'll listen, he can show 'em how to end their smallpox, if they'll do exactly like he says. We'll have 'em move the ones with pox to a separate place an' burn all the clothing. The ones with red spots have to stay off to themselves for several weeks."

"It's the way they done it in New Orleans," Seth remembered aloud. "Tell 'em we can stop it from spreadin' if they'll listen an' do what we say."

Augustine turned to the chief. He began speaking Kiowa, and to Eli it sounded no differently than when it was spoken by the Indians. But even while the naked priest was talking, most every Kiowa was watching Seth closely.

"Nearly makes me wanna laugh," Seth whispered in Eli's ear. "Anybody who thinks I'm an Injun medicine man has gotta be a bit on the crazy side. Appears they never heard of no black slaves."

As soon as Augustine finished his explanation, Chief White Mountain pointed to Seth's rifle.

"Pe-ie. Nah-ich-ka."

Augustine spoke softly. "He wants to hear the medicine rod make a loud noise. I'm sure it will frighten them and I pray you won't shoot anyone during the demonstration."

Seth adopted a serious look. "Tell the chief I'm gonna fire it up at the sky, to kill the evil spirits causin' them to die of smallpox. Only remind him, they'll have to do what we say to get rid of it."

Augustine nodded. "I understand. These Ki-was are difficult to turn aside from their primitive beliefs." He turned to Chief White Mountain and spoke rapidly in the Kiowa's tongue.

The moment Augustine fell silent, Seth aimed the muzzle of his Whitney skyward and drew the hammer back. A few Indians standing close backed away; however, the chief stood perfectly still watching Seth's every movement.

To put on a better show, Seth threw back his head and let out a yell. "Hallelujah!"

When he pulled the trigger, the Whitney's explosion sent Indians running in every direction. Only Chief White Mountain stood where he was without flinching, looking up at the sky as though he expected to see something fall from it. As the thunderous noise echoed and faded away, the chief closed the palm of his right hand over his heart and said, *"Su-vate."*

"He believes you now," Father Augustine said.

Chapter Twelve

Seth's rifle shot had an understandable effect on the Kiowa women. They ran in all directions, shouting to each other while some hurried to gather small children in their arms before they disappeared into their tents. Men who had been frightened by it stayed back a safe distance. A few remained close to Chief White Mountain staring at the Whitney's muzzle, or at Seth. As cries the women made died down, a silence spread over the camp.

Seth spoke to Augustine. "Tell the chief I want that rope taken off your neck. Tell him you're gonna help us get rid of the sickness. If he believes I'm some sort of holy man then he oughta do like I say."

The priest seemed doubtful. "I'm not at all sure he'll do that. He is convinced I'm the cause of all the evil that has befallen his people."

"Tell him that I'm orderin' it. You can say I won't lift a finger to help 'em unless they let you go." To emphasize his point, Seth looked at the chief and made motions with one hand that clearly showed he wanted the collar removed.

"You're pushin' mighty hard, Seth" Eli said softly. "Let's see if it works. . . ."

Augustine spoke to Chief White Mountain. As the priest was talking the chief never took his eyes off Seth or his gun. After a lengthy explanation, again there was total silence. For a time Chief White Mountain stared up at Seth without uttering a word or moving a muscle.

Seth sensed the chief's indecision. "I'm gonna do a little more convincin'," he said, pulling his pistol from his belt. He aimed over his head, drew the hammer back, and fired before Eli could argue against it.

The clap of igniting gunpowder from another object startled Chief White Mountain. He flinched as soon as the gun went off, then he blinked twice, looking from the Paterson to Seth's rifle. When he spoke his tone was grave. *"Cona pah-mo. To-oh po-haw-cut che-ak. Suvate."*

"What did he say?" Eli asked.

Before the priest could answer, Chief White Mountain turned. In two short strides he reached Augustine, and with a flash of steel, he used the knife Eli had given him and sliced the plaited rawhide rope off at the collar.

The priest's eyes were bulging with a knife so near his neck, and he gasped as the severed rope fell to the ground. He needed a moment to collect himself before he said, "He is letting me go because of what he believes he has seen . . . he calls it magic. He says the black giant's magic is very powerful, with smoke and fire coming from his thundersticks. He doesn't know what to call a gun and thus he applies his own terms to describe what he believes they are. He says he knows the black giant's medicine is very strong. Otherwise, he could not make thunder and fire come from either hand."

Eli let out a quiet sigh. "Then it's okay if you come with us?"

"He is giving me to the Negro as though I were a piece of property," Augustine replied, "because he is afraid of the black man's magic. It isn't fear in an ordinary sense. These people are afraid of nothing earthly; however, they do fear the wrath of their pagan gods. Chief White Mountain fears the Negro may have the ability to incite his gods against him. He says I am free to go with you. May God be praised that you came here. My prayers have been answered at long last."

The priest took a few uncertain steps toward Eli, his legs trembling with weakness.

"You can hardly walk," Seth observed. "We'll fix you some food, soon as we get away from here."

Augustine reached Eli and put a shaky hand on his shoulder to steady himself. "They only fed me scraps, what they wouldn't eat themselves, the entrails and such. I'm afraid I can't last much longer without nourishment. The past few days I've been so weak and dizzy I could not stand up unassisted." He looked at Seth. "Thank you, dear friends, for what you've done. I feel I owe you my very existence now. In a few more days I would have perished."

Chief White Mountain was watching them, paying the closest attention to Seth. Eli decided to take advantage of the chief's benevolent mood. "Before we leave to look for Father Bolivar, I want you to ask White Mountain somethin' for us. Tell him we've brought knives an' beads to trade with his people for the right to run beaver traps here this winter. Tell him we got plenty of trade goods. All we ask is they leave us alone to run our traplines."

Augustine hobbled around with the help of Eli's shoulder until he was facing the Kiowa chief. He began saying clipped words, strung together in seemingly senseless order, using one frail, bony hand to make gestures while he talked. Eli felt the priest's trembling weakness as he gripped his arm. His legs were so bony his knees looked outsized, too large, and his slender arms were like reed stalks, all his muscles eaten away by starvation.

As soon as Augustine ended his explanation, Chief White Mountain grunted. *"Te-bit-se mon-och. Sic-bah-ton."*

"He wants you to return in one sun, in one more day. He says you will be allowed to trap beaver . . .

they have no use for these animals, finding the meat too tough and tasteless. His principal concern is when the Negro will begin making his good medicine so the sickness will end. He hopes it will be very soon, before more of his people die."

Eli glanced over to Seth. "We can begin separatin' them in the mornin', the sick ones from them that's healthy. If we start at first light, it shouldn't take all day."

Seth nodded. The beginnings of a grin tugged the corners of his mouth. "They think I'm magic, Cap'n." Now his face turned serious. "Have to be real careful not to touch none of them open sores or we'll get the pox ourselves. That's what Bessie told me a long time ago . . . touchin' was what made it spread. Don't touch none of their clothes, neither."

"Let's shove off," Eli suggested, remembering Bolivar and his cart. "We need to warn Father Bolivar what's in store for him up this river. White Mountain made it real plain he ain't got no use for priests."

Seth tucked his pistol in his belt. He gave the village a final look and turned for the canoe, wading into shallow water before he climbed inside and took his paddle, resting the rifle on his lap.

Eli helped Father Augustine to the stern, holding him up in places where deep mud caused him to falter. Moving one of the packs forward allowed just enough room for the priest to sit in front of Eli.

The Kiowas and their chief watched them paddle backward and then begin rowing slowly downstream with the current. Not one of them moved until the canoe floated out of sight around the bend.

Eli noticed the priest's jutting ribs and backbone. "I've got an extra shirt an' some pants I'll give you, Father. You've been out in the sun so long your skin is burnt pretty bad."

"They tied me to a stake in the middle of the village. They taunted me and hurled stones at me every time they walked past. I was treated worse than the low-

liest animal." He lowered his head and started to pray.
"Hail Mary, full of grace, the Lord is with Thee. Blessed
art thou among women, and blessed is the fruit of thy
womb, Jesus. Holy Mary, mother of God, be with us
now and at the hour of our death. Amen." A moment
later, he began sobbing quietly, his thin shoulders shaking with every soft cry until soon, he was gasping for air.

"It's over now, Father," Seth said from the prow,
paddling. "You'll be safe with us, an' we'll fix up somethin' for you to eat soon as we find Father Bolivar."

Augustine straightened his bony spine. "I'm sorry,
gentlemen, for behaving like a child." He sniffled once
and made no more crying sounds.

Seth chuckled softly, without real mirth. "You's just
glad to be alive. Seems mighty natural to be happy 'bout
it. Truth is, when Father Bolivar first told us 'bout you
buildin' a church way up here, we didn't expect to find
none of you alive when we got up this river. We was told
by a couple of trappers who came here last winter that
these Kiowa Injuns are plenty mean, things don't go to
suit 'em."

"They are a warlike people. We believed by teaching them principles of Christianity, it would change
them. Unfortunately we never got the chance."

The canoe drifted easily in swifter current toward
the fork where this smaller river joined the Red. Eli had
only been half listening to Father Augustine's story, remembering their encounter at the village. Seth's physical appearance was a part of the reason for their success
making an arrangement with the Kiowas. They feared
him because of his skin color and unusual height. And
the noise made by his guns. Perhaps for the first time in
Seth's life his Negro ancestry had been a blessing rather
than a curse. Most Negroes were slaves, and only benev-
olence on the part of a landowner's widow allowed Seth
to live as a freedman.

Eli's thoughts returned to what they had seen at the
village, an outbreak of smallpox. "If we aim to set our
lines here this winter we'll have to do all we can to stop

those pox from spreadin'. We'll have to make 'em understand they've got to stay away from the sick ones. That'll be up to you, Father, seein' as you're the only one speaks their language. Word'll have to be sent to other tribes to stay clear of them that's sick. You'll have to explain it."

"It has already spread to branches of the Comonses and one Osage band. As far as we are able to tell, there are five bands of Ki-was, which is what they call themselves. Spanish soldiers dubbed the Comonses, Comanches, although some Ki-was call them by another name, Sata Teichas. Apparently all of them are susceptible to smallpox epidemics. While they seem a very hardy people, they succumb quickly to smallpox."

"I think you avoided answerin' my question," Eli said, with his paddle acting as a rudder now. "Will you go back with us so they'll understand what they have to do after the rough treatment they gave you?"

Augustine needed very little time to answer. "I will. If we are successful, perhaps they will listen to Christ's teachings. I have not given up establishing our mission. Misfortune cost us dearly, the lives of five dedicated priests, but I am not without hope. If this Father Bolivar is willing, we shall try to establish Mission San Miguel on our own. A solid foundation has been laid in stone. If he brought the seeds I requested from Father Tomas, we can plant a garden there next spring."

"He lost some of them seeds," Seth recalled. "When those two soldiers looted him an' killed his partner, they took most of the seeds an' supplies. Seems he claimed he still has a few."

"It will be enough," Augustine said firmly. "We shall grow whatever he has."

They came to the river's mouth and swung downstream along a quiet stretch of the Red, paddling past cattails and willows and brush.

"Don't see no sign of that jackass," Seth said, scanning the bank downriver. "He sure is travelin' slow today."

Eli rummaged through a canvas pack until he found a broadcloth shirt and a pair of pants with patches on the knees. "You can wear these," he said, handing them to Augustine, "only I'd wait 'til we get ashore before you put on them britches, so you don't tip this canoe over wigglin' around."

The priest looked over his shoulder, and when he spoke to Eli his voice was thick with emotion. "God surely sent you to me this day. I'm very grateful."

Seth laughed. "That's the second time a priest has said we was sent some place by the Almighty. Hell, all we done is paddle up a river lookin' for furs. . . ."

Chapter
Thirteen

Eli witnessed a touching meeting between Father Augustine and Father Bolivar when they went ashore. Augustine looked like anything but a priest dressed in Eli's pants and shirt, but when the two met they embraced and held each other as soon as Eli told Bolivar who the stranger was. Augustine began to cry.

"What has happened to your monk's habit, Father, and what is that dreadful collar around your neck?" Bolivar asked, stepping back, concern narrowing his eyes. "Why, you are nothing but skin and bones. . . ."

Augustine sleeved tears from his cheeks. "It is a very long and tragic story, Brother Bolivar. I have been a prisoner of the Ki-was. Things have gone terribly, terribly wrong at the mission and all the others are dead. There was an outbreak of smallpox among the Indians, for which we were blamed. More than a hundred have died and it is spreading to neighboring villages, even to other tribes." He fingered the collar around his throat. "They took me prisoner and kept me at the end of a rope, starving me, hoping to appease their pagan gods by torturing me. Five of our brethren were butchered so savagely I could never describe it to anyone. When I sent my diary to San Antonio, requesting supplies and seeds from the bishop's commissary for our future needs so we might sustain ourselves with gardens, things seemed to be going well. The Indians were peaceful and we truly believed we could begin making a significant number of conversions."

As Augustine was talking, Seth walked up behind him with his knife. "Hold still, Father, an' I'll cut this thing off so's you can breathe. I'm gonna fry up some pan bread an' put on a pot of beans. The bread won't take long. Meantime, come get a strip of jerky so you won't have them shakes so bad."

When the collar fell from his neck, Augustine turned around and spoke to Seth. "I'm so grateful to you and I don't even know your names."

"I'm Seth Booker, an' this is Elias McBee. He goes by Eli. I go by Seth, seein' it's the only name I got."

Bolivar said, "These two men also spared me from starvation, Father. And I fear the story of my travels to reach you is just as tragic. Brother Esteban, my lifelong companion, was killed by two soldiers escorting us north when they heard of the declaration of war made by the Texans. I escaped death by running away to hide in the woods. Most of the supplies and seeds were stolen and there is very little left, a few ornaments for the altar at the mission, a wooden crucifix blessed by Bishop Delgado, and some candles. They took our silver chalice and candle holders, all of the things having monetary value."

Augustine motioned for Bolivar to join him sitting on the riverbank. "I'm afraid I'm almost too weak to stand. Sit with me. We have much to share." He slumped against the trunk of a willow tree and rested his head. "We have both been through a tremendous ordeal in the name of God. We are being tested, both as men and as priests."

Bolivar took a strip of jerky Seth offered and gave it to Augustine, who began chewing it hungrily, muttering "Thank you Mr. Booker" around brittle pieces of dried beef. Eli gathered armloads of driftwood and sticks to begin a fire. The donkey grazed at the end of a rope, still harnessed to its cart shafts. Seth was preparing tinder for a fire, grinding pieces of dry leaves into a powder that would ignite easily.

"We were both fortunate to be met by these kind gentlemen," Bolivar said. "God has directed them to us as surely as He gives forgiveness to repentant sinners. Our lives are spared by the grace of God, in the form of two kind fur trappers."

"Yes," Augustine said, closing his eyes before he swallowed a mouthful of jerky. "It is clearly Divine intervention. It is a sign that our work is blessed, despite the terrible prices some have paid in its behalf. We must go on, Brother Bolivar, and see to God's work at Mission San Miguel."

"Has the sanctuary been built so quickly?" Bolivar asked.

Again, Augustine closed his eyes. "No. We had just begun. A foundation of stone was laid by devoted Brothers named Donivan, Paul, Oscar, Angelo, and dear sweet Reynaldo, a tiny man who had more strength than those twice his size. Their bones still lie among the rocks, unsanctified by last rites. I was dragged away as soon as they were killed . . . slaughtered. I can still hear their cries in the night as they begged for their lives. The Ki-was had no thoughts of mercy, believing they were destroying the cause of their illness by killing us. Ofttimes, as I prayed for the souls of my brothers, I wondered why my life was spared. God surely has a purpose for me on earth, unfinished work which must be done."

"Sounds like you was plain lucky," Seth said, adding a few sticks to a crackling blaze beside the river. "On the other hand maybe you wasn't so lucky after all, bein' tied up by the neck, gettin' starved like that. An' look at your feet. They's cut up somethin' awful."

While it appeared to pain him some, Augustine smiled. "You may choose to see it as luck, my friend, that you came along when you did. Others will insist it was the hand of God."

"Perhaps we should turn back," Bolivar suggested. "If these heathen Indians cannot be reasoned with, there is little hope our mission will succeed."

Augustine wagged his head slowly. "Then so many lost lives will have been for naught. We are sorely needed here. Women and children are dying of small-pox, along with a number of Ki-wa men. A most curious thing happened when our two friends arrived at the village. They have never seen a Negro, nor have they seen anyone so large and imposing. They believe he is some form of messenger from their gods, sent from the after-life to help them heal their sick. Even their bravest chieftan, White Mountain, showed the greatest respect for Mr. Booker . . . a type of fear that unless he is appeased in some way, they may all die of the sickness. With his help, we can quarantine those individuals with visible signs of the disease from the others."

"That's how it spreads," Seth said quietly, tending to his fire. "The runnin' sores can't be touched by no-body, an' their clothes has gotta be burnt. There was this big epidemic down in New Orleans back in twenty-nine, an' that's how they stopped it. Burnt all the sick folks' clothes an' put 'em off by themselves, like they was lepers. Some got better on their own. Some of 'em died, but that stopped it from spreadin' all over cre-ation. I was there, an' so was Eli."

Eli remembered. "It was an awful thing to watch. They had to burn the bodies, like they weren't much more than firewood. Only it didn't seem like all that many died from it, best I can recall, but it sure as hell made everybody who had it sick."

Augustine bit off more jerky. "Chief White Moun-tain has agreed to have us return tomorrow. He said he would do whatever Mr. Booker asks. The Ki-was seem to fear his retribution if they do not comply with his wishes. It will be an opportunity to show them how helpful we can be, a major step toward regaining their confidence."

"They think I'm magic," Seth remembered, grinning. "When I fired a couple of shots in the air, they was lookin' up at the sky like they figured to see somebody fall off a cloud. Wasn't a cloud in the sky, but they was lookin' up anyways."

Bolivar still seemed worried. "If we fail, they may kill us as they did the others."

Seth's heavy eyelids lowered a fraction. "We ain't likely to fail, if they listen. Meantime, me an' Eli are gonna run our traps up these creeks an' fetch more beaver pelts than anybody ever saw this winter. That chief agreed we could trap here, an' if he do go back on his word, we may have to put a little of them magic lead balls through their skulls to remind 'em of our deal."

"Let us pray that won't be necessary," Augustine said. "It would be sad indeed if guns were used on them. They are a very primitive race. Superstition plays a big role in their daily lives. They carry eagle claws and bear teeth and all manner of natural objects in small pouches, believing they have magic in them. They call it medicine, spirit medicine, and when they see things they do not understand they often attribute them to spiritual origin. As with you, Mr. Booker. They are afraid of your magic because they have never seen a man like you, nor have they seen or heard a gun. It would be a tragedy to shoot them over a misunderstanding. They have only primitive weapons made of flint rock and fire-hardened wood."

Now it was Seth who wagged his head. "You sure have got a forgivin' nature, Father, after what they done to you. Most men would be mad as hell over bein' mistreated like you was."

"I am a priest," he replied. "We devote our lives to God's work and His commandments. Thou shalt not kill is but one tenet of Christian doctrine. I have forgiven the Ki-was for what they did to me and my Franciscan Brothers. If we can teach them how to pray, then God will also forgive them for their sins. They cannot be held accountable for sins they do not understand. This is the very reason why we have come, to teach Christianity."

Seth looked across the flames at Eli. His expression was hard. "Don't appear I'd make much of a Christian, Cap'n," he said. "When some son of a bitch tries to kill me I'm gonna kill him if'n I can, an' I damn sure won't be askin' nobody for any forgiveness over it."

Firelight danced among the trees. Overhead, a clear sky beamed bright with stars and a waxing moon. Bullfrogs croaked endlessly from marsh grasses. The canoe bobbed up and down with rippling currents below the limb of a willow. Fireflies winked through forest shadows. Eli felt a sense of peace as he watched the river flow past, although his thoughts were elsewhere, back at the Kiowa village and what they had seen there.

"If I live to be a hundred I'll never forget bein' so close to those people," he said during a lull in the priests' conversation. They had been talking without pause even while they ate beans and frybread about their journeys here, the hardships they faced, and of unfamiliar things such as bishops and something called a diocese, which Eli learned was an area controlled by one bishop who was in charge of church affairs there. The war in Texas was expected to change some of this, they said. "I never will forget how much they reminded me of somethin' wild, like animals, only they're men. I had the feelin' that if Seth hadn't been along, they'd have killed us just for the hell of it. It was real easy to see they didn't have no use for us."

Augustine spoke around a mouthful of bread. "They are very primitive. When we arrived, they seemed puzzled by the wheels on our carts, watching them turn like they couldn't understand how they actually worked. They use a simple device to haul belongings, a pair of poles tied behind horses, over which they afix buffalo skins. It drags behind the horse and soon wears out. A wheel is a thing of wonderment to them."

"We saw another bunch of 'em eat raw liver right out of a buffalo they killed," Seth said. "Downriver a few miles there's another bunch. Appears they's Kiowas too, by the way they wear their hair. An' there was this girl with 'em, a real pretty one who sure caught Eli's eye. She spoke a few words of English an' she said she learned it from a priest. *Powva* was the word she used for a preist, I think."

Augustine turned to Seth when he heard this. "It must be the same girl, a woman from Lone Wolf's tribe. Her Ki-wa name is Senatey, and she learned English very quickly. She came often to the mission, before the sickness began, and she seemed to develop a special fondness for Brother Paul. She was able to speak some English in only a few weeks, and she was eager to learn more. We believed she was an important link to establishing good relations with Lone Wolf's band, until smallpox started among her people. I'm quite sure it was Senatey you met. None of the other women were allowed to come to the mission on a regular basis. She was somewhat taller than the others . . ."

"That's gotta be her," Eli said, recalling the girl's face and her smile. "She was damn sure pretty. She an' some other women came with an old man. They brought us three buffalo skins as a way of thankin' us for savin' their village from a bunch of Osages. We heard 'em screamin' from the river, so we left our canoe an' went to see what was causin' all the ruckus. We found this bunch of Osages usin' clubs on some women an' kids back in a clearing real close to the river. We ran them Osages off when we shot two of 'em. They took off like their britches was on fire as soon as they saw what our rifles did. That girl showed up the next day with the old man an' a few more women. That's when she said somethin' about how it was good that we killed Nah-taih, an' we figured they meant those Osages. Two men who trapped up this river before said Osages shaved their heads, an' the ones we saw usin' clubs on those women was shaved bald as goose eggs."

"Nah-taih is the Ki-wa word for Osage," Augustine said as he put down his tin plate. "They are Ki-wa enemies. They have been in fierce battles with each other for many years. They hunt in the same regions. White Mountain and Lone Wolf are continually at war with them. If only the illness had not begun when it did, Senatey would have a key to improving our relations with the Ki-was."

"You mean her bunch has got the smallpox too?" Seth asked.

Augustine nodded. "I'm afraid it has spread among all of the tribes here. Even the Comonses, the Comanches, have experienced a large number of deaths. They fall victim to it easily and it spreads very rapidly. This is why they sought to destroy us and our mission."

Eli listened to a coyote's cry coming from somewhere across the river. "Leastways they're givin' us a chance to show 'em how to stop it," he said thoughtfully. "I reckon tomorrow we'll find out if they mean to listen to what we say. So long as they think Seth's got some kind of magic, maybe we'll have time to keep it from killin' the rest of 'em. . . ."

Seth grunted, his broad face webbed into worried lines. "It may take more'n magic to convince 'em," he said, "but if we don't run out of gunpowder an' shot, we sure as hell will have a mess of beaver pelts come spring."

Chapter
Fourteen

Smoke hung in filmy layers across the village. Fires burned where meat racks were tended by women. Curls of smoke came from small openings at the tops of tents. A buffalo-hide flap fastened to a pole allowed smoke to rise from the tent floor through a hole in the top where tent poles were joined. Eli supposed the flap performed like a fireplace flue, drawing smoke and heat when adjusted properly in concert with prevailing winds. The Indians entered their tents through a circular hole covered by buffalo or deer skin. Each tent bore a number of paintings, designs that he surmised identified its owner. As they paddled upriver toward the village an hour past sunrise, Kiowa men emerged from their lodges and came toward the riverbank to watch the canoe approach. Although a number of them still carried bows and slings full of arrows, there was no visible show of hostility or fear this morning. The Kiowas merely watched the canoe glide upstream as though their visitors were expected.

Eli's gaze wandered from one side of the village to the other. The meadow full of animal-skin tents, surrounded by trees bright with fall colors, was a scene he could never have fully described. A tribe of primitive people who had never seen a wheel or iron objects were camped in a clearing beside the Washita River and just the sight of it, of their village and its half-naked people, stirred something in him, a feeling that they were witnesses to a part of the past that had somehow survived untouched by a civilized world around them.

"They ain't actin' agitated today," Seth observed, swinging the prow toward shore. "They ain't hidin' behind trees the way they was yesterday."

"Chief White Mountain told them we were coming," Augustine explained. "I suspect that because of the illness they will be looking forward to our return, waiting for your magic to begin."

"Won't be no magic to it," Seth said. "All they's gotta do is listen to what we tell 'em to do an' burn the clothes on them that's sick."

Augustine's voice was much stronger after a night of rest, with food in his stomach. "As supersitious as they are, they may view the fires as offerings to their gods. Burning sweet bark, which they call *kinnikinick,* is often done to please a god known as Earth Mother. They believe the earth itself is a god, a being they worship in ritualistic ceremonies. The sun is an important god in their religion, a belief quite common among Indian tribes in Mexico."

Eli continued to watch the village as they came closer to shore. Last night he had dreamed about the girl, Senatey. If they were successful stopping smallpox with Chief White Mountain's people, he wondered if Senatey's tribe might also ask them to help. "The problem's gonna be how long it takes," he said. "It'll be weeks before we'll know if it's stopped spreadin'."

"I'll try to explain," Augustine said. "They speak of time in terms of suns and moons. The passing of a moon's changes is one month, as with the sun's passage marking a day's end."

"You seem to speak their language real good," Seth observed, slowing his paddle strokes in shallower water. "Make sure you tell 'em it takes time to get rid of them pox, an' that some's already so sick they maybe gonna die anyway. All we can do is separate 'em an' tell 'em they can't mix. Sick folks gotta stay off by themselves 'til it runs its course.''

As the canoe slowed to a crawl where bulrushes and marsh grass grew, Seth stepped out carrying his rifle to guide their boat to land.

"You won't need your guns today," Augustine suggested.

Seth didn't bother to turn around when he replied, "I ain't goin' no place 'round here without 'em, just in case they's in need of a reminder how my magic works.''

Eli cradled his own rifle in the crook of his arm. "I'm of the same mind on it. Won't hurt to be ready if anythin' happens to go wrong.'' He stepped off in muddy water, helping Augustine out of the boat when his feet were firmly planted. "I'm takin' along a few more beads. We'll offer 'em to the chief, just to prove we mean business about our arrangement to trap here this winter. Father Augustine, you explain to them again what we want. Beaver pelts is all we're after.''

"I have a favor to ask," Augustine said, struggling to shore holding firmly to Eli's shoulder while casting an eye around the village. "If we are successful halting the illness, I'd ask that Mr. Booker speak to Chief White Mountain in favor of Mission San Miguel. If he tells the chief we have his blessing, so to speak, they may grant us peace to build our church. It is quite clear they believe Mr. Booker is a holy man and his word will carry a great deal of weight.''

Seth was watching Indians edge closer, although they stayed back a safe distance, twenty or thirty yards. "We came here for beaver pelts, Father. Long as we get what we want, I'll tell 'em anythin' that suits you.''

A murmur of quiet conversation spread through the Kiowas at the river. There was no sign of Chief White Mountain among them, and that began to worry Eli a little. "Where's the chief?" he asked Augustine.

"Looks like he shoulda been here to meet us if he's keepin' his word."

"It's a form of Ki-wa protocol. He waits for any visitor inside his lodge a few moments before he comes to greet them. I can't tell you why. It's a custom. Be patient. I assure you he will come soon. He won't risk inciting the wrath of Mr. Booker by insulting him. He fears his magic and he wants an end to the disease killing his people."

"Remember to tell him 'bout Father Bolivar comin' along in his cart pretty soon," Seth said. "So they won't start shootin' at him."

"I assure you they already know he's here, Mr. Booker. Very little takes place in this territory they don't know about. They send out scouts who keep watch for enemies, the Osage and a tribe called the Arapaho."

From a slightly larger tent near the center of the village a man stepped into the sunlight wearing deerskin leggings and a vest adorned with porcupine quills. A bonnet made from eagle feathers covered his head, a row of red-tipped white feathers arranged so they stood erect in a circle around his skull, then trailing down his back to a point almost touching the ground.

"Yonder's White Mountain," Seth remarked. "I never saw so many feathers in all my borned days."

"He is wearing his best apparel, a sign he considers you an honored guest," Augustine said. "The headdress is a mark of his leadership among the Ki-was. He is showing you his highest form of respect, coming dressed this way."

Seth muttered under his breath, "He looks more like a bird than a man in that getup. Maybe he figures them eagle feathers stickin' up in the air makes him look taller."

Eli watched White Mountain stride toward the river. By the way he walked he appeared to have his shoulders thrown back and was making an effort to draw attention to himself. "The best way to do this is to have 'em line up, women an' kids an' all the men so we

can see which ones have got the pox. If you'll explain it
to the chief, me an' Seth can look real close at every
one, so we can decide which ones have to leave. The
sick ones will have to move their tents to some other
clearing upriver, an' that's where we'll burn their clothes
an' bedding. The rest can stay here."

"I understand," Augustine replied as White Mountain came down to the water's edge. "It may be important to note if he is one of the healthy ones. He won't
take it well if he has to be moved along with the sick."

"Depends if he's got them sores," Seth said when
the chief was only a few yards away.

Augustine spoke first when the chief arrived. He
began a lengthy speech, using a number of gestures,
pointing to the north now and then, mingling sign language with Kiowa words. But as Augustine talked,
White Mountain kept glancing to Seth as if he expected
to hear him say something.

When Augustine hesitated, the chief held up a
hand and then pointed to Seth. *To-oh tivo ein mah-su-
ite.*"

"He wants to know if these are your words," Augustine said. "He still does not trust me and he blames
me for the illness. If you say something . . . say anything, he will believe you have spoken to him through
me."

"He wants a little showmanship, Seth," Eli said
quietly. "I think it's time you fired another round up in
the air. You gotta give him somethin' that looks like
magic to him."

Seth nodded, looking past the Indians to a fire
where meat was smoking. "I got a better idea than a
rifle shot. I'll toss a pinch of gunpowder on them flames
yonder . . . it'll make a hissin' noise and a big puff of
smoke." He turned to Augustine. "Tell the chief I'm
gonna call up some magic spirits from that fire an' he'll
know the fires has got magic in 'em if I say so. I'll yell
hallelujah real loud, like I done yesterday. That oughta
convince 'em."

Augustine looked a bit worried. "It's trickery; however, I suppose it might work." He spoke to White Mountain, pointing to the fire, then the sky and a ball of morning sun rising above the treetops.

White Mountain grunted, as though it satisfied him. He took a step back out of Seth's way . . . feathers in his headdress rustled softly when he moved.

Seth ambled slowly through the assembled Kiowas to the fire, taking a pinch of powder from his powder horn as he walked to the edge of the firepit lined with stones. Eli stood back a few feet in anticipation of what would follow.

Resting the butt of his Whitney against his thigh, Seth threw back his head and shouted, "Hallelujah!" toward the heavens. But as he did so he tossed a few grains of gunpowder into the flames while attention was drawn to his mighty shout.

A ball of fire and smoke erupted from the firepit, boiling upward, making a crackling, hissing sound. Smoke lifted in a great, ten-foot spiraling cloud above from the flames, surrounding the meat rack briefly until it rose toward the sky.

Every Kiowa in the village seemed to gasp or flinch when the ball of igniting powder sounded. Some of the women cried out and cringed, gathering children about them.

"Hallelujah!" Seth yelled again, spreading his arms toward the heavens. Then the turned slowly to Chief White Mountain and gave him a malevolent stare.

"Po-haw-cut," the chief said, almost a whisper. *"To-oh tivo po-haw-cut."*

Augustine was standing behind Seth. "The chief says you are a powerful medicine man, calling up spirits at your bidding. He will instruct his people to do whatever you ask. Your trickery has worked. He no longer has any doubts."

"Tell 'em all to form a line," Seth said. "Me an' Eli will find the ones that's got pox. When we find 'em, we'll send 'em to that bare spot beside the river. Tell him the rest can stay where they are."

Augustine began explaining again what Seth wanted. Chief White Mountain stood stoically, devoid of expression, listening to what was being said.

When Augustine finished talking, White Mountain shouted to several men standing around them. In twos and threes, the Kiowas began forming a line behind the firepit where Seth had put on his demonstration.

Eli's attention was suddenly drawn to a tent on the far side of the village. A slender, wiry Indian came out and stood in the sun wearing an outlandish costume made from wolfskins. A wolf's head was tied across the Kiowa's skull so that from a distance it appeared he carried a dead wolf on his head and shoulders. The Indian's skin was dusted with ashes from head to toe, making him look almost as dark as Seth. He carried a strange object in his hand, a stick with feathers and fox tails and other objects tied to one end.

"Who's that?" Eli asked, catching Augustine by the arm. "It looks like he's wearin' a wolf's hide with the skull for a hat."

Augustine looked across the village where Eli was pointing. "His name translates to Sitting Bear. He is a Ki-wa medicine man serving this tribe. He is in disgrace now because his medicine will not stop the illness. He covers his body with charcoal as a sign of mourning for the dead. He carries their sacred *taime,* an idol or a religious ornament which they believe possesses great healing power. Because Sitting Bear has failed to stop the pox from spreading with his incantations and ritural dancing, he has more or less been banished from the tribe. They allow him to be here and to carry the *taime;* however, he has lost his position of power among them. White Mountain no longer listens to him. He won't be happy to see an outsider end the illness when his best efforts have failed. As you must have guessed, his medicine is nothing more than superstition and foundless belief in spiritual healing performed by their pagan gods."

Seth was watching Sitting Bear too. "He looks plumb ridiculous wearin' that dead wolf tied over his head."

"It's a skin," Augustine explained. "It has been cured and the skull has been fashioned into headgear, a tradition among the Ki-wa medicine men I have seen. Each tribe has its own spiritual healer. Since the smallpox epidemic, most of them have been cast out of their villages or shunned by their people. Failure is not tolerated, among warriors or shamans. They believe it is better to die than to fail at anything. Should the smallpox have gotten much worse, I'm quite sure White Mountain would have ordered that Sitting Bear be killed by his own people for failing them."

Seth cast a worried glance back at Eli. "I 'spose that means they'll try an' kill us too, if too many more of 'em die."

Eli shrugged, noting that most of the Indians were standing in line now. "All we can do is try. There ain't but one way I know of to stop it from spreadin'. Let's get started findin' the ones who've got sores."

Chapter
Fifteen

S ome of the women showed a genuine fear of Seth when he came close to examine their skin . . . a few drew back, wild-eyed, staring up at him as though they believed he meant to harm them somehow. But fears began to calm after it became clear Seth and Eli were only looking for the sores. Some younger women were reluctant to pull down the tops of their deerskin dresses, turning away bashfully or covering their breasts with cupped hands until they had been examined.

"This one's got 'em," Seth announced, indicating a somewhat pretty Kiowa maiden whose body was covered with angry red spots. "Send her over yonder."

Augustine spoke to the girl and she lowered her head as if in shame, trodding slowly toward a group of children, women, and men standing by the river.

Eli came to a powerfully built young warrior with open sores oozing pus on his face and chest. "This one goes too." He went farther down the line to a thin, older woman who had three children gathered around her. She looked into his eyes as he bent to examine a child.

"Tivo am-a wau paph. Nah-chich. Wa-hat tivo sic-ba-ton mu-ash taum."

The woman's voice was so soft Eli had trouble hearing her.

"She says she has never seen a white man with red hair, Mr. McBee," Augustine explained. "She wonders where you come from, and she has never seen eyes the color of a sky. Light-eyed races are virtually unknown to them. It is also rare for them to see men with hair on their faces. She says two men came last year who had hairy faces. They trapped farther north, up the river. As you can see, Ki-wa men are almost hairless. That is one reason why they remember seeing the other white men, because of their unusual whiskers. Ki-was have very limited experience with outsiders. As you know, Mr. Booker is the first Negro they have seen."

Eli smiled, finding the woman and her children showed none of the sores. He took a step closer and reached for her hand. At first, she refused him, until he touched his matted red beard and pointed to it, indicating she could touch it if she wished. "The two men who came last year were trappers who told us about this country," he said to Augustine, still looking at the woman.

Very slowly, hesitantly, she placed a fingertip lightly on his whiskers, then drew her hand away. *"Am-a-wau,"* she said, and she returned his smile.

"It's their word for red, also meaning apples. Very often their words have several meanings."

Eli pointed toward the village where the healthy Kiowas were being kept. The woman bowed her head and led her children away.

"Must be two or three hundred of 'em," Seth said, walking to another Indian waiting to be inspected. "I figure we's gonna be here most of the day. We can set the fires tonight, after we get the ones with sores moved upriver."

Augustine nodded. "It does go slowly; however, it is far too important not to miss any diseased members of the tribe to hurry the job."

Eli came to another older warrior. He could see

fever in the old man's eyes and his body was covered with red rash. But before Eli could show him the direction to walk, the Kiowa looked down and shuffled off toward the river as if he knew he was one of the sick or dying.

Seth found a boy covered with rash standing in line and gave him a nod toward the river. When Augustine saw the boy walking off he shook his head.

"I remember that particular youth. His name is Owl. He was one of the first to come to the mission to listen to the word of God, and it saddens me greatly that he has the illness. He told me once that he believed there was only one true God. I believed then he would be one of the first to be baptized and soon, others would follow his example. Now, because of the smallpox and their belief that we were the cause, bright young men like Owl and most of the others have turned against me. Owl had even begun to learn a few words of English."

From the corner of his eye Eli saw the medicine man, Sitting Bear, watching at a distance with the *taime* in his fist. Just a look at the Kiowa's blackened face was enough warning. The medicine man was their enemy . . . they were a threat to his power in the village. He stared at Seth and Eli with hatred in his eyes. If he could, Sitting Bear would see to it their quarantine failed. Eli was convinced of it.

Seth came to a woman with two small, naked children hiding behind her skirt. Both her offspring were covered with red spots and one, a tiny girl of two or three, appeared to be shivering.

"These has gotta go," Seth said, pointing to the river.

The woman let out a piercing shriek, wagging her head side to side. Then she cried, *"Nei ka habbe we-ich-ket!"* backing away as though she meant to run.

"What's she sayin'?" Seth asked.

Augustine's eyes filled with sorrow. "She says she doesn't want to die."

Before the crying woman could pull her children

out of line, a stocky warrior strode toward her, uttering
a string of harshly spoken words. He reached her and
swung his hand in a vicious arc, slapping his palm across
her face. She screamed and fell on her back, kicking,
moaning as she clutched her left cheek.

"Na-miso!" the warrior cried, pointing to the river.

Seth looked as though he might intervene, taking a
step in the direction of the downed woman, when Augustine quietly warned him against it.

"It isn't wise to interfere in family matters, Mr.
Booker, no matter how brutal they may seem. He told
her to hurry to the river. He is her husband. . . ."

The woman got up slowly holding her cheek, then
took her children by the hand and walked toward the
group of Indians being sent from the village.

Chief White Mountain waited until all his people
had been examined before he stepped in front of Seth.
It was almost dark by the time the Kiowas had been
separated. Baring his chest, he stared into Seth's eyes
with a look Eli might have called defiance, as though he
dared him to find smallpox on his body.

Seth's flat expression gave no hint of his feelings.
His gaze drifted down, across the chief's chest, then
back to his face. "No sores," Seth announced in his res-
onant voice. "He can stay here."

A moment Eli had been dreading passed without
incident.

Huge bonfires lit up the night. Towering flames
roared in a small clearing upriver, fed by cured buffalo
robes and deerskin garments tossed into the fires by
those who were ordered by Chief White Mountain to
destroy their clothing and bedding. Towering columns of
smoke and sparks rose into an inky sky sprinkled with
stars, while the crackling of flames grew so loud it
drowned out the hum of conversation among Kiowas in
the clearing. Augustine said none of the Indians understood why their belongings were to be burned. However,

upon orders by their chief they did so without protest, feeding giant fires long into the night as Eli and Seth and the two Franciscan priests looked on from a spot on the riverbank where the canoe was tied. Bolivar's donkey and cart waited by the water's edge. Naked Indians sat near the flames to escape a deepening night chill. The looks on their faces showed how bewildered they were complying with Seth's order to burn everything.

Bolivar, who had arrived shortly after noon, stood watching the fires consume the Indians' belongings. He spoke to Augustine in a hushed voice. "Some of the women are weeping."

"Understandable. We have asked them to destroy virtually all their worldly goods. Because they do not understand how a disease spreads, they act as though Mr. Booker is punishing them for being sick. My limited knowledge of their language does not permit me to explain it fully, other than to say it is necessary and it is ordered by Mr. Booker. They believe he is a messenger from their gods and it would appear they are willing to do what he asks of them, regardless. They are convinced they will die, otherwise."

"But what of Christ's teachings and the word of God? Have they chosen to ignore what you tried to teach them before this happened?"

Augustine's face fell. "They no longer trust me. In time, perhaps with the help of Mr. Booker, we can begin again. They will listen to what he says, and if the epidemic can be stopped soon, they will credit him with it. I have prevailed upon Mr. Booker to speak in behalf of our mission and he has agreed; however, it will be to no avail if the epidemic continues."

Eli watched the fires a moment longer before he spoke to Augustine. "We counted eight-seven sick. By the looks of 'em, a few will die before it runs its course. Explain that to White Mountain tomorrow mornin' . . . that the disease is too advanced in some cases for anythin' to work."

From the shadows between bonfires a slender boy

was watching them. He started walking toward the river. Unlike so many of the others his face was not downcast . . . he approached with no sign of hesitation or fear.

"It is Owl," Augustine whispered. "He must have something he wants to say."

The boy, fourteen or fifteen years old in Eli's estimation, came to a halt a few yards from Seth and stood with his shoulders squared. He looked up into Seth's eyes, ignoring the others.

"Mo-pe," he said. *"Ta-quoip tao-yo-vis-ta."*

Augustine translated. "He is telling you his Ki-wa name is Owl, and he asks if you will talk with him, even if he is only a boy, not yet a warrior."

"Tell him I'll talk. Ask him what he wants," Seth replied.

"Ta-quoip," Augustine said to the boy.

Owl seemed to think a moment. *"Nie habbe we-ich-ket?"*

"He asks if they are going to die, the ones who are here."

Seth shrugged. "Tell him some's gonna live an' some ain't. I reckon it's up to the Almighty an' how sick they get."

Augustine gave Seth's answer, using his hands to add emphasis now and then.

Again, Owl appeared thoughtful. The other Kiowas watched the exchange in silence. *"Ein Tatoco ta-quoip?"* he asked.

"He wonders if you are truly a messenger from the gods, or if you speak for the gods of their ancestors." Augustine's brow furrowed. "I'd be careful how I answered, Mr. Booker. It may be important that they believe you have some sort of spiritual power if you want their cooperation. You won't be speaking a falsehood if you say we intend to pray for them. There are prayers for the sick."

Eli offered his ideas. "You won't be lyin' to 'em if

you say you have the power to stop the sickness. All we gotta do is keep 'em separated a few weeks."

Seth gave it a moment's thought. "You can say I'll speak to the Almighty about their troubles, that we'll be doin' a bunch of prayin' for 'em, only they gotta do like we say an' stay in this here place 'til the sickness stops. I'll put a little more of my magic dust in their fires once in a while so they'll believe I'm sendin' a message to the spirits. All we's after is beaver pelts this winter. Tell him that, so they'll understand why we came in the first place."

Augustine began a lengthy dialogue, pointing to the night sky once in a while. He required several minutes to explain things.

As soon as Augustine fell silent Owl nodded once, although he looked puzzled. *"Pa-uh-ma?"* he asked. Then he uttered a few more words quietly.

"He doesn't understand why anyone would want a beaver skin," Augustine explained.

Owl grunted and started back to the fires.

"I told him you were God's messenger," Augustine said as they watched Owl vanish into the dark. "In a manner of speaking, Mr. Booker, you are. You've come at a time when only God could have directed you here. Owl will tell the others what you said, and if God is willing the epidemic will end and Brother Bolivar and I will continue our work at Mission San Miguel."

Seth made a face and turned for the canoe. "Just so long as they let us run our traps peaceful, I don't s'pose it matters who they think I am. We came here for furs, not no job helpin' build a church in the middle of nowhere. Me an' Eli ain't lookin' to get in the preachin' business. We's fur trappers, not preachers or nothin' of the kind."

Augustine cast another glance across the Kiowa camp. "Owl said one more thing. Perhaps he meant it as a warning. He said if you were a powerful medicine man, you would send their illness away, to villages of the Nah-taih, their enemies. He was speaking of the Osage

tribes and he wonders why you haven't driven off evil
spirits here so they would kill the Nah-taih. Unless this
epidemic ends, I wouldn't count on being able to trap
beaver in Ki-wa territory this winter."

Seth looked at Eli as they shoved their canoe into
shallow water the color of ink.

"Maybe we oughta figure on settin' lines someplace
else, Cap'n," he said. "We found ourselves right in the
middle of a whole lot more'n we bargained for, these
Injuns bein' sick."

"We're stayin'," Eli said. "Let's move upriver an'
find a place to camp for the night. We ain't leavin' this
good beaver country unless they don't give us no other
choice."

Chapter
Sixteen

E li dreamed about Senatey again, vague dreams of an Indian girl he'd only seen once and yet it was as if he knew her. She appeared in his vision several times, beckoning to him, and he did his best to follow her through a cold gray mist that seemed to envelop her each time he was close enough to touch her hand. In his dream she was so very beautiful, more striking in some hard-to-define way than Marybeth or any other woman he had ever known. Long raven hair framing an oval face with high cheekbones, full lips, and obsidian eyes with a playful sparkle mirrored in their dark depths like lights reflected in precious gems. When he awoke just before dawn he sat up and rubbed his eyes, recalling visions of her loveliness as though she'd only left him a few moments ago. He reminded himself it was only a dream, that he'd seen her from a distance . . . he had imagined the playfulness in her eyes, details of her face, almost everything. To rid his brain of it he shook his head and took a look around him.

Their campsite in an oak grove beside the Washita was quiet, still at dawn's first light. Across the river wood ducks hunted shallows for small fish, their white-banded bodies radiant even in pale skies brightening

with daybreak. A gray crane stalked through stands of
bulrushes searching for prey, and for a moment, Eli sat,
enjoying the river's peace, its beauty. They were camped
less than two miles upstream from the Kiowa village,
and as he awakened fully his mind drifted back to the
sick members of White Mountain's tribe.

So many of them will die, he thought. He wondered
if their truce with Chief White Mountain would last if
too many succumbed to smallpox. As they paddled upstream last night they passed three more feeder creeks
in the darkness, all bearing evidence of beaver activity
along their thickly wooded banks. But would the chief
allow fur trappers to stay in his territorial lands when
scores of his people died? If the sickness continued to
spread? The chief believed in Seth's magic and there
was no magic, only a quarantine, a pinch of gunpowder
cast into a fire, and a couple of gunshots.

"It's like gamblin'" he told himself softly. "You
take the best odds an' play 'em out to the end." The
Indians' belief in Seth's magical powers might be
enough to hold them through most of the winter . . .
unless the quarantine failed.

Seth sat up in his bedroll. "Heard you talkin' to
yourself, Cap'n."

"Just wonderin' out loud if they'll let us stay here."

"No need wonderin'. We can move farther west up
the Red if things don't work out. This is the best beaver
country I ever did see an' I ain't gonna be inclined to
give up an' leave it on account of some mad Injuns. We
move west, maybe it gets better."

"That boy Father Augustine called Owl said it
pretty plain last night. Unless the pox leaves their village
an' goes someplace else, like to their enemies, the
Osages, White Mountain is gonna quit listenin' to us.
Maybe try to lift our hair."

"It'll spread, if it ain't already. Remember what
that old priest said . . . it's spread to them Comanches
an' one bunch of Osages. Seems like Injuns ain't got no
natural ability to get over it the way some folks do.

When they get sick, they up an' die from it mighty easy. Most likely, the ones we moved upriver are gonna die. Some of 'em was covered with sores. Didn't see nobody with pockmarks scabbed over or healed up like they done back in New Orleans in twenty-nine. Folks who got over it had scars after the sores dried up. I never saw a one of them Injuns who had pockmarks showin' they was healed."

Augustine rolled out of a blanket borrowed from Seth. "I've been listening to what you were saying," he said sleepily. He yawned. "I can assure you the Ki-was are unusually susceptible to death from smallpox. They die at an alarming rate as though they somehow lack the capacity to recover from it. Their children are the most likely to die in its early stages, when fever is the most common evidence they have contracted it. These people have little understanding of disease, almost as if they never experience it. I believe this is why they have blamed me and my brother Franciscans for what is happening. Until we came here, smallpox was apparently unknown to them, a most unfortunate coincidence for the furtherance of our mission to teach them Christianity."

Seth gave the Washita a lingering look. "Can't exactly say it's our fault, Father Augustine, that they ain't got whatever it takes to get over it." He watched ducks swim against the river's current for a moment. "Best I remember, the pox takes a spell to stop on its own."

Augustine nodded. "We had outbreaks in Mexico City several years ago. I wish I could remember more of what happened. The bishop sent us to minister to the sick and dying in poorer parts of the city where the illness seemed worst. I gave last rites to so many; however, the disease seemed to run its course and then it stopped. Physicians dealt with all forms of treatment. We were there to minister to their souls."

Eli looked downstream, toward the village. "We'll know in a few weeks, I reckon. 'Til then, we'll scout for beaver dams an' a place to build a shelter for the winter.

Stop by the village every now an' then to see if the pox
have stopped spreadin'. I don't see much else we can
do."

"Word will spread to other Ki-wa bands of Mr.
Booker's magic and we should expect them to come,
seeking his help. If you intend to remain in Ki-wa lands
this winter you'll be asked to help them as well. Your
reputation as a medicine man will soon reach the other
bands."

Seth got up slowly, stretching, watching the sunrise.
"Got no objections to helpin' them others," he said quietly, thoughtfully, "so long as it don't interfere with
trappin' beaver. If bein' a Kiowa medicine man includes
gettin' all the beaver pelts me an' Eli want, then I'll
make as much magic as I can . . . 'til the gunpowder
runs out."

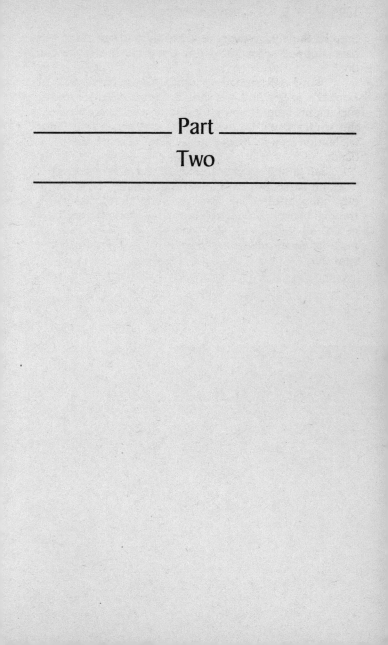

Part
Two

Chapter
Seventeen

They were summoned by a horseback messenger who spoke to Augustine rapidly, shouting and pointing to the east as though something of importance was taking place. Eli had stopped work on their lean-to to listen carefully to what the Indian said, although in the two weeks they'd been camped in Kiowa territory he had only learned a few simple words from both priests. But when Father Augustine told them what the messenger wanted, he'd turned to Seth and told him to gather up their guns. A large party of Osage warriors had been sighted entering Kiowa lands and Chief White Mountain expected a fight, an attack on their village, asking that Seth return as quickly as possible to perform some sort of magic that would allow his weakened people to defend themselves.

"He don't understand," Seth had said as they shoved their canoe into the river, leaving Father Bolivar behind. "Only magic we've got is havin' a good aim an' a steady pair of hands with a rifle."

"Maybe we can scare 'em off," Eli suggested, "shootin' up in the air, or wingin' one or two. Hadn't bargained on gettin' no Indian war, but if we aim to stay we'd better do what we can to help White Mountain's people."

They paddled down to the village in a scant quarter hour with the current pushing them, watched closely by the messenger who rode along the riverbank. Passing the quarantined group, Eli noted a few tents had been erected, a dozen or more. And as their canoe drifted by he saw Owl standing near a leafless oak tree beside the river, staring at them as they rowed past. His upper body and face were covered with red pockmarks and his skin appeared to be stretched across his ribcage. While he carried a bow and a sling of arrows, he didn't appear to be in any fighting condition if his village came under attack.

"Some of 'em's gettin' worse," Seth observed, pausing with his paddle raised above the water. Between two trees, a row of corpses lay covered in buffalo skins. "I see more dead bodies over yonder. Damned if it don't seem all of 'em's gonna die from it afore it's done."

"Owl looks sicker," Eli said, steering around a bend where the river swept past White Mountain's camp. He gave the boy a final glance and turned his attention downstream when he saw men on horses gathered along the bank. Fifty or sixty Kiowa warriors sat their ponies carrying weapons and crude buffalo-hide shields. He noticed their faces were painted—streaks of yellow and red and white drawn across their cheeks below their eyes. Even their ponies were painted, flanks sporting red handprints or designs, feathers tied into their foretops and tails. The warriors' hair was braided into a solitary strand with pairs of eagle feathers tied to it near the base of their skulls.

"Hell of a sight, ain't it?" Seth asked. "You ain't gotta know nothin' 'bout Injuns to know they's ready to put up one hell of a fight with somebody, an' we've got ourselves square in the middle. We came up this river to get away from trouble an' live peaceful. Appears we guessed wrong. They look mighty ferocious painted up like that."

Augustine said, "Tribal warfare is as old as time between them and most neighboring tribes. They see it as necessary, to protect their territory and belongings. We couldn't persuade them otherwise in the short time we were here."

Eli saw Chief White Mountain sitting on a pinto pony near the water's edge. His face bore streaks of black and yellow paint below his eyes. He watched the canoe approach without moving, like a statue carved from copper-colored stone wearing a headdress of eagle feathers trailing off his pony's flank. In full regalia he was a fearsome figure. Eli had fought his share of men over a lifetime, and he judged the chief would be a wily adversary, quick, deadly if he had an advantage. "Wish we wasn't expected to lend a hand," he said, thinking out loud as they turned for shore, "but maybe a few gunshots will turn them Osages back before real trouble starts. The others we saw back down the Red took off soon as we dropped that pair clubbin' those women. Maybe it was the noise scared 'em. If we're lucky it'll be that easy this time."

Seth stepped out of the canoe and pulled it ashore, balancing his rifle in one hand. White Mountain watched Seth's every move carefully, as did all the other Kiowas gathered around him. Eli got out and helped Father Augustine to the bank, cradling his own Whitney in the crook of an arm.

Augustine approached the chief and began to speak. For some time White Mountain said nothing, until the priest fell silent.

"Nah-taih sic ba-ton. To-ho-ba-ka ma-way-kin."

"He says the Osages are coming, that there are many and they are few because of the illness. He asks you to use your magic to help them," Augustine explained, speaking to Seth.

Seth looked over to Eli, and when Eli nodded Seth spoke to the chief. "Tell him we'll help. Ask him to show us where he figures they'll be comin' from, so me an' Eli can find a spot to shoot. Tell him to let us use our magic

before he sends his men off to fight. We'll see if we can
scare 'em off with a dose of lead an' gunpowder."

Augustine translated for White Mountain, halting
now and then when he wasn't sure of a word. White
Mountain's eyes went from the priest to Seth, flickering
occasionally to the rifle or Seth's belted pistol or the
long knife sheathed at his waist.

The chief spoke, pointing to the northeast.

"He will show us the direction from which they will
come and he warns they are very close now. He also
wonders if your magic will be powerful enough to stop
them because there are so many of the Osage warriors . . . more than a hundred, his scouts tell him."

Seth stared up at the chief. "You can say he ain't
got all that much to worry 'bout. Me an' Eli been up
against long odds before. Won't be our first one-sided
fight. Me an' the Cap'n's had our share of experience
evenin' things up."

A wooded slope ran down to a winding creek flowing through a shallow valley. Fall leaves added their colors to dry grasses blanketing every hillside. All was
quiet. A stirring rustled leaves when breaths of wind
swept along the valley floor. Seth and Eli stood behind
thick oak trunks high on a hilltop overlooking the valley.
Along ridges on either side of them, Kiowa men sat
their ponies just below the horizon, out of sight from
below. Eli studied every movement, every swirl of air
turning leaves or bending branches along the stream.
An hour passed silently. Up and down the lines of Kiowa warriors, occasionally a pony stamped a hoof or
pawed the ground as though the animals sensed a presence close by, the nearness of danger. Chief White
Mountain sent scouts across the valley when they first
arrived, and as yet, they had not returned.

Augustine spoke softly from his hiding place behind a tree. "White Mountain sent messengers to Lone
Wolf's band asking for help. The Ki-wa tribes are widely
scattered this fall preparing for winter and he doesn't

expect help to arrive in time. This is why he asked you to come. He doesn't trust Sitting Bear's spirit medicine any longer. He believes Mr. Booker has the counsel of Tutoco, their Great Spirit."

Seth chuckled mirthlessly. "All I's got is a Whitney rifle an' good eyes, Father. Don't reckon there's no need to tell him that just now. Me an' Eli will let our rifles do the talkin'."

Eli studied a wooded slope across the valley. "They can call it spirit medicine or whatever they want," he said quietly. "Let's just hope too many of 'em don't rush us all at once, so we'll have time to reload. . . ." He was interrupted when a rider galloped over a distant ridge, then another horseman came right on his heels. "The scouts are comin' back," he muttered, "an' it looks like they saw somethin', ridin' hard as they are." He felt his hands grow damp around his rifle stock. "I 'spect it won't be long before the shootin' starts."

Seth shouldered his Whitney, peering through its sights for a moment. "Let 'em come," he whispered savagely, as muscles hardened in his cheeks. "They come lookin' for a fight. We'll give 'em plenty."

A distant cry echoed across the valley as the scouts pushed their ponies down to the stream. Splashing across, they swung in the direction of Chief White Mountain, drumming their heels into their ponies' sides.

Suddenly the far side of the valley came alive with swarms of mounted Indians. Multicolored ponies swept over the crests of hills, darting between trees, galloping full speed down every slope and ravine toward the bottom of the valley. Yipping cries like coyote calls accompanied the charge. Osage warriors, their clean-shaven heads bobbing up and down with their ponies' gait, clung to the backs of their horses as the animals dodged trees and rocks at a breakneck run to reach the stream. Eli felt his chest tighten. These Indians would make difficult targets while on the move, racing back and forth like they were. He wondered how many times he would miss.

A group of Osages started upslope after the pair of
Kiowa scouts. Seth spoke to Eli over his shoulder as
screams from the valley grew louder. "I'll take the bastard on that white pony, Cap'n," he said, swinging his
sights to the left where a shouting warrior leaned over
the neck of a bounding white horse with a bow and
arrow in his hands.

Eli put his sights on a rider aboard a calico dun,
moving the notch so his muzzle sight rested on the warrior's chest. He thumbed back the Whitney's hammer
and waited, holding his breath. It would be a tricky shot,
but not impossible if he allowed for just the right
amount of drop to account for distance, yet he waited
longer, making sure, listening to the cries swelling down
below and the drumming of pony hooves moving steadily closer.

The crack of a rifle made him flinch . . . he hadn't
expected Seth to take a shot at this range. A puff of
cottony smoke boiled away from Seth's gun barrel, and
in the same instant a sharp cry arose from the slope.

The Osage riding the white pony was torn from the
back of his horse as though he'd run into some invisible
barrier. He flew backward, tossing his bow and arrow
into the air to clutch his chest, tumbling ball-like off the
rump of his pony, spinning for a moment in midair before he fell to the grass and disappeared.

Eli corrected his aim slightly and nudged the Whitney's trigger as gently as he knew how. The butt plate
slammed into his shoulder when gunpowder exploded.
The roar of the gun hurt his ears. A breath of smoke
spat from the muzzle just fractions of a second after the
recoil ended. Eli blinked, waiting for gunsmoke to clear
in front of his eyes.

The Indian perched on the spotted dun's withers
floated off to one side, kicking and screaming, pawing
his stomach as the force of the impact carried him away.
He fell hard on his back, skidding through tangles of
deep grass—his pony swerved and broke stride to

change directions, forcing another mounted Indian to swing wide to avoid a riderless horse.

Seth was reloading as Eli fingered a fresh firing cap onto the nipple. Osages charging toward the trees were looking over their shoulder following the pair of gunshots. One slowed his horse and stopped, staring back at his downed companions like he couldn't quite believe what he had seen. Others halted their ponies to look backward, and for a moment their charge was broken just long enough for Seth and Eli to reload.

Before Eli could take aim again, Seth's rifle thundered. A bare-skulled warrior yelped, tumbling off his sorrel pony just as the winded little horse bounded to a stop near a patch of bloodstained grass where the first warrior had fallen. All but one of the Osages halted there . . . a single Indian riding a sleek black pony continued at a hard gallop toward the trees with an arrow fitted to his bowstring.

Eli turned the muzzle of his rifle and took careful aim. In a matter of seconds he squeezed the trigger . . . fate caused the pony to stumble and his shot went high, whining harmlessly over the warrior's head.

Seth swung around the tree trunk with his Paterson aimed up at the Osage's face. The crack of igniting gunpowder drowned out the drumming of hooves. The Indian's right cheek puckered where Seth's ball struck him, and his head twisted violently, turning him backward amid the snap of splintering bone. The black pony snorted and lunged past the tree as the Osage slid off its back and fell, landing disjointedly on his belly a few feet away from Seth.

Confusion and a touch of fear ran through the Osages coming upslope when they heard guns and saw warriors falling. They reined their ponies to a halt all across the valley to look up at the spot where Seth and Eli were shooting. Their war cries ended and for a moment things were still, silent as more than a hundred Indians abruptly halted their charge.

The coppery scent of blood drifted past the tree

where Eli stood, and he wrinkled his nose, hurrying to
reload his rifle. A pony snorted somewhere behind him
when it too caught the smell of fresh blood.

Unexpectedly, Seth slipped off his sleeveless cotton
shirt and stuck his pistol in his belt; then he walked
away from the oak tree toward the Osage warrior he
shot. Standing out in plain sight of Indians downslope,
he bent down and lifted the Osage in his arms. Eli's lips
formed to shout a warning, when Seth did the strangest
thing of all.

Hoisting the dead warrior above his head, thick
muscles rippling in his arms and chest while blood from
the Indian's wound dribbled over his face and body,
Seth threw back his head and bellowed "Hallelujah!" at
the top of his lungs. Then he gave a mighty heave and
threw the body as far as he could downhill.

The corpse flew a dozen feet and landed with a
thump where it began rolling through matted grass. It
rolled a few feet more before it finally came to a halt.

Seth drew his pistol, glaring down into the valley.
He gave another roar, "Hallelujah!" and fired the Paterson over his head.

Perhaps it was the unfamiliar color of his skin,
along with his booming voice and being witness to gunshots killing members of their tribe that made the
Osages start backing away. A few at a time, then in
groups, mounted warriors turned away from Seth and
began a slow retreat toward the valley floor.

Chapter
Eighteen

It was a sight Eli knew he would never forget, when a sudden end came to the Indian attack after only a few shots were fired. There was an eerie, surreal quality to what went on in the valley now, as a hundred fierce Osage warriors quietly pulled back down gentle slopes without firing an arrow or using a lance. Three of their dead lay in blood-smeared patches of grass, and they seemed mystified by it—how death could occur from a distance without an arrow. Several warriors hesitated near the first two corpses at the bottom of the hill to stare at their wounds before they rode off.

Seth watched them retreat a moment longer, then returned to the tree and picked up his rifle. Blood from the Osage he shot at close range ran down his arms and chest. He grinned weakly. "They's mighty superstitious, Cap'n. Otherwise they'd have come at us so thick we'd never have driven 'em off. It's the ruckus these guns make. Don't appear they can figure it out, how a bangin' noise can kill a man. We's lucky they never saw no guns before."

Eli heard Father Augustine praying softly. "I don't reckon it matters why they backed down." He watched several warriors at the stream talking among themselves, pointing uphill. "It may not be over yet. Some are talkin' down yonder like maybe they're thinkin' about tryin' us again."

Seth gazed into the valley. "Workin' up some courage," he wondered.

White Mountin slid off his pony's back. He walked over to Seth, then spoke to Augustine, gesturing toward the valley as he uttered a string of clipped words and grunts run together in such a way Eli couldn't distinguish where one ended and the next began.

"Chief White Mountain says Mr. Booker's medicine is strong, too strong even for so many Nah-taih. He says you are truly a messenger from Tatoco, a powerful warrior and medicine man. No mortal man can have your strength or cause an enemy to die by calling on thunder and lightning to come from your fire rod at will, and he wonders if Mr. McBee is also a medicine man sent by Tatoco because he controls the powers of thunder and lightning to kill enemies of the Ki-wa."

Eli continued watching Osages gather along the stream bank to talk about what had happened: "Maybe you oughta tell him it may not be over just yet. It may take a little more convincing. . . ."

It appeared Eli's concerns were justified when several Osage warriors swung their ponies back toward the ridge, fitting arrows to bowstrings. They began moving in groups up slanting hillsides at a slow trot.

"Here they come again," Eli warned. "This time it may not be so easy to discourage 'em." He raised his rifle and rested it against the tree trunk.

Seth knelt down, gazing toward the advancing Indians. "If I get just the right shot, I'll drop one early, maybe three hundred yards if this wind don't pick up. Looks like you was right about it takin' a bit more convincin'. Good thing these here Whitneys have got some range."

More and more Osage warriors started uphill, only now there were no more war cries, only silence and what seemed to be grim determination to get to the ridge.

White Mountain wheeled and swung back on his pony. He spoke to warriors on either side of him, who began readying bows and arrows and lances when they heard his voice.

"They'll come harder this time," Seth warned. "Won't be quite so easy to turn 'em back, I'll wager."

Several Osage ponies broke into a lope. Others quickened their strides to keep up. Once again the scene below was a mass of colorful ponies bearing armed Indians toward Seth and Eli's firing positions.

"I'll take the first shot I think I can make," Eli said as his hands tightened around the rifle stock.

Seth was reloading his Paterson pistol with his rifle across his knee. "I just knew it was too easy before, Cap'n. A little voice inside my head said fightin' men don't quit so quick like they done."

Eli studied the movements of an Indian aboard a strawberry roan near the front of advancing warriors. It was an impossible shot at this distance unless everything was right. He drew back the hammer and steadied his rifle barrel against the tree as best he could, aiming above the warrior's head while hoping he wasn't allowing for too much drop when the ball lost velocity. "They ain't doin' all that whoopin' this time," he muttered, knowing it made no real difference.

Galloping ponies began the steepest part of the incline to reach the ridge, hooves whispering across a blanket of grass. Eli took in a breath, pressing the butt plate to his shoulder. Following the bobbing motion of his target as the roan pony labored upward, he lowered his sights a fraction and pulled the trigger with a feather-light touch of his fingertip.

The report banging from his Whitney's muzzle abruptly ended the valley's silence. Gunsmoke blinded Eli briefly. The whine of a speeding rifle ball followed the explosion, then he heard a distant yell.

The Osage atop the strawberry roan jerked, twisting, bending over his pony's neck. He dropped his bow and clung to his pony's mane with both hands while the little horse continued to run. A moment later the Indian disappeared, slumping to the ground in a jumble of arms and legs when he fell, bouncing along in the wake of his horse for a few yards before he began to slide and finally skidded to a halt in deep grass.

Eli hurried to reload. As he forced a ball and wadding into the muzzle he heard Seth's gun roar. A horse cried out in pain. At the front of the charge a spotted pony went down on its chest, tossing its rider in the air.

"Aimed too damn low!" Seth cried angrily, rodding a patch and ball into the smoking muzzle of his rifle.

Eli readied his Whitney and took aim at a stocky warrior on a chestnut horse bounding toward him with an arrow drawn tight in his bowstring. The Osage's face was twisted with hatred, a look so fierce it made Eli's mouth turn dry. He waited, moving his gun muzzle up and down in time with the pony's galloping strides. When the V-notch was perfectly placed, Eli curled his finger ever so slightly, bracing himself for the Whitney's kick.

A clap of igniting gunpowder rocked him back on his heels as the butt plate jolted against his shoulder—no matter how many times he fired the heavy rifle he was never quite prepared for its recoil, or the noise. Down below, a shriek of pain gave all the evidence he needed of a perfect shot while gunsmoke cleared in front of his sights.

The chestnut's rider took flight off his horse's withers in a backward arc, halted by molten lead passing through his shoulder. Eli saw his bald head turn in an unnatural way as though his neck might be broken before he fell. The Osage went out of sight behind his horse, plowing through stands of bending prairie grass marking his landing place.

Seth's rifle roared and the muzzle lifted despite his great strength. A stabbing finger of bright flame spat from the barrel and quickly vanished in a cloud of smoke. Amid a wavering line of Indians charging toward the ridge a rider dropped from sight into a mass of flying legs and pounding hooves. A pony stumbled in the middle of the pack and went down, tossing its rider off to one side when it collapsed on its chest.

Eli rodded another ball into his rifle, burning his fingers on its heated barrel when he loaded too hastily, without his usual caution. Osage warriors were closing the distance to a hundred yards, and he'd be lucky to get off more than one or two rifle shots before they reached him. Then he and Seth would depend on pistols for their lives, five shots each, not nearly enough to halt so many attacking Indians.

He aimed quickly, feeling his heart race, sweeping the gun muzzle back and forth until he found a target. When his sights were centered on a bronze-skinned horseman, he held his breath a moment, making doubly sure, knowing each shot must count now.

Seth's rifle barked before Eli's, although the shots came so close together they sounded almost as one. An Indian riding a mouse-colored pony dropped his bow to reach for his thigh, and an instant later, he fell.

A warrior at the front of the charge raised his hands to his throat, letting a feathered lance fall to the ground. He rolled off his pony's rump, clinging to his neck with blood pumping from between clasped fingers.

Movement on either side distracted Eli as he rammed a ball into the fiery hot barrel of his Whitney. Screams echoed from the forest as White Mountain led his warriors from the trees, a series of war cries so chilling Eli was reminded of the shrill scream of a swamp cougar before making a kill. Kiowa riders flashed over the top of the ridge like a giant tidal wave armed with bows and lances and shields. Bounding ponies dashed past him carrying painted Indians in a headlong rush toward the Osage attack. Before he could get a firing cap in place and take aim, White Mountain's warriors blocked his view of the enemy.

They came together in a crush, a collision of ponies

and men in war paint running at top speed. Arrows flew,
whistling in all directions, some whacking into tree
trunks where Seth and Eli stood watching the battle.
War clubs and lances sought targets on both sides, and
the noise was a cacophony of yells and thumping blows
and whickering horses, thudding hooves and cries of
pain, coyote calls and clubbing sounds when weapons
landed on buffalo-hide shields. Warriors tumbled to the
ground, some bleeding from mortal wounds, others
stunned by blows to the head or the fall of a wounded
pony. Men staggered through the melee seeking a horse
or a weapon, many of them bleeding so profusely they
collapsed from blood loss and shock.

"Can't find nobody to shoot at!" Seth cried, sweeping his gun back and forth.

Eli faced the same dilemma . . . Indians from
both tribes were locked in mortal combat, making it
impossible to pick an Osage from a Kiowa without risk-
ing killing the wrong man. He watched the fight help-
lessly, rifle ready, unwilling to take a shot he couldn't be
sure of.

White Mountain's warriors fought with animal-like
ferocity despite being outnumbered. They charged fear-
lessly into groups of mounted Osages swinging war clubs
and lances. Arrows were fired from the backs of galloping ponies with surprising accuracy as more and more
Osage warriors were downed. Loose horses ran back
and forth trailing jaw reins, adding to the confusion and
the difficulty of taking a rifle shot from the ridge. Thus
Eli and Seth watched the battle rage, listening to war
whoops and screams and the crashing of weapons
against shields, unable to do anything for the moment to
help the Kiowas turn the tide.

Suddenly Seth knelt and fired at an Osage kicking
his pony toward the trees. His shot missed, taken too
quickly, and just as Eli swung his rifle to fire at the
Osage an arrow flew from a stand of oaks to the west,
followed by a piercing war cry.

The arrow struck the Osage below his ribs, burying

itself in the warrior's belly as his pony continued charging toward Seth. Eli glanced in the direction from which the arrow had come. He saw a slender Kiowa clinging to the back of a sorrel pony dashing from the trees, fitting another arrow to his bowstring. And Eli recognized him immediately . . . the boy named Owl, his skin dotted with smallpox sores, raced into the battle at full speed shouting a war whoop.

The Osage Owl wounded tried to turn his pony when he was a few yards from Seth. Blood poured from his side, spilling down his leg, splattering across his pony's back. Seth drew his Colt and fired just as the little horse began to turn.

The bullet struck at a distance of forty yards, lifting the Indian off his pony's withers. He made a twisting dive toward earth and disappeared behind clumps of tall grass.

Owl fired an arrow as his sorrel gathered its forelegs for a leap over a downed pony. The arrow flew toward an enemy's belly and found its mark, shaft quivering, spilling an Osage. A shout that could be heard above the others sounded shrill, victorious when it came from Owl's throat.

Eli triggered off a booming shot at a horseless Osage racing uphill. The Indian staggered and fell, clutching his chest where a dark hole appeared suddenly, blood erupting from his back as the ball exited. Now shouts and screams grew to such a chorus it filled the valley with noise. Whickering ponies, terrified by the smell of blood, fought the pull of jaw reins, bounding away in every direction out of control.

Seth's pistol roared. A slender Osage carrying a spear went to his knees. While Eli was reloading his rifle the Indian fell on his face and lay still.

Farther downhill groups of Osage warriors began to pull back toward the stream, leaving the battle in utter confusion, ignoring the plight of their tribesmen where the fight was being waged in deadly, hand-to-hand combat. In twos and threes more Osages joined the retreat.

"They's turnin' tail!" Seth shouted, pointing to the creek.

Eli readied his Whitney and nodded, watching larger bunches of warriors wheel their ponies away from the fight.

"Maybe this time they won't come back," Eli said, glancing across the stream where dozens of Osage warriors galloped toward hills on the far side of the valley.

Slowly at first, the war cries lessened. Victorious Kiowas gathered in small groups, pointing to the Osage retreat. Then an eerie silence returned to the slopes as the last mounted Osages hurried their ponies over the valley floor, leaving scores of dead and wounded behind.

Chapter Nineteen

Seth balanced his Whitney in a palm, gazing across the scene below. "This time we took the fight out of 'em," he said. "They lost too many, an' they still can't figure out these guns."

"Appears you're right," Eli agreed, paying close attention to the beginnings of strange actions on the part of several Kiowa warriors gathered around Chief White Mountain. Men were dropping from their ponies near downed Osages, pulling flint knives before they knelt over the bodies. "Can't quite figure what those Kiowa aim to do. . . ." His wondering ended abruptly when he saw a Kiowa bury his knife in a dead man's belly. More Kiowas joined him on the ground as he began pulling the Osage's intestines out amid a chorus of raucous screams. Tossing bloody entrails about like slippery purple ropes, the Kiowas shouted, some holding loops of intestine aloft as though they represented some sort of grisly trophy.

"Sweet Jesus," Eli whispered, feeling his stomach begin to churn. "They're gonna mutilate 'em . . . cut 'em up like they did those dead buffalo."

Father Augustine took a deep breath and turned away from the sights they witnessed on the slopes. "Perhaps now you understand why they are called savages, my friends. And you can also see why it is so terribly important to teach them about Christianity. These are the practices of animals, not men, like a pack of wolves tearing into a carcass after a kill. It's an abomination to defile the dead in such a manner. They must be taught otherwise if their immortal souls are to be saved."

Seth grunted. "I ain't so damn sure they's got any such thing as a soul, Father. If you aim to teach these people how to act like civilized folks, you've got your hands full."

More and more Kiowas began cutting into the bellies of Osage corpses. Suddenly, a piercing shriek came from a stand of tall prairie grass when a wounded Osage staggered to his feet clutching a chest wound. He stumbled a few steps while surrounded by Kiowa warriors holding bloody knives and spears, and the Kiowas seemed to be taunting him, shouting, even laughing as the dying man tried to flee. A warrior tripped him from behind, sending him sprawling on his face. Others started kicking him while more laughter echoed from the valley floor.

"I ain't gonna watch no more of this, Cap'n," Seth said as he turned away. "We done what White Mountain asked us to do an' there's no need stayin' to see how they's celebratin'."

Eli cradled his rifle and swung away from the tree. "Don't reckon I got the stomach for it either," he muttered, walking into deeper woods running behind the ridge to return to their canoe. Augustine came quietly behind him with a waxy pallor to his face.

Moments later they heard the thump of hooves. A pony came after them bearing a Kiowa rider. Eli halted to see why they were being followed.

"It is Owl," Augustine remarked. "I wonder what he wants with us?"

Owl drew his sorrel to a halt when he caught up to them, and for a time he merely sat his pony with a scowl on his face as if he were trying to remember something.

"Why you go?" the boy asked, speaking faltering English Eli could barely understand.

Augustine answered him in Kiowa, pointing back to the valley now and then before he spoke to Eli and Seth in English. "I told him we do not condone what they are doing to dead men. I said it was wrong, being against the teachings of our God."

Owl still seemed puzzled. *"Nah-taih nie habbe we-ich-ket."*

"He says the Osages came here seeking death. He does not understand why it matters what is done to a dead man who came here to kill them," Augustine explained. "It is ritual and they believe it will serve as a reminder to other enemies that Kiowa territory is forbidden ground. They intend to leave the bodies there as a warning of what will happen to others who come to their lands."

Eli shrugged. "How can you tell someone about an idea from a religion they don't know nothin' about. They ain't none too likely to listen."

"That was the purpose of our mission here, until the smallpox ended everything."

Seth examined the spots on Owl's skin. "Best you tell this boy to get back to where he belongs. He can make the others sick if he don't stay where he's supposed to be."

Augustine spoke to Owl, gesturing toward the river. But as soon as Augustine ended what he was saying, Owl replied in angry tones and shook his bow.

"He says he thinks he is going to die anyway from the pox and he wanted to give his life for his people in battle, not by lying in his buffalo robes waiting for death to come while he slept. It is important to him that he dies bravely, not like an old man or a coward. He says he and the others know they will all die, the ones you sent away."

Eli understood. "Tell him it's over now, an' it's important that he stays away from them who ain't got the spots. We saw how bravely he fought a while ago an' so did his chief, but now it's time he went back. An' you can say it ain't necessarily true the ones we sent upriver will die . . . it's only to keep the rest of his people from comin' down with the pox."

Augustine started to explain, when Owl stopped him with a wave of his bow. "*Mo-pe* go now. Medicine of *to-oh tivo* strong." He kicked his pony to a trot and rode past them into the woods, quickly disappearing in forest shadows.

"He's a brave kid," Eli observed, continuing back in the direction of the river. "Too bad he ain't gonna make it past bein' sick."

Seth wagged his head thoughtfully, looking up at the sky as he said, "I ain't so sure 'bout that, Cap'n. If I was gamblin' on any one of them sick Injuns pullin' through, it'd be that boy yonder. He's skinny, but he's damn sure tough an' he don't act scared of nothin'."

Eli remembered the epidemic in New Orleans. "Bein' scared ain't got much to do with whether he lives or dies from the pox. It's if he has the constitution for it. No way to know ahead of time. If he's lucky, he'll pull through. If he ain't, there ain't a damn thing anybody can do to save him."

Behind them, as they resumed their slow walk back toward the Kiowa village, more excited whoops and yells reached them on soft winds. Eli tried to shut the scene from his mind. Seth's remark lingered in his memory . . . it seemed nigh onto imposssible to teach a band of wild men respect for the dead. White Mountain's tribe apparently viewed the mutilations as some form of celebration for a victory. Eli doubted anything Father Augustine could say or do would change them.

At the village news of the Kiowa victory had already reached scores of women and children and older men—laughter came from a number of groups gathered by the river near the canoe. But when the Indians saw Eli and Seth enter a clearing around the village, silence spread quickly. Then a half dozen women emerged from one of the tents carrying armloads of buffalo robes, clay pots, and curiously shaped fans made from eagle feathers. The women came toward them, bowing their heads meekly, and before Seth reached them their gifts were placed on the ground, blocking Seth's path to the canoe.

An older woman spoke to Augustine, speaking in a soft voice while looking at the ground.

"The woman is one of White Mountain's wives," Augustine said. "Like many of the most powerful Kiwas in his tribe, he has several wives. It is White Mountain's wish that offerings of buffalo skins and food be given to Mr. Booker. They believe in the power of his magic, his spirit medicine, and they have seen proof his spirit medicine was strong enough to defeat their worst enemies, the Nah-taih."

"We don't need no more buffalo robes," Seth began.

Augustine raised a hand. "They will be offended if you do not accept their offering, Mr. Booker. They are unable to understand why anyone would do something in their behalf without expecting something in return. My advice to you is to take the robes and food. It will be a long, cold winter and the robes will be valuable. The cooking pots contain a mixture of acorn bread, to which they add wild berries and nuts. It is actually quite tasty, and as I said before, White Mountain will be offended if you refuse them."

"We'll take 'em along," Eli said quietly. "An' tell the chief we're grateful, only we ain't gonna take no part of any more wars between Osages an' his tribe. We came here to live peaceful trappin' beaver, an' that's the way we aim to spend the winter here. We ain't soldiers."

Augustine nodded as though he understood. "The only problem with your peaceful intentions is that they now believe Mr. Booker was sent to help them by their spirit ancestors. War is as much a part of their lives as gathering food. Should you refuse to help them in the future, Chief White Mountain may see it as some form of disfavor from their spirits." He glanced in the direction of Sitting Bear's tent where the tribal holy man stood watching them, arms folded across his chest. "And you have an enemy among them now. Sitting Bear will look for any excuse to discredit you with his chief in order to enhance his position within the tribe. I understand you wish to live peacefully among these people, Mr. McBee. However, as you have already seen today, they have a very limited view of peaceful relations with their neighbors."

"We didn't paddle all the way up this river to get involved in no Injun wars," Seth argued, scowling when he too saw Sitting Bear watching them. "We're in the fur-trappin' business an' by God, that's the way we intend to stay. There's a thousand other creeks leadin' into the Red. We'll move farther west if they won't let us live here peaceful."

Augustine looked worried. "I'm afraid going west won't be the direction to travel, Mr. Booker. West of Ki-wa territory lies the land of the Comanches. If any tribe of western Indians is more warlike than the Ki-was, it will be any one of the five Comanche bands. While I have no personal knowledge of their habits, we have heard reports that they are even more brutal and unreasoning than their Ki-wa allies."

Seth looked at Eli. "We made up our minds to leave that damn Mississip' on account of all the trouble. Don't seem we've found what we was hopin' for here." He fingered his rifle. "It ain't that I'm against killin' another man, Cap'n. You've seen me do it more times than either one of us cares to recall. But I had it figured we'd find us some empty land out here where we had a chance to make a livin' without spillin' any more blood. I was aimin' to live quiet the rest of my days without no more dead men to add to a tally book."

Eli watched the Kiowa women walk away from the piles of gifts. "About all we can do is ask Father Augustine to explain it to 'em as plain as he can. We didn't come here to fight, just to trade for the right to run our traps. If the chief can't be made to understand, then we'll give up on that lean-to we're buildin' an' go somewheres else. I'm of the same mind on it as you . . . we done about all the killin' any man oughta, mostly to save loads of bad whiskey an' staples headed up the Mississip'. If livin' peaceful don't suit Chief White Mountain, then we'll move on an' take our chances with those Comanches."

As they were talking, a lathered pony galloped from a grove of trees north of the village bearing a rider clad in deerskin leggings. He jerked his pony to a bounding halt near the river and began shouting to some of the older men standing around the canoe.

"What's goin' on?" Seth asked, casting a worried look in Augustine's direction.

The priest's face darkened. "I'm afraid there is more bad news, gentlemen. The rider is a messenger from Lone Wolf's tribe where another battle has taken place. While Lone Wolf and his hunters were out gathering buffalo meat for the winter, the village was attacked by another Osage band. The village was not prepared for war with their fighting men off on buffalo hunts. A terrible toll has been exacted against Lone Wolf's people." He fell silent long enough to listen to more of what the rider was saying. "The messenger says women and children were killed by the Nah-taih, and their heads were cut off. The heads were put in clay cooking pots as a declaration of all-out war between the Nah-taih and the Ki-was. I fear the peace you were hoping for is quite impossible now. White Mountain and Lone Wolf will call a council with all six Ki-wa tribes. A terrible Indian war is sure to follow, gentlemen. This territory will become a battleground and nothing short of a miracle can prevent it. The Ki-was will unite to fight off an Osage incursion and to seek revenge for what has happened to Lone Wolf's tribe."

Eli immediately thought about the girl, Senatey. "I hope the woman who spoke English to us that day escaped somehow. You said her name was Senatey . . ."

Augustine didn't appear to be listening, paying closer attention to what the messenger from Lone

Wolf's band was saying to Kiowas gathered around him.
"He says the slaughter was by far the worst in recent
memory, since trouble began between the two tribes.
Women and children and older men left behind for the
hunt were dismembered and beheaded."

Again, Eli thought of the girl. It was foolish to
think he might have feelings for a young Indian woman
he'd only seen once, and yet something deep within
caused his heart to ache as Father Augustine described
what had happened at Lone Wolf's unguarded village.

Chapter Twenty

Even Seth, who was usually calm in the face of any kind of trouble, had grown edgy as days passed. Since their fight with the Osages they spent long hours finishing a lean-to above the Washita, aided by Father Bolivar and Father Augustine. A crude shelter of trimmed tree trunks and branches provided a break from growing winds as fall slowly gave way to the first signs of winter. Nights grew colder. During the day sunlight warmed forested hills around them, but when darkness came, a deepening chill swept down from the north as winds shifted with a change of seasons. No word had come from the Kiowa village since Seth and Eli and Father Augustine returned. Eli continued to think about the news they heard from an Indian sent to White Mountain's village, of an attack on Lone Wolf's people—women and children beheaded and cut to pieces by an Osage war party while Lone Wolf and the men of his village were off hunting buffalo. He couldn't keep his thoughts from wandering to a recollection of the Kiowa girl, Senatey, wondering if she had been a victim of the Osage attack.

"Seems like your mind is someplace else," Seth said when Eli didn't answer a question late one sunny

morning. A smoldering fire burned near the front of the
lean-to, causing Seth's eyes to burn when wind swirled
smoke near his face. "We's in the heart of good beaver
country an' you don't act like you give a damn 'bout no
beaver pelts lately."

"I was thinkin' about that girl from Lone Wolf's
tribe, if maybe she was one who got killed."

"A blind man can see you're broodin' over somethin'. This ain't like you, Cap'n, to get soft over a
woman. Not since you was with Marybeth. Strangest
part is, you only seen her that one time an' you act like
it was somethin' special. She hardly said a word to you."

Eli finished lashing a bundle of branches to the
roof where sod would be added later, to make it as
waterproof as possible. "I don't reckon it does make
much sense. There was somethin' about her. Maybe it
was the way she sorta half smiled when she spoke to us."

Seth glanced across the river. He'd been unusually
vigilant lately, watching for Osage warriors approaching
from the east. A couple of nights ago while seated
around their fire he'd wondered aloud about the council
Father Augustine said would take place among the six
Kiowa bands to plan a war against Osage villages. "She
was a right pretty woman," Seth agreed, scanning forests to the east. "But if what Father Augustine overheard was the truth she may have got her head cut off
an' put in one of them clay cookin' pots."

"I've been wonderin' about it," Eli sighed, bending
down for another bundle of oak limbs.

"Best you get your mind on traplines 'stead of
women. We came here for pelts, if you'll remember."

They heard the creak of cart wheels coming
through a wooded ravine to the west. Bolivar and Augustine were out gathering limbs for the roof all morning, and as noon approached, Eli had begun to worry
some. "I ain't forgot why we came, Seth. Spent too
many years dreamin' about this to let a woman or an
Indian war take my mind off business. It's just that she
was so pretty an' she had a pretty smile."

Seth grunted, watching the two priests approach leading the donkey pulling its loaded cart. "It's the Injun war that's got me a touch on the jumpy side. If those two bunches start fightin' it could get mighty dangerous workin' traps up some of these creeks should we get caught between 'em. Like I said before, we hadn't oughta be takin' no side in it like we done. Let them do the fightin' an' we'll take our profits back to New Orleans without no extra holes in our skin."

"Father Augustine says White Mountain will ask for your help if the Osages come again. They believe you've got supernatural powers."

Seth shrugged and went back to tying a bundle of limbs to a roof support with a piece of twine. "All I's got is good aim," he said quietly.

The priests came along the bottom of the draw, and Eli took note that they both looked worried. Before the cart rolled to a halt Augustine began to speak, pointing over his shoulder.

"We have been followed," he said, looking up the ravine they had traveled. "Four or five mounted Indians keeping to the woods behind us. They were letting us know they were there, making no real attempt to hide themselves. I'm not quite sure what to make of their behavior."

Seth moved quickly to his guns, sticking the Paterson in the waistband of his pants before Eli made it to his rifle.

"How far back is they?" Seth asked, stepping over to a tree trunk behind the lean-to while peering up the ravine.

Father Bolivar said breathlessly, "They are very close, only a few hundred *varas.* I believe they are Kiwas. I'm very sure they did not have shaved heads."

Eli checked the firing cap on his Whitney before he put his pistol in his pants, squinting into the sun's glare to see if any horsemen came from the draw. The past days of quiet had given him a false sense of security. "If they're Kiowas they shouldn't give us any trouble," he

said, as much to reassure himself as to convince anyone
else.

Then he saw them, counting seven riders as they
emerged from a line of trees and brush choking the
floor of the ravine. He held his breath a moment, looking for signs of aggression or any weapons held in a
threatening way.

"They's Kiowas," Seth observed, "only don't none
of 'em look like White Mountain's bunch. Don't recognize no faces, 'cept for maybe one. Look at the one
ridin' way back, Eli. It's a woman, an' damned if she
don't look like the girl who's got you so moonstruck."

He recognized Senatey at once. Another girl rode
beside her on a dappled mare. The women stayed back
while all five warriors rode slowly toward their camp
beside the river. The men carried bows, but no arrows
were fitted to the strings.

The Indian riding in front was a curious figure, a
young man with fierce black eyes and rippling muscles
underneath his copper skin. He had a pair of scars running down one cheek as though he had been cut severely with a knife sometime in the past. His pony was a
piebald stallion prancing under the restraint of a jaw
rein. And Eli noticed he carried an iron knife in a belt
around his waist, rusted by weather and improper cleaning. Could the knife be a trade item from Mose and
Frenchy last year? he wondered.

"Their leader, the one riding the spotted horse, is
Chief Lone Wolf," Augustine said in a hushed voice.
"He is said to be very unpredictable. The girl who came
to the mission is there on a black pony, the one named
Senatey."

Lone Wolf stopped his pony near the back of the
priests' cart. His cold stare lingered on Seth a moment.

"To-oh tivo po-haw-cut Tatoco," he said, addressing
Seth as though he understood.

Augustine translated. "He is asking if you are the
black medicine man sent by the Great Spirit."

Seth looked at the priest. "What the hell do I say? I'm no medicine man."

Augustine appeared thoughtful. "I suppose he was told what the two of you did to help Chief White Mountain against the Nah-taih. In their eyes, you have strong medicine because your guns killed so many of their enemies in ways they do not understand."

"You can say I'm the same one who helped White Mountain's people, only you'd best explain we ain't interested in doin' no more fightin' for nobody."

Augustine began speaking Kiowa. Father Bolivar cowered at the front of his cart as though he expected arrows to fly at any moment. While Augustine was talking, Eli let his eyes drift back to the girl.

She wore a short deerskin dress pulled high on her thighs by the way she clung to her pony's back with her legs. Her black hair fell below her shoulders, surrounding the most unusual face he had ever seen. Her cheekbones were so high and broad as to give the impression she was smiling, but her mouth was drawn in a thin line and there was no friendliness in her eyes. She stared at Eli, then looked away while Augustine continued to talk.

Lone Wolf seemed displeased by what the priest said. He spoke sharply, pointing to the river, then to Seth, making a number of small gestures with one hand. His eyes passed over Eli quickly. When he fell silent it was clear by the expression on Augustine's face there was bad news.

"Lone Wolf is angry, demanding to know why you helped his brothers with Chief White Mountain and now you say you will not use your magic to help his people against the Nah-taih. He is asking for your blessing, I think, rather than help from your guns. These people believe in magic, and if they think you have given them some sort of magical powers in battle by asking the Great Spirit to intervene, they will be victorious. He has never seen a man with black skin before and attributes your color to Ki-wa legend, that a dark

messenger from the spirit world below ground will come
to save them from being driven from their ancestral
lands by enemies. As you've already seen, they are very
superstitious people. He wants to know if Mr. McBee is
also a medicine man, and why his hair is an unusual
color."

Seth glanced over to Eli. "I suppose I can tell him
I'll do a little prayin' for him, Cap'n, but I sure as hell
don't want no part of this war brewin' an' neither do
you. As to the part about the Cap'n, you can say he's got
as much magic as me."

"We want to avoid any more fightin' if we can," Eli
said. "Have Augustine tell Lone Wolf you'll use all your
influence with the Great Spirit, but that we're done
fightin' for now. Have him say we came to trap beaver,
an' that if they'll leave us alone to run our traplines
you'll cook up as much magic as you can to help 'em."

Seth turned to the priest. "Tell him exactly what Eli
just told me, that I'll pray to whatever spirits they want
for his victory. Explain that we're after beaver skins, an'
if they'll leave us be to run traps up these creeks this
winter we'll give 'em more knives like the one he's got
an' strings of beads. I'll talk to them spirits an' ask for a
Kiowa victory over his enemies."

The priest appeared uncertain before he began a
translation of what was said. While he was talking, Eli
rested his Whitney against his leg to watch the girl
again, without making himself too obvious about it.

Senatey was looking at him too, but when she felt
his eyes, she looked away. The girl seated on the gray
pony beside her said something quietly, before she too
looked away.

He marveled at the smoothness of her skin,
rounded places underneath her dress, the shape of her
legs. She was every bit as beautiful as he remembered . . . perhaps even more so when he examined
her features more closely.

When Augustine finished talking, there was a moment of uneasy silence. Chief Lone Wolf stared at Seth, then at Eli, all but ignoring the two priests.

"He wasn't happy with your answer," Augustine whispered. "I fear we may have fallen into disfavor with him now."

Seth sensed the same uneasiness between him and the chief. He placed his rifle against a wall of the lean-to and took a pinch of gunpowder from his ammunition pouch. Lone Wolf watched him closely, suspicion on his face. Seth approached the fire and held his arms in the air.

"I'll try yellin' hallelujah again," he said to Eli as he tilted his face toward the sun. "It worked the other time, only this time I'll use a little bit more . . ."

Seth's booming voice echoed from trees surrounding the camp when he cried "Hallelujah!" He swept his palms back and forth over the fire twice, then a ball of flame and smoke erupted from the bed of coals, accompanied by a loud bang.

The Indians' ponies snorted and tried to whirl away from an unexpected sound. The girl beside Senatey lost her balance and fell to the earth when her gray mare bolted to escape the noise. Chief Lone Wolf's pony, being closest to the explosion, reared on its hind legs and attempted to run off until he brought it under control with a sharp jerk on its rein.

A moment was required for the Indians to settle their horses as the cloud of gunsmoke boiled into the air. The girl with Senatey swung back up on her mare. Seth stood quietly at the edge of their firepit with no expression on his face. As the ponies calmed, Seth turned to Lone Wolf.

"Tell the chief I just brewed up some real powerful magic so his people could win a war with their enemies," Seth said, and now his voice was hard, like a growl. "You can say he won't have no trouble winnin' his fight if he'll leave us alone to run our lines this winter. But I also want you to say that if he don't keep his word, them spirits will be angry as hell. Tell him all of what I said, Father." Seth's face turned mean. "An' tell him if he don't listen, I'm liable to use my magic against him. Be real damn sure you tell him that!"

"It might not be advisable to threaten him," Augustine said in a voice so small Eli barely heard it.

Seth turned his malevolent stare on the priest. "You say it anyway," he warned.

Augustine swallowed and began a careful translation, pausing every now and then to think of a word. As he spoke, Eli noticed how a subtle change had come to Lone Wolf's face, not altogether a look of fear, but perhaps the beginnings of it.

Lone Wolf held his pony in check while the priest finished delivering his message. Then he made a sign, a closed fist over his heart, before he turned his pony back up the ravine and rode away with his warriors and the women.

Once, just as Senatey was about to ride out of sight into the trees, she looked over her shoulder. Eli couldn't be sure, but it did look like she flashed him a trace of a smile before she disappeared into deep forest shadows.

Chapter
Twenty-One

"What do you make of it, Eli?" Seth asked, the silhouettes of Lone Wolf's band vanishing in the ravine, melting into dark places away from the sun where oaks thickened.

Eli thought a moment. "He was damn sure surprised by the gunpowder. . . ."

Augustine cast them both a worried look. "If things do not go well in their battles with the Nah-taih they will come back. I had hoped Brother Bolivar and I could begin our trek up the river to our mission. However, with an Indian war beginning in this region I wonder if it would be wise to leave your protection at the moment."

Bolivar sleeved sweat from his brow, still watching the ravine as if he expected the Kiowas to return. "If Mr. McBee and Mr. Booker are in agreement, Father, I wish we could stay here with them until matters between tribes are settled. I am neither a brave man nor a coward, but I am quite sure these people would show us no mercy if they find us there."

"You're welcome to stay," Eli said, returning his guns to a pile of packs in a corner of the lean-to, convinced that for now the trouble had passed. "You're

earnin' your keep by helpin' us with this shelter an' it's a
help to have Father Augustine here to tell us what
they're sayin' when they show up."

Augustine seemed somewhat embarrassed. "We
should continue building the mission as soon as we can,
although I quite agree with Brother Bolivar that it may
be too dangerous just now. If you do not mind our presence here, perhaps it would be best if we stayed through
a part of the winter, the first few months. We learned
the Ki-was are less inclined to make war when the
weather is inclement. They remain in their lodges for
the most part and show few aggressive tendencies. I
sometimes wonder if they view war as something akin to
a sporting contest, like kickball. They prove themselves
on a battlefield, it would seem, yet they do not often
enter into open warfare when weather is bad unless they
are on raids to gather food. Horses are the prize among
almost all of these tribes, most especially the Comanches to the west. Ki-was are close kin to Comanches in
that regard and their usual raids appear to be designed
to enlarge their horse herds in spring and summer, adding to their wealth as a tribe."

"I think we should stay," Bolivar added, with a
hopeful glance to Seth and Eli. "We can offer our ser-
vices with the completion of the shelter and possibly
even be of some use in running animal traps, despite the
fact I know nothing of such things. We can learn, and
someone will need to gather firewood for winter and
help with other chores. I feel safer here. These gentlemen are obviously capable of taking care of themselves
in a dangerous situation and this helps ensure we will
be . . . alive to continue our work at the mission this
spring."

"You can stay long as you like," Eli said. "We could
use the help with cuttin' wood an' gatherin' food for the
cold months ahead. Might was well stay here where we
can look out for each other."

"We'll be most grateful," Bolivar said with obvious

relief. "And I assure you we will do anything we can to assist you."

"Then it's decided," Eli remarked, walking to the cart for more bundles of cut limbs to add to the roof. "We can begin mixin' mud to sod this roof by tomorrow. Takes a while for it to dry an' we'll need to cut some tall grass to bind it together on this framework."

"I'll gladly cut whatever grass is necessary," Bolivar continued. "And if you'll show me how to mix the mud required I'll prepare it. We have clay pots the Ki-was gave us and we can use the cart to ferry it from the river. It sounds very similar to mixing adobe for brick in San Antonio."

"No caliche 'round here," Seth observed. "We'll have to make do with this red river clay an' hope it works like it's supposed to."

Eli hoisted an armload of branches to the framework, where he began tying it down. "Sure was glad to know that girl wasn't one of them who got her head cut off. Too bad she don't speak no more English than she does."

Augustine spoke, wrinkling his brow in memory. "She understands more than she speaks, Mr. Booker. Actually, she learned very rapidly."

"I was sorta wonderin' why she was with the chief just now," he added. "Maybe she's one of his wives— you said some of 'em had more'n one."

As Augustine unloaded more limbs from the cart he said, "If memory serves me well she is the daughter of Lone Wolf's brother, a man who was killed several years ago. It is Ki-wa custom for other members of a family to raise children when a parent dies. She was a very good student of our language and I was so hopeful she would become an important connection between us and her tribe in the introduction of Christianity."

Seth was still a little nervous over the arrival of Lone Wolf. "I ain't all that convinced we've seen the last of them. A puff of gunsmoke won't be enough to help 'em win a war with them Osages. I still say we oughta stay out of it if we can, Cap'n.'"

"That's what we're doin' now, Seth. Gettin' ready for cold weather so this lean-to will keep us from freezin' to death, cut a store of firewood an' such. Pretty soon we'll start hunting up some game so we can smoke deer an' turkey and fish. Then we'll begin scoutin' creeks for beaver dams so we know where the best beaver trappin' will be. If those Indians fight their war someplace else, we shouldn't be caught in the middle."

Augustine piled more branches near the roof frame. "There is one more thing to consider, Mr. McBee. If the smallpox gets any worse, if it continues to spread, White Mountain will be back asking for your assistance again." The priest frowned. "I'm sure you've considered another possibility as well. He may find a way to blame you for its spread as he first blamed us for it when his people began to die. Let us hope and pray the quarantine works."

Seth shook his head. "Seems like we run into more'n we was lookin' for out here. Frenchy and Mose warned us 'bout Injuns, only they didn't say we'd find ourselves in no Injun war or in the middle of a pox epidemic."

Eli considered what Seth said. "But on the other hand, we found streams so rich in beaver it's like no other place we've ever seen. This is uncharted wilderness an' a man's got to be ready for a few surprises."

Bolivar hefted an armload of limbs from the bottom of his cart. "We are, I suppose, among the first civilized people to visit this region. I confess I was quite unprepared for these savages here, their complete disregard for human life unless it is a member of their own tribe. While I have vowed to dedicate myself to the fulfillment of our mission, I have a number of serious doubts we will ever be successful converting them to any Christian principles. The value of life is meaningless."

Augustine turned to Bolivar. "Wars no less inhumane have been fought between civilized nations around the world since the beginning of time and we must not allow the savage appearance of these people to discourage us."

"Please forgive me, Father," Bolivar said softly, "but I find I am thoroughly discouraged by what I have seen. I shall pray for the strength to continue and seek forgiveness for my doubts."

Seth chuckled. "Prayin' for the strength to keep goin' may not be enough, Father. Maybe you should learn how to shoot a gun just in case all your prayin' don't work."

"We do not believe in violence, Mr. Booker. Men who devote their lives to the priesthood could never take another man's life no matter how dire the circumstances."

The humor left Seth's face. "Then I 'spect you oughta think 'bout what it'd be like to have your head chopped off an' put in one of them pots like that messenger said happened to Lone Wolf's band. They may get my head too, but it ain't gonna be 'til after I take a few of 'em down with a gun."

Augustine waved Bolivar silent to end any further discussion of it. "If we keep the faith in our mission and seek the Lord's blessing, we shall prevail, Brother. Often, faith is tested in a most unusual way under the most trying circumstances. With the consent of our kind hosts we will remain here until difficulties between the Ki-was and Nah-taih have ended. Then we must start anew building our mission and establishing new relations with the Ki-was. Until then I suggest you provide these gentlemen as much assistance as you can without discussing differences in our beliefs."

"I understand, Father," Bolivar said quietly, hurrying over to the cart for the last armload of limbs.

Eli twisted twine around a bundle of sticks. Down deep he gave the two priests little chance of success converting Kiowas to Christianity, but then what did he know of such things?

* * *

A Kiowa boy on a buckskin pony rode up to camp at sunrise. He spoke to Augustine, using sign language between words, pointing downstream toward Chief White Mountain's village.

Eli listened until the boy finished. Augustine nodded and began a translation.

"A Ki-wa council has been called. Five of the six tribes are gathering at Lone Wolf's village to mourn for the dead women and children and to prepare for war. Chief White Mountain and Chief Lone Wolf ask if Seth will come, to cast your magic spells so that their warriors will defeat the Nah-taih in battle. You will be given presents of food and buffalo robes and Lone Wolf gives his word there will always be peace between the Ki-wa and the two of you. You will be allowed to hunt for beaver as many seasons as you wish. It is a very generous offer on the part of two powerful Ki-wa chiefs. The boy says you will not be asked to fight with your thundersticks, only to call upon the spirits to give them victory banishing the Nah-taih from their lands. And Chief White Mountain promises to make you a gift of many ponies if you agree to come."

Eli gave Seth a questioning look.

"Sounds okay with me, Cap'n, so long as we ain't gotta be in no fight."

Eli spoke to Augustine. "Tell Chief White Mountain and Chief Lone Wolf we will come in the canoe tomorrow morning. We agree to help them with whatever magic show Seth can perform, but make sure they understand we won't fight."

The priest began his explanation. The young warrior sat on his pony, expressionless, listening. When Augustine said no more, the boy whirled his pony and struck a trot down the riverbank. In a few moments, he was gone.

"We can look at the ones with pox while we're there," Eli said. "Not that there's much more we could do."

Seth wore what might pass for a grin. "We could

run out of gunpowder before spring," he said dryly. "I been tossin' more in a campfire than we shot huntin' somethin' to eat. I reckon it don't make no difference, seein' as they's gonna let us stay. If they keep their word, we can come back every year. We'll be rich men afore you know it, Eli."

"Don't start countin' profits yet," Eli warned. "There's still a hell of a lot of Osages runnin' through this part of the country. We could lose our scalps to the other side if we don't stay real watchful."

Bolivar spoke up quickly. "This means I'll be left alone to watch things here, with the three of you away at their council. I sincerely hope none of the Nah-taih show up while you're gone."

"It's a gamble," Seth agreed. "You'd be safer if you let me show you how to shoot a pistol."

Rather than argue the point again, Bolivar gave Augustine a helpless shrug and carried a bucket down to the river to begin mixing mud for their sod roof.

"Maybe I'll get a chance to see Senatey again," Eli wondered aloud.

Seth actually grinned now. "You can't get that Injun gal outa your head, can you? Damned if I ever expected to see you make such a fool of yourself over a woman again."

Eli refused to argue against it. "Never saw one so pretty since Marybeth, even if she is a wild Indian."

Augustine lent a word of caution. "Ki-wa men are known to be very protective of their women. If I were you I would be very careful making any sort of advance toward Senatey. Her uncle might find it objectionable since they almost never intermarry with other tribes."

"Hadn't planned on askin' her to marry me," Eli objected as he toed the ground with his boot. "But it'd be nice to get to know her better."

Augustine continued, "They also take a dim view of women who indulge in infidelity, Mr. McBee. Ki-wa women who consort with men other than their husbands have their noses cut off as a reminder to everyone who sees them from that day forth of their infidelity."

Seth made a face. "Sounds like one hell of a price to pay for a little bit of fun."

Eli wasn't listening, remembering a woman at White Mountain's village who had her nose cut off even with her face. He pondered what sort of people could have such a strict code for a woman's behavior, while men delighted in cutting the bodies of their enemies to shreds in a victory celebration. The longer he thought about getting to know the girl better, the more he found himself wondering why. These Indians were truly savages, and no matter how beautiful Senatey was, she was still a wild creature who belonged where she was . . . in this wilderness.

Chapter
Twenty-Two

At dawn Eli and Seth and Augustine bade Bolivar farewell as they loaded guns and a few trade items in the canoe. Bolivar was uncharacteristically nervous about being left alone, since no one knew how far they must travel to reach Lone Wolf's village or how long it would be before they returned.

"I will pray for your safety," Bolivar promised as they put the canoe into deeper water. He was wearing his monk's robe in spite of its tattered appearance. Augustine still wore the shirt and pants Eli had given to him.

Augustine smiled gently. "And I shall pray diligently for yours, Brother. Have no fear. We have been shown God's mercy by our chance meeting with Mr. McBee and Mr. Booker and we must be assured this is God's will . . . that we will prevail and go forth with our mission. Surely you cannot believe we both were saved from starvation and death by accident. We are in God's hands now and you must keep your faith strong. Doubts are the handiwork of Satan. Trust in the Lord, my gentle friend."

A flush colored Bolivar's cheeks. "Forgive me for

having any doubts, Father. I promise to say rosaries for you and our kind shepherds while you are away."

Seth assisted Augustine into the canoe. Since they first found the priest in White Mountain's village he had grown much stronger, eating regular meals. Many of his cuts and bruises had begun to heal.

Eli pushed the canoe away from shore, then stepped lightly into it. A small bundle of beads and knives lay at the bottom of the boat beside his rifle and ammunition.

Bolivar waved as they paddled away, before folding his hands in prayer. He watched them swing into stronger currents near the middle of the river, where Eli and Seth began rowing slowly downstream.

Augustine sat cross-legged in the center of the boat with bony fingers clutching each side. He spoke to Eli. "Brother Bolivar is unaccustomed to the hardships here. He has much to learn if he is to adapt to life among the Ki-was. His heart is good, and given time, I hope he will come to understand how important it is that we succeed."

Eli left unsaid how little confidence he had in any mission to convert wild men to Christian religion. He paddled harder on the portside of the canoe to bring it full into the slow power of the current moving downstream toward Chief White Mountain's village.

Drifting past the quarantined Kiowas, they saw groups of Indians seated by firepits. Lodges of buffalo hide had been built in the clearing, and where grass grew, dozens of ponies grazed on thinning grass. Even from the river Eli could see pockmarks on the Kiowas' skin—and more bodies cloaked in worn buffalo robes spread between rows of trees away from the center of camp.

"Looks like more of 'em died," Seth said tonelessly, paddling to keep the prow aimed downriver. "I can't find Owl among 'em. Sure do hope that boy ain't layin' over yonder with them that's dead."

"I sorta figured he'd make it," Eli remarked. "In spite of his small size, he seems tough."

"Toughness is rarely ever enough," Augustine remembered, as the canoe sliced through muddy water around a bend. "Some of the strongest died easily. It took a terrible toll among small children when it began to spread."

Seth pointed to a spot half a mile downstream. "Appears they's waitin' for us, Cap'n. Injuns all over the place yonder 'round that next turn."

Mounted warriors lined the riverbank. Eli saw feathered lances and shields, decorated ponies, bows with feathers tied to both tips.

"Kinda scary, just lookin' at 'em," Eli said. "They've got every able-bodied man armed an' ridin' a horse this mornin'."

Seth wagged his head. "Let's hope they didn't get none of 'em outa the quarantined bunch. If they did, we can count on havin' that smallpox spread like a prairie fire amongst them who ain't got it."

Augustine spoke up. "I explained everything very carefully to them. If they've broken their promise to keep the sick off by themselves, there isn't much we can do."

As they floated closer to the village, Eli noted how small some of White Mountain's warriors were. A great many appeared to be boys of twelve or thirteen, mounted on ponies, carrying bows and slings of arrows, wearing feathers tied in their braided hair like the older men.

"Damn, Seth," he said under his breath. "I'd nearly swear some of them ain't hardly more'n kids."

Before Seth could answer, Augustine said, "Manhood occurs in these people early. Before they are half grown they are asked to demonstrate bravery in battle. As mere children, boys go through a rigorous training period to prepare them for war. It was hard to understand when we first arrived, how they could expect young children to become fighters before they entered their teens. It was difficult for us to believe the rites into manhood were put in place while they were so very young. Children are only given adult names after they have proven themselves in battle, symbols of their courage or a particular deed they performed or a vision they experienced before adulthood. It seems odd; however, it has been a practice among the Ki-was for many years."

Eli recalled his own boyhood. "It don't give 'em much time to be a kid. When I was the age of some of those Indians I was learnin' how to skip rocks across a pond an' keep a spinnin' top goin' with a buggy whip. Seems mighty hard to ask 'em to grow up so sudden, just so they can start killin' Osages."

Augustine nodded thoughtfully. "Ki-wa society teaches them difficult lessons quite early, both their young men and women. It is, they believe, necessary for their survival in a hostile world. By introducing them to Christianity we can show them how to live in peace with their neighbors."

"You got your work cut out," Seth said from the prow as he dipped his paddle deeply for another long stroke. "From what we've seen of these Injuns, livin' peaceful is the last thing on their minds."

By the sound of Augustine's voice he remained hopeful. "I quite agree they are a primitive race. Being here is like being a witness to the past of mankind. History teaches that all races began in much the same manner. The development of civilization among western Indians has been slow. There have been few outside influences to lead them toward change. They exist in virtually the same way as they have for centuries, gathering food, moving from place to place. Our mission here was to show them a better way of life, how to farm and live in harmony with other tribes by converting them to an understanding of Christian principles and faith in the salvation of their souls through baptism and the acceptance of Jesus Christ as their savior."

"You sound mighty damn willin' to forget what they done to you, Father," Seth said. "Wasn't that long ago they had you tied up by the neck like a dog, starvin' you half to death. You still got the marks they gave you an' you ain't nothin' but skin an' bones."

"I have forgiven them, Mr. Booker."

"Most men ain't built that way," Seth added, by his tone making sure Augustine knew he wasn't as willing to forgive.

Eli saw more mounted Indians ride to the river-bank from the village, crowding closer to shore, watch-ing the canoe for its arrival. "Appears we've drawn a crowd down yonder. Let's hope we don't have far to go to get to Lone Wolf's village. This weather is gonna change pretty soon an' we'd best be ready for it. Before it turns cold we'd better have that shelter built or we'll freeze."

"Brother Bolivar understands what is needed to sod the roof in the manner you described," Augustine said. "His work will continue while we are away."

The canoe swung toward shore when Eli used his paddle for a rudder. Chief White Mountain stood on the bank in front of his pony and Eli aimed for a spot in front of him to bring the boat to land. White Mountain was wearing his best deerskins and his eagle-feather headdress, but at the moment he wore no streaks of paint on his face, nor did any of the others.

He felt the bottom of the canoe brush against water plants growing in shallows. Seth stepped out in water below his knees to bring the prow to land. Chief White Mountain stared at them until they got out and walked ashore, paying particular attention when Eli and Seth removed their guns from the bottom of the boat.

Augustine carried the small pack filled with trade items to the bank, clutching it before him.

White Mountain spoke. *"Mea mon-ach. Poke mea-dro."*

"He says we are going a long way," Augustine ex-plained. "He is bringing ponies for us to ride."

Seth was first to shake his head. "Never was much on ridin' no horse. Tell him I'll walk."

"Same goes for me," Eli added. "I spent most of my life on a boat an' the notion of ridin' a pony wherever we're goin' don't suit me. Tell the chief we'll walk."

As Augustine was translating, three rawboned ponies were led to the river by two older women. White Mountain seemed puzzled by the refusal of his offer.

"Ein mah-ri eh ah-wit."

"He wonders why any man would walk when a pony can carry him easily. He does not understand."

Seth looked at Eli and Eli stared back at Seth. Suddenly, Seth grinned.

"You can say a real medicine man who's got big magic travels by a river or on foot," Seth said to Augustine. "Tell him it's how these things are done by men who come from his spirit world, wherever the hell that is."

Augustine's face paled somewhat. "I won't tell him all of what you said, Mr. Booker." He turned to the chief. When he spoke he did so carefully, halting often as though he needed time to phrase what he was saying.

White Mountain looked at Seth, then Eli. He made a sound deep in his chest and waved the women and ponies away. When he said more to Augustine it was softer, gentler.

"He asks us to follow him. He will lead us to Lone Wolf's village where the council will be held. He also said Lone Wolf is offering both of you gifts for agreeing to help them in their war with the Nah-taih. You will be given several ponies, or two women from Lone Wolf's tribe are being offered to you as wives, if you want them."

"We wasn't in the market for no women," Seth said. "Not no Injun women, anyways. All we's after is beaver pelts. An' you was supposed to say we didn't aim to help with no fightin'."

"They understand you will not join them in battle, Mr. Booker. The horses or the women are merely being given as presents for the magic powers he believes you possess. Lone Wolf was prepared to offer you horses, until I told him what you said, that you only traveled by river or on foot."

Eli wondered how any race of people could view horses and women equally as trade goods. "Tell the chief we're grateful, but that it ain't necessary to offer us anythin' more than the right to run our traps this winter. That's all we want."

"I shall explain. However, you must be prepared in case Lone Wolf is offended by your refusal to accept his gifts. It can be considered an insult if someone refuses an offer from a Ki-wa chief."

Eli chewed his lip a moment, feeling Seth's eyes on him as he was thinking. "I reckon you can tell him we'll talk to Lone Wolf about it when we get there. Right about now a couple of women would only get in the way an' we hardly got any use for horses."

Augustine nodded and began speaking to White Mountain. But as Eli was listening he wondered if Senatey might be one of the women they would be offered. His decision to refuse the women would be far more difficult then. . . .

"We'd be better off with horses," Seth muttered, as though he could read Eli's mind.

Chapter
Twenty-Three

A silent procession wound its way through deep woods across beds of fallen leaves, moving north-east under a darkening sky as gray clouds drifted up from the south on gentle winds. Eli and Seth and Augustine walked behind Chief White Mountain's pony and a group of older warriors. The Kiowa men hardly spoke to each other. Most seemed to wear a look of grim-faced determination while others watched hills and gullies around them. Eli supposed they were looking for signs of a party of Osages. Scouts rode out in front reading the ground for pony prints. Others spread out far and wide, disappearing from view altogether as they rode a circle around the main body of warriors. Eli guessed White Mountain's band numbered close to one hundred, ranging in age from twelve or thirteen to older men approaching fifty. Trudging along through piles of dead leaves and yellowed fall grasses, he and Seth spoke softly to each other now and then.

"Last thing we need is a couple of Injun women," Seth said. "Maybe we could use a couple of gentle packhorses to carry furs down from our traps to the river. Horses ain't near as much of a handful as most women. Women are temperamental as hell where a horse usually ain't. A horse can be persuaded with a buggy whip while there ain't nothin' on earth can convince a woman to change her mind when it's made up. I sure as hell hope you don't decide to let 'em give us no women."

"It'll be a long winter, Seth. Havin' some company an' a woman to share our blankets might not be all that bad, if you think about it."

"What'll we do with 'em come spring? Take 'em downriver to New Orleans with us? What'll folks think if you an' me show up with a couple of half-wild redskinned gals?"

Eli sighed. "I reckon I hadn't thought that far ahead, to tell the truth about it. We couldn't just leave 'em up on the Washita 'til we got back, could we?"

Augustine overheard their conversation. "You can leave them at the mission with Brother Bolivar and me if you wish. We could teach them English and perhaps use them as cornerstones to begin rebuilding relations with Lone Wolf's tribe. We felt we had made great strides with the girl, Senatey, until the epidemic ruined everything. She could read a few passages from the Bible before she stopped coming to the mission and she was capable of carrying on simple conversations in English."

Seth looked over at Eli. "Eli sure is taken with that gal. Lately, he don't hardly talk 'bout much of anythin' else an' I see it on his face when he's thinkin' 'bout her."

Walking out in a clearing surrounded by barren oaks, Eli shook his head. "It was a notion that popped into my head, how I'd like to get to know her. Just a notion is all it was."

He pushed thoughts of the girl from his mind. Seth was right. The last thing they needed this winter was a couple of Indian women to take care of.

They made camp after sunset in a dense forest. The Kiowas built no fires. Some of the men passed out strips of dried meat that appeared to have been pounded flat.

The meat smelled of smoke. It was brittle and hard to chew, although it had a good flavor reminding Eli of beef jerky.

"I reckon this is buffalo meat," Seth said quietly, sitting on his haunches with his back resting against a tree. "It don't taste all that bad. Sure as hell could use some salt."

Eli turned to Augustine. "Ask the chief how much farther it is to Lone Wolf's village. We didn't bring any bedrolls an' it's gonna get cold tonight without no fire."

Augustine arose from his resting place against a tree trunk and walked slowly through the darkness to White Mountain. He spoke a few moments and got a terse reply. When the priest came back he knelt and said, "It is only a few hours more. We are waiting here because one of his scouts reported finding a number of pony tracks ahead, possibly a raiding part of Nah-taih. We are waiting for other scouts to come back to tell us it is safe to proceed."

"My feet's sure tired from all this walkin'," Seth complained. "I'm grateful we ain't got much farther to go."

Eli chewed a mouthful of brittle meat in silence. If they ran across an Osage war party, he and Seth would have no choice but to fight them to save their lives. Once again they found themselves in a possible war they wanted to avoid. It had begun to seem that everywhere they went, trouble loomed on the horizon like the dark clouds blackening skies above them now, blocking out the stars.

He judged it was close to midnight when they crossed a dark ridge above a sprawling meadow filled with tents and glowing campfires. There were hundreds of buffalo-hide lodges spread across the clearing below, and the smell of smoke lay heavy in the cold night air.

A handful of mounted warriors rode up from the village to White Mountain and a few words were exchanged. Eli turned to Augustine to learn what was said.

"They welcome Chief White Mountain to the council fires and asked if *To-oh tivo,* the black medicine man, and the other spirit messenger with hair the color of fire are with them. Lodges are prepared for the chief and for us. Food is ready. Two more of the Ki-wa bands have already arrived from the north. A council of war will begin tomorrow morning."

While Augustine was speaking, the line of riders began moving forward again, down a gradual slope toward the village.

"There's damn sure a bunch of Injuns here," Seth whispered as they walked softly through clumps of dry grass. "Nobody said how many Osages there is 'round here, but if both bunches run up on each other there's gonna be a hell of a lot of killin'. Let's make sure we ain't here when that happens."

"You'll put on your magic show for 'em tomorrow and holler hallelujah a few times, then we'll start back on our own. All you gotta say is that you asked their spirits to help 'em win this war an' then make some gunpowder go off. Can't see no reason why we'd have to stay any longer than that."

"Suits the hell outa me, Cap'n. Bein' 'round so many Injuns makes the skin crawl on my neck. Too many of 'em. An' there's just the two of us."

The closer they came to the village the more detail Eli saw because cloudy skies hid the stars and moon. Tents were spread for half a mile or more in both directions. Fires flickered in small clusters between the tents, and now he could see men seated around them wrapped in buffalo robes. A huge horse herd grazed in the darkness at the northeastern end of the clearing, held in a group by mounted Indians riding in slow circles around them. A few camp dogs barked somewhere in the village. Some of the pale buffalo-skin lodges glowed eerily with fires burning inside that made them appear translucent, like milky glass. No women or children were anywhere in sight, and had he been a superstitious man he would have said there was a heaviness in the air, a feel-

ing of danger looming above this place that he could
almost touch.

Passing among some of the tents Eli smelled odd
scents, a sweet odor like fruit, then a musky smell reminding him of bark trimmed from a tree. When he
peered inside some of the lodges he saw tiny firepits
lined with stones at the center. Smoke from the fires
rose through a flap at the top of the tent. Shadowy
forms sat around some firepits, faces aglow in light from
red embers and dying flames. In places, Indians stood
between the lodges to watch White Mountain's band
walk through camp, and as before, particular attention
was paid to Seth due to his size and the color of his skin.
Some Indians spoke softly, pointing to Seth or Eli as
they followed White Mountain toward the center of the
village, and Eli judged they were commenting on how
strange their visitors looked . . . a white man and a
black, something they apparently had never seen.

They were shown to a pair of lodges where a group
of women stood near both entrances carrying clay bowls
of food. White Mountain slipped off his pony's back,
giving its jaw–rein to one of Lone Wolf's warriors.

A brief conversation was held, until heads turned
toward two figures walking toward White Mountain in
the darkness. In light from a campfire Eli recognized
Chief Lone Wolf, and with him was a much older man, a
bowlegged Indian clad in fringed buckskins and deerskin boots almost reaching his knees.

"Who's that with Lone Wolf?" Eli asked Augustine
softly.

Augustine replied over his shoulder, listening to an
exchange of greetings between White Mountain and the
others. "He is Chief Red Eagle, an elder statesman for a
small band from the easternmost Ki-wa tribe. They are
continually at war with the Arapaho and the Nah-taih
and their numbers have been dwindling. He is respected
by the other chiefs and his words will be listened to
carefully. As far as we knew the smallpox had not yet
reached his tribe." Augustine paused to hear more of

what was being said by the chiefs. "Red Eagle says he has heard about the powerful black giant who calls upon thunder and lightning to kill enemies of the Ki-wa and he has come to hear what the medicine man has to say, and to see him work his magic."

Eli noticed most of the Indians around them now were staring at Seth. As much as his skin color it was his unusual size that seemed to interest them.

Chief Red Eagle looked past White Mountain to the spot where Seth and Eli stood. In light from nearby fires Eli saw the old man's eyes narrow as they traveled up and down Seth's frame. He then examined Eli, paying particular attention to Eli's hair and beard.

Another figure came between tents to the south, walking with a swinging, almost clumsy gait. It was apparent from his dress, elegant deerskins, and strings of bear and eagle claws around his neck that he was some sort of leader. He walked up to Chief White Mountain and they spoke to each other.

"He is Chief Ten Bears," Augustine replied. "They range to the north of Ki-wa territory, and from the beginning he refused to allow any of his people to come to the mission. He warned the others we were evil and that we should be driven from Ki-wa land. Alas, they believe his warning contained great wisdom because of the pox which came shortly after we arrived. His wishes will be listened to closely by the other tribes."

Chief Ten Bears, much heavier than the other chiefs, gave Eli and Seth a passing glance. When he spoke to White Mountain his voice was harsh, grating, as though he was angry.

"What's he sayin'?" Seth asked, fidgeting a little, his hand tightening around the stock of his rifle. "Whatever it be, I don't much like the sound of it."

"He says no Ki-was should listen to words from strangers who are not from their own people. He warns against listening to what either of you have to say and he reminds the other chiefs that it was me and my brother Franciscans who brought the terrible sickness to their people." At that, Augustine swallowed, and when he spoke again, his voice sounded strained. "Ten Bears says they should kill us now, before we bring evil spirits into the hearts of brave Ki-wa warriors before they battle the Nah-taih."

"Will the other chiefs listen to him?" Eli asked, suddenly feeling trapped by the circle of Indians around them.

Before the priest could make a guess, White Mountain began to talk animatedly, using his hands to make gestures while he continued a lengthy speech describing something neither Eli nor Seth understood.

"What the hell's he sayin'?" Seth wondered. He looked over at Eli and whispered, "Get ready, Cap'n, on account of we may have to shoot our way outa here."

Augustine shook his head. "Chief White Mountain is telling the other chiefs how the two of you killed dozens of Nah-taih by using thundersticks—his term for your guns—and how Mr. Booker can call upon thunder and smoke to erupt from the ground at will. He describes what he has seen in his own terms, calling it magic, since he knows of no other explanation. He told Chief Ten Bears that both of you can kill an enemy without arrows or spears, that you call upon the spirits to strike down the Nah-taih with bolts of lightning. You must remember he merely describes what he has seen."

"It don't sound like Ten Bears believes it," Seth offered.

Augustine listened awhile longer to what the chief was saying. "White Mountain promises that tomorrow, with all Ki-was watching, you will give them a demonstration."

Eli still saw doubt on Chief Ten Bears' face, and even Red Eagle seemed doubtful. But when Chief Lone Wolf spoke, the two listened closely to what he had to say.

Lone Wolf's voice carried throughout the village, and as he talked, a silence gripped his listeners. Lone Wolf pointed to the west, toward the Washita, then folded his thick arms across his chest. Firelight danced across the scars on his cheek while the others simply stared at him.

Eli waited impatiently for Augustine to explain.

"Lone Wolf said he has seen the fire and lightning come from the ground at Mr. Booker's bidding. He believes the two of you are messengers from the spirit world. He warns Ten Bears and Red Eagle that if they anger you, the Nah-taih could defeat them in battle and place their severed heads in the women's cooking pots as they did when the Nah-taih attacked his village. He asks the other chiefs to listen and watch your demonstration tomorrow."

"We'll shoot somethin' an' I'll toss some powder in a fire," Seth said, "only I sure as hell hope that's all they want."

Augustine turned to face Seth, and his expression changed. "You could use this opportunity to ask the Kiwas to seek peace with the Nah-taih and other tribes, Mr. Booker. You could be an instrument of God by urging them to abandon these senseless wars to live peacefully."

"I don't reckon they'd listen, Father. Killin' other Injuns is all they're interested in."

"But you can't be sure unless you try. . . ."

Seth was growing impatient. "Look, Father, we didn't come here to settle no Injun wars between Kiowas an' Osages. All we want is beaver skins. I'm leavin' the preachin' up to you. We got no stake in this otherwise."

"You have a stake in the future of mankind, Mr. Booker. You could use your influence to change the way they live and quite possibly save many lives."

"I ain't no preacher. I's a riverboatman who got tired of fightin' pirates an' hard times. Me an' Eli came out here to be away from trouble, not look for more of it."

Augustine looked to Eli for support. "Don't you

see how the opportunity is in your hands, Mr. McBee, to
end years and years of bloodshed?"

"They ain't gonna pay attention to us when it
comes to bein' in a fight with their enemies. They won't
stop just because we tell 'em it's a good idea."

The priest lowered his head. "Please consider it,
gentlemen. You may have been given a chance to end
conflicts which have cost countless lives. It would cost
you nothing to say that war is against the wishes of their
spirits. In a way, it is the truth, no matter what form they
believe the one true God has."

Chapter

Twenty-Four

It was Eli's first experience inside a Kiowa lodge, and as he examined it, lit by a small fire casting wavering shadows across walls of buffalo skin, he found it larger than he imagined. They sat on piles of buffalo skins eating a stew made from deer meat and a softened white root resembling a potato. Two Indian women came with bowls of stew and a crumbling piece of cake, baked in a dish of clay, that tasted a bit like pecans and berries.

Outside the camp was quiet. Occasionally a dog barked off in the distance or a muted voice spoke in one of the tents close to theirs.

"I was starvin'," Seth said, his cheeks stuffed with food.

Augustine ate more slowly while staring thoughtfully at the fire. "I must ask you again. You have a chance to do what I and my Franciscan brothers could not accomplish," he said. "You may be able to convince them that war is a waste of human lives. They will listen to you if events go well tomorrow. I beg you . . . please use your influence to stop this retaliation against the Nah-taih before more killing occurs."

Eli swallowed another mouthful of stew. "There's

no way to be sure they'll listen to us," he said. "If they want revenge for the women an' kids who were killed by them Osages, I don't see no way to stop 'em with a few gunshots an' some gunpowder or havin' Seth yell halle-lujah loud as he can."

"The point is this . . . they are superstitious and they believe you and Mr. Booker have come from a place where their ancestors live to bring a message from their spirits. If you use this as a means of ending the slaughter of women and children and ending meaning-less wars between them, how can it be wrong? You are reasonable men. Why not use their superstition to bring a peaceful end to so many years of bloodshed over the ownership of horses and buffalo herds? Does it not seem a worthwhile cause?"

Eli took a bite of bread. "Worthwhile, but probably a big waste of time. These people don't appear to be-have the way most men do. They cut open their victims an' toss their innards all over the ground. This ain't ex-actly the way a man who's got all his senses behaves. You act like you forgot these are wild men, not a hell of a lot different than a pack of wolves. Talkin' to 'em don't seem to do much good."

"Eli's right," Seth said, glancing to the tent flap leading outside. "These Injuns ain't like regular people. They live by a whole different set of rules, if they's got any at all. They can kill each other as long as they like, so long as they let us be to run our traps this winter. What you're askin' us to do is be like preachers, tryin' to convince 'em to change. We ain't in that business, Fa-ther. That's what you claim to want to do an' I wish you the best. Only, don't try an' get me an' Eli involved in none of it. We're fur trappers."

"But you have this special opportunity to do more," Augustine argued. "With a few words you can do what we could not in a year of hard labor. Is it asking too much for you to tell them that war is wrong?"

Seth turned a look toward Eli. "I don't reckon it's

askin' so much, only it might get us in the middle of somethin' we ain't got no part of. Right, Cap'n?"

Eli gave it considerable thought. "I suppose it wouldn't be all that much trouble to say that fightin' ain't what the spirits want. If they don't listen, it's not any fault of ours. We can say their ancestors ain't happy on account of all the women an' kids who're gettin' killed. Heads chopped off an' such. Maybe they'd listen if we said it was a message from the spirits they believe in so strong."

"It can't do any harm," Augustine insisted.

A soft footfall outside the tent interrupted their conversation. Two figures bent down to enter through the flap, and in the dim firelight, Eli saw Lone Wolf follow White Mountain inside.

"Cona gi-kai ke-ne." It was Lone Wolf who spoke.

"The chief says a council fire will begin at dawn tomorrow. He is asking you to come," Augustine explained.

"Tell him we'll be there," Seth remarked. "An' I reckon you can tell him we's got a message from their spirits havin' to do with this war."

The priest almost smiled, then he turned to Lone Wolf and began a translation, requiring almost a minute to complete it.

Lone Wolf said something to Augustine. His dark eyes went back and forth from the priest to Seth while he talked. Only once did he glance at Eli, after he finished what he wanted to say.

"The chief asks how many ponies you want for bringing good medicine to his people. He offers each of you a woman from his tribe as a sign of respect for powerful medicine men."

Seth looked to Eli for a response. When Eli spoke he did it carefully, giving his answer a great deal of thought. "Thank the chief for his offer. Tell him that we'll consider it. We got no use for horses 'til spring. Maybe then we'll take a few. As to the women, you can say we'll think about that too. You could say we've gotta talk to the spirits about it . . . about havin' a woman. Be sure he understands we ain't sayin' no to either one, only that we're gonna think on it some. Meantime, we'll show him all the magic we can with guns an' some gunpowder tomorrow. Then I want you to say we gotta get back to our camp so it'll be ready before it snows."

Augustine began a long translation, gesturing, having more difficulty than usual finding the right words. Both chiefs were watching Eli as the priest explained what he said.

Minutes later, without another word, Lone Wolf and White Mountain left the tent. Augustine lowered his voice.

"They seem to be satisfied, gentlemen," he said. "Let us hope that tomorrow the influence of Chief Ten Bears is not too strong to give the others doubts. Red Eagle is a wise man and I believe he will listen to you. If the Lord is willing, tomorrow may be the beginning of an end to war between the Ki-was and the Nah-taih. Should this occur, it will be nothing short of a miracle."

Seth lay back on a pile of buffalo robes. "Hope you'll be pardonin' me for not believin' in no miracles, Father. If you ask me, what happens tomorrow will have a hell of a lot to do with dry gunpowder an' steady hands." He rested his rifle beside him and closed his eyes with a fist wrapped around the grips of his pistol.

Minutes later, exhausted from walking all day and almost half the night, Eli drifted off to sleep, his guns within easy reach.

Hundreds of Kiowa men formed around a big firepit at the center of the village. Seated close to the fire, Chief White Mountain, Chief Lone Wolf, Chief Red Eagle, and Chief Ten Bears watched Seth and Eli and Augustine sit cross-legged near the flames as sunrise bathed the village in golden light. Eli had been awakened by the slow beat of drums at dawn, and when he and Seth emerged from their tent they were greeted by a sight so unexpected they said nothing to each other for several minutes.

Indian warriors, dressed in painted deerskins, shuffled in a circle around a blazing fire. It could have been called a dance step of sorts wherein the men hopped on one foot, then the other, while uttering chants in a singsong voice, holding fans of white and red feathers or shaking rattles made from hollowed gourds. The drums beat continuously, never changing their rhythm, nor did the dance steps change. Several dozen dancers moved around the fire chanting and singing. The chiefs sat beyond the ring of dancers watching the ceremony. Several hundred Kiowas crowded as close to the fire as they could to witness what was taking place. None of the onlookers carried weapons. No women were in sight.

"Whatever they's doin', it looks plumb crazy to me," Seth said.

Eli had no explanation. "Some sort of ritual, I reckon. It must make sense to them."

Augustine came from the tent. He watched the dancing for a moment, listening to drumbeats. "They have begun a ceremonial dance to attract the attention of their gods. In Ki-wa religion all things in nature are seen as spirits. Earth Mother, the moon and stars, the four winds, and the sun represent the physical presence of their Great Spirit. The dancing is meant to show respect for the spirits. We were never allowed to watch one of these ceremonies. They believe only a Ki-wa can be in touch with their gods and the presence of others causes disfavor among the spirits. We are being honored to witness this ceremony. If it were not for their belief that you are messengers from their gods they would not allow it. We would all be killed."

Now, as they sat watching the dancers, Eli tried to measure attitudes of the chiefs seated across the fire. Lone Wolf wore a serene expression. White Mountain stared into the flames as if he were in a trance. Red Eagle had his eyes closed, listening to the drums, swaying back and forth keeping time to the beat. But when

Eli looked at Ten Bears he felt the stocky Indian's mistrust and resentment. Ten Bears stared back at him without blinking, a hard look in his unwavering, obsidian eyes.

"Ten Bears don't want us here," he whispered to Seth. "He's the one we'll have to convince."

Seth merely nodded. "Can't say as I like the son of a bitch anyways, Cap'n. He keeps lookin' at me like that an' I'm liable to lose my temper."

"We're surrounded by Indians, Seth. Don't do anythin' dumb. All we promised to do is put on a magic show. Make some smoke an' shoot a few rounds. Don't let him make you mad."

Seth's heavy eyelids drooped, the way they did when he got really angry. "I ain't forgot we's outnumbered, but if I put a ball square between his eyes, he wouldn't be lookin' at me like that. Injuns or no Injuns, if he don't wipe that goddamn look off his face I'll do it myself."

"Remember, you're the one who keeps sayin' we didn't want no part of this fight. If you shoot him, there's no way we'll make it out of here alive."

At that, Seth lowered his head. "You's right, Cap'n. We got no stake in this. No reason why I should give a damn how some Injun looks at me. If I had my way I'd never look at one more Injun myself. What's got my temper up is how we got ourselves in this fix in the first place. No reason why we let a bunch of wild men drag you an' me into a war that's got nothin' to do with us. I gotta keep remindin' myself the reason we's here is beaver skins. Let 'em kill each other if that's what they got their minds made up to do. It ain't nothin' to us."

Drums continued to beat out a slow rhythm while dancers made endless circles around the fire. The chanting grew noticeably louder as the ceremony went on.

Augustine leaned closer to Eli to be heard. "The dancing will end soon. Then each chief will deliver a talk about the reasons for making war on the Nah-taih, reminding everyone of the women and children who

were killed and beheaded. Senatey told us it is polite to
listen to what the chiefs have to say. You won't understand it, but it is best that we sit and listen until each
chief has had his say. Chiefs consider themselves great
orators, possessing wisdom denied everyone else. Only
after they have talked will you be allowed to speak."

Eli felt his uneasiness growing. Seth's rising anger
over the way Chief Ten Bears was staring at him was
something he had not counted on. In the past he'd seen
Seth's rage result in all manner of bloodshed. They were
encircled by four or five hundred Kiowa warriors preparing for war. If Seth lost his temper now, Eli was sure
the consequences would be disastrous no matter how
sincerely the other Indians believed Seth was some sort
of holy man.

At a time when the drumbeats and chants had
grown monotonous, suddenly a shrill cry ended everything. Dancers stopped where they were and the drums
halted.

Chief Lone Wolf came to his feet. Silence spread
through the village. All eyes were on Lone Wolf. He
held his arms in the air and waited. Shafts of morning
light turned his skin a bronze color.

When Lone Wolf spoke his voice rang out.

"Nie habbe we-ich-ket!"

A murmur spread through the crowd around him.

"Tuh-yah may-way-kin!"

"What's he sayin'?" Eli asked Augustine.

Augustine's color had changed, pale even in the
glow of a rising sun. "He says he is ready to die. That he
prefers death to losing more of his women and children
to an enemy."

"Then he's tellin' his people he wants war," Eli remarked. "He'd rather die than forget about what happened to his people."

"That's what he said," the priest whispered.

Seth overheard Augustine's reply. "Then there
ain't no sense askin' 'em to forget about makin' war on

them Osages. It sounds like Lone Wolf's already made up his mind."

"They might listen to you, Mr. Booker. After you make the smoke and fire your weapon, they might listen."

Seth's gaze wandered across onlookers assembled near the fire. "I ain't no judge of human nature, but I don't see a one of 'em who looks inclined to pay no heed to what I've got to say 'bout keepin' peace."

Eli had no choice but to agree. From the looks on faces all around the firepit, peace was the last thing on anyone's mind.

Chapter
Twenty-Five

Chief Lone Wolf walked closer to the fire. His face was a mask of hatred. He began speaking in a voice that was almost a shout, shaking his fist in the air, appealing to Indians around the firepit. There were nods of approval and murmurs from some warriors while Lone Wolf continued his impassioned speech.

Eli watched White Mountain and Red Eagle for their reactions to what was being said. White Mountain remained devoid of any expression. Red Eagle's face was also blank.

But when Eli looked at Ten Bears he saw the smoldering anger in his eyes. The chief watched Lone Wolf attentively. Muscles in his cheeks and neck were taut, like corded ropes.

Augustine translated in a soft voice. "He says the deaths of his children and women must be avenged. The Nah-taih will be back to strike again unless they are punished for what they did at his village. He is asking the council to follow him in a war against the Nah-taih that will be unlike any other war before."

"We's wastin' our time here," Seth muttered, watching Lone Wolf pace back and forth as he continued to shout so that everyone could hear him.

"The other chiefs have not spoken yet," Augustine reminded. "All will be allowed to talk. One important chief is missing. A bullish man named Sees Far has not arrived yet."

"Don't see how it'll make any difference," Seth said. "Any fool can see they's wantin' to make war."

Unexpectedly, Lone Wolf turned to Seth and Eli. He pointed across the flames and spoke in a softer voice.

"What's he sayin'?" Eli asked under his breath. "Why the hell's he pointin' at us?"

"He is telling the others that two powerful holy men have come to the Ki-wa ceremony, that all can see how different you are in appearance. He is telling them you make powerful magic and that you control thunder and lightning. He calls the guns you carry thundersticks and he is describing how they can kill from a great distance, making a loud noise like thunder in a storm. He says that the black giant, Mr. Booker, can make balls of fire and smoke come from Earth Mother at his command. He asks the others to watch a demonstration, and he promises that you have agreed to call upon the spirits to help them win battles against the Nah-taih."

When Lone Wolf fell silent, Ten Bears came to his feet with his stare fixed on Seth. He spoke sharply, angrily, making gestures, pointing to the sky, then the earth, and lastly to the spot where Seth and Eli sat.

"Whatever he said, it don't sound good," Eli whispered.

Augustine hesitated a moment. "Ten Bears says he has seen other men with white skin and he has heard their thundersticks make loud noises killing buffalo. He does not believe that you, Mr. McBee, can be a holy man, that you are simply from another race of people he has seen from a distance a long time ago. But he agrees he has never seen anyone like Mr. Booker. . . ."

Red Eagle spoke quietly without standing up. He said only a few words.

"Red Eagle is reminding Ten bears of Ki-wa legend, that a dark messenger will come from the spirit world to save the Ki-was from a terrible enemy. He says he believes Mr. Booker is a holy man, although he asks to see the demonstration whereupon fire and smoke comes from the ground at his bidding."

All eyes were suddenly on Seth.

"It's time you put on your magic show," Eli told him in a whisper. "Better make it good."

Seth rose to his feet. When Indians around the fire saw how tall he was, there were more murmurs from the crowd.

Seth rested the stock of his rifle against his hip with the barrel aimed skyward. With his free hand he reached into his ammunition pouch, a movement so slight no one noticed. Now Seth drew his lips back across his teeth in what appeared to be an angry snarl. He turned his head slowly, glaring into the eyes of those standing near the firepit.

Seth circled the fire, a few steps at a time, showing off his height and the vicious look on his face. He said nothing, pausing here and there to make sure everyone saw him.

When he came to the seated chiefs he stopped, staring down at White Mountain, then Red Eagle, and lastly into the hardened eyes of Ten Bears. For several seconds he met Ten Bears' level gaze without blinking, frozen in his tracks with the rifle on his hip. A moment later he spoke over his shoulder to Father Augustine.

"Tell this fat son of a bitch I could kill him before he draws another breath!" Seth cried. "Tell him I speak for the spirits of his ancestors, an' that they ain't happy with all this talk about war! I'm gonna prove I talk for the spirits by makin' smoke an' a ball of flame come from that fire yonder, an' if I do it's the angry voices of his dead kinfolks tellin' him to get his ass back to his village an' stay peaceful this winter. An' you can tell him that if he don't, them Osages are gonna come to his village an' cut off the heads of his women an' kids. Maybe his own head to boot. Tell him what I just said,

Father, an' make damn sure you don't leave nothin' out."

"I'm not sure that would be wise, Mr. Booker," Augustine said.

Seth gave the priest a chilling stare. "Say it anyways. Then tell him this here thunderstick is beggin' me to shoot him with it, only I ain't gonna do it if'n he goes home an' behaves hisself."

Augustine swallowed. He began a careful translation of what Seth said while Seth was standing over Ten Bears gazing down at him through slitted eyelids.

Ten Bears showed no evidence of fear—he simply sat there listening to Augustine explain what Seth said. As soon as the priest's translation ended, Seth made a half turn toward the firepit.

He threw his head back, staring up at a cloudless morning sky, and cried "Hallelujah!" Then he shook his rifle in the air to take attention away from his other hand as he tossed grains of gunpowder into the flames.

A whooshing sound preceded a loud bang. A billowing cloud of smoke belched upward, rolling, boiling, crackling with hundreds of tiny sparks. The smoke lifted, swirling, changing shape as it dissipated, becoming a filmy wisp of blue before it vanished.

Eli had been watching Red Eagle and White Mountain. Both men jumped when the banging noise occurred, and in unison they watched the smoke cloud rise above them.

Ten Bears took his eyes off Seth when the gunpowder erupted, and for a time he stared at the smoke. Although his expression did not change, he would not look at Seth afterward, letting his gaze wander across the faces of warriors standing nearby.

"Hallelujah!" Seth shouted again.

"He's got their attention now," Eli muttered, speaking to Augustine.

Seth brought his rifle to his shoulder. Aiming at a treetop near the edge of the clearing, he thumbed back the hammer on the Whitney and fired.

The explosion seemed magnified in the morning quiet. A loud concussion hurt the ears of several Indians close by as it echoed across the Kiowa camp. A leafless limb atop a gnarled oak tree snapped and fell, tumbling to the ground after Seth's well-aimed rifle ball broke it off.

Lone Wolf stood at the edge of the crowd with his eyes glued to Seth and his rifle. But it was Ten Bears who drew the attention of Seth after the sound of the gunshot faded to silence.

Seth stared down at Ten Bears, and Eli knew by the droop in Seth's eyelids he was prepared to kill the Indian if events did not go the way he wanted.

Seth spoke. "Tell this Injun he'd best pay attention to what I said. If them Osages come back to harm any of his women or kids, I'll kill the sons of bitches for him, only he'd better do like I say an' go back home for the winter, 'stead of makin' war. If that don't work . . . if he won't listen, then we ain't gonna take no side. Tell him we won't lift a finger to help any of 'em if they won't do like I say an' forget about fightin' them Osages 'til spring." He looked over at Eli. "We'll be headed back to New Orleans by then, Cap'n, an' neither one of us will give a damn what they do to each other after we's gone."

Augustine began explaining what Seth said, speaking to each of the chiefs while he talked. Eli tried to read their faces to see if any one of them appeared willing to listen to a call for peace through the winter.

White Mountain eyed Augustine with suspicion. Red Eagle listened passively, nodding every once in a while and with some relief. Eli believed the older Kiowa was more or less in agreement with the terms of Seth's bargain. Ten Bears remained stoic throughout the priest's translation, and Eli found it impossible to guess what he was thinking.

Before Augustine finished, Seth turned to Eli.

"Some of 'em out yonder has got smallpox, Cap'n," he said, with a jerk of his thumb toward the crowd of warriors around them at the council fire. "If they don't get separated from the rest they's sure to make it spread."

"I'll ask Father Augustine to explain what oughta be done to the other chiefs so they'll understand. If they won't listen it's a good bet more'n half these people will die an' there's a chance we'll be blamed just like those priests were, before they killed 'em."

Seth ignored the Indians for now. "We can always go up the river aways. Seems like makin' a deal with these here Injuns is gettin' to be more trouble than it's worth. There has to be more beaver upriver someplace."

"Father Augustine claims Comanches up the Red are worse'n Kiowas when it comes to dealin' with outsiders. I say we stay for a while. See if maybe they'll leave us alone through the cold months. We'll be out of here in early spring an' then it don't matter what happens. Unless we aim to come back . . ."

Augustine ended his translation, and once more all eyes were on Seth. It was Red Eagle who spoke first, and as he began his talk, he came to his feet.

Red Eagle spoke softly, his voice thinned by age, but when he spoke no one else made a sound. For a few minutes the old chief talked quietly, pointing several different directions during his speech. Ten Bears still refused to look at Seth while Red Eagle offered his opinions on what had been said.

Augustine leaned closer to Eli. "Red Eagle is asking his brother Ki-was to hear what the black medicine man has to say. He believes Mr. Booker is truly the dark messenger they were told would come to them. He says he does not agree, that postponing an attack on Nahtaih villages until spring is not the traditional way of their people. He does, however, believe Mr. Booker is speaking for the spirits and if this is their wish, all men of wisdom should listen."

When Red Eagle ended his quiet speech, he sat down in Indian fashion with his knees bent. White

Mountain stood up, casting a glance at the men around him.

"Po-haw-cut To-oh tivo ho-kai-kee-ne."

"He says he has seen the magic of Mr. Booker and he knows it is very powerful," Augustine said. "He has seen Mr. Booker fight and he knows his heart is brave, that no enemy can defeat him in battle."

White Mountain spoke again, waving an arm eastward. He made a gesture toward Seth, then he talked for several minutes more.

"He says the Ki-was have a terrible sickness, the red spots which kill so many of his people. He believes the winter will be a good time for the illness to end, and he hopes his people will grow stronger by springtime. He is telling the others that those with red spots must be separated, according to Mr. Booker, and it is the only way the others without red spots will be spared from slow death."

"He's got that part right," Eli agreed.

The priest's expression turned grave. "Even with a quarantine it may be too late to save them, Mr. Mc-Bee."

"We're doin' all we can. There's no other way to stop it that we know of."

"I quite agree. However, until more time has passed we have no way of knowing if the quarantine works."

White Mountain continued to talk to the tribesmen, making a great many hand signs to punctuate the words he used. As before when Red Eagle spoke, everyone listened closely to White Mountain's opinions.

"The chief believes Mr. Booker's advice is sound, that to wait for spring is advisable. That way, more of his warriors will be strong enough to join the battle. As you can see, none of their chiefs is willing to consider peace a permanent proposition between the Ki-was and the Nah-taih. It goes against many decades of tradition."

"Some folks are naturally inclined to fight, Father,"

Eli said. "If I ever saw a whole race of people who take a likin' to makin' war, it's these Kiowas."

"They know little else, my friend. It was our hope to show them another way of life according to God's teachings."

"Maybe you bit off more'n you could chew?"

"We believe in our purpose here and nothing short of death will discourage me."

Eli wondered if Augustine understood just how close he was to dying if he continued to interfere in Kiowa customs. What the priest failed to comprehend was that some men were born with a mix of fighting blood in their veins and that only a dose of lead or a knife could stop them.

Chapter
Twenty-Six

C hief Ten Bears came to his feet. A hush spread
through the assembled warriors. Ten Bears stared
at Seth a moment, looking up into his eyes. A sap
knot popped in the fire's embers, sending a shower of
sparks above the flames.

*"To-oh tivo mah-von-et tani-har-ro. Ta-es-na-ba
kah."*

"Ten Bears says the black medicine man asks them
to wait for spring to make war," Augustine told Eli quietly. "He is against it, saying war should be made now."

Eli had been certain all along that Ten Bears would
be the one to push for immediate retaliation against the
Osages.

Ten Bears turned to the other chiefs and spoke angrily for several minutes.

"He believes Mr. Booker is asking them to behave
like women and cowards. He reminds Lone Wolf what
happened to his village while they were away hunting
buffalo. He is urging them to reconsider, that a strike
against the Nah-taih now will teach their enemies a les-
son. The Nah-taih will think all Ki-was are weak if they
let the attack on Lone Wolf's people go unpunished. He

wants war before the first snows come and he says only
women hide in their lodges during the cold months."

Eli watched the faces of Lone Wolf and White
Mountain, but it was Red Eagle who shook his head
first.

"Ka! Ka! To-oh tivo tep-pe Tatoco!" Red Eagle's answer could be heard throughout the village.

"Red Eagle says he will not fight until spring, for he
believes Mr. Booker speaks for the Great Spirit now."
Augustine sounded relieved. "If the others follow Red
Eagle, Ten Bears will have no support. It would appear
Mr. Booker's speech and his demonstration have con-
vinced Red Eagle. Now, it is up to Lone Wolf and White
Mountain to decide who they will believe."

Lone Wolf spoke softly. *"Ka. Ka."*

"Ka," said White Mountain, glancing across the
firepit to Seth.

Augustine whispered to Eli, "The others have decided not to make war until spring. Ten Bears stands
alone. He knows he will not be able to win a fight with
the Nah-taih. Only Sees Far remains as a potential ally
for Ten Bears and he has not come to the council. It
would appear a major war has been averted, at least
until the winter passes."

"That'll give us enough time to cure our pelts an'
get the hell outa here," Eli said. "It ain't a permanent
solution, but I reckon it's a start."

Seth walked over to Eli. "What's happenin' over
yonder?" he asked.

Augustine explained. "Three of the chiefs have decided not to fight until the snow melt. Only Ten Bears
still wants a war and he cannot win it without their
help."

Seth's shoulders dropped. "Then I say we get back
to camp. We done what we came to do. Tell the chiefs
we's grateful they listened. Then you'd best explain how
them that's sick has gotta be separated from the rest."

Eli saw Lone Wolf rise and come toward them. He
spoke to Augustine so his words could be translated.

For a few moments Lone Wolf talked quietly; then he turned to Seth while Augustine gave him a lengthy explanation.

"I told Chief Lone Wolf what you said. And I explained how the people with pox must be kept apart from the others until the spots disappear. He says he will send warriors to our camp on the Washita with gifts for both of you."

"We don't want no women," Seth said with certainty.

Augustine smiled. "Lone Wolf did not say what the gifts would be, only that they would arrive in two suns . . . two days."

Eli came slowly to his feet, working stiffness from his knees. "It probably ain't smart to question him over what he aims to give us. Whatever it is, horses or women, I reckon we'll take 'em an' make the best of it. It wouldn't be smart to refuse him if we aim to live in their territory this winter."

"A wise decision," the priest agreed, struggling to his feet with noticeable effort, dusting off the seat of his borrowed pants. He looked at Lone Wolf and Lone Wolf nodded. "We're free to go back now." He gave Seth a sideways glance. "You are to be congratulated, Mr. Booker. You have succeeded where all our previous efforts failed. Your magic demonstration has convinced them that you are . . . in their view, supernatural. It is not all that important that simple gunpowder is all that was needed."

Kiowa warriors backed away to provide an opening in their circle. Eli noticed several near the back of the group had red sores on their faces and chests. He spoke to Seth quietly as they walked among the Indians, heading west to leave the village for a long trek back to the river.

"I count several dozen more with the pox. Gettin' 'em together like this could cause it to spread faster'n it might otherwise."

Seth cast a look backward. "We done all we can to

show 'em what to do," he said, loading a powder charge and ball, then a bit of wadding into the muzzle of his Whitney as they walked. He rodded the charge and placed a cap on the nipple before balancing the rifle in his hand.

Near the edge of the village they were met by four Indian women carrying strips of dried buffalo meat. Eli's heartbeat quickened when he noticed one of the women was Senatey.

She looked at him and smiled, waiting near the last tent west of the village, extending the meat in her hands. He came over to her and returned her smile while he took the handful of buffalo jerky.

"Thank you," he told her gently, trying to sound as proper as he could.

Her brow furrowed slightly. "Is . . . meat?" she asked, as if she was not sure of the English words.

"Yes. It's meat. Buffalo meat. My name is Eli. Father Augustine told me your name is Senatey."

She looked at Augustine and her scowl deepened. "Him bring bad thing to Ki-wa. Many die. No can go place where him teach read book. Is bad place."

Before Augustine could respond, Eli said, "It isn't a bad place. Your people have a sickness. We've shown Chief White Mountain and Chief Lone Wolf how to stop it from spreading. A priest or a place did not cause it to happen."

Clearly, the girl did not understand.

Augustine began a translation in Kiowa, using sign language to make a point now and then. Senatey listened, although she had a clouded look in her eyes.

"No can go back," she said, shaking her head. Then she took a closer look at Eli's hair and beard. *"Am-a-wau,"* she whispered in a tiny voice.

Eli remembered it was the Kiowa word for red. "It's red. I had some Irish ancestors. My pa had red hair."

Again, Senatey did not fully comprehend. Her lips formed in a slow, careful way, then she said, "Red."

"That's right." He thought quickly of a way to get to know her better, for as he stared at her now he found she was even prettier than he imagined. "You could come to our camp on the river if you wanted. It ain't a bad place an' I don't think Lone Wolf would mind."

Augustine spoke to her in Kiowa, telling her everything Eli said. While she listened, a hint of color crept into her cheeks and the corners of her mouth turned up slightly in the beginnings of a smile.

"Maybeso come," she said, looking down at her soiled deerskin dress.

"I hope you will," Eli added. "Nothin' bad will happen to you there. You got my word on that."

She glanced over to Seth a moment, then asked Eli a question. "To-oh tivo speak for spirit of dead Ki-wa?"

"I'd be careful how I answered that one," Augustine warned. "Right now it may be important for them to believe Mr. Booker is a true messenger from their spirit world. If peace is to be had this winter, they must believe it is what their ancestors want and that Mr. Booker's message is the truth. In a way it is the truth. God wants peace for all His people, peace on Earth. It won't be a complete falsehood to say he speaks for the spirits of their dead when he asks for peace in the name of God."

Eli thought about his answer while he looked Senatey in the eye. "To-oh tivo speaks the truth," he said finally.

"For spirit of dead Ki-wa?" she persisted.

He felt cornered by her question. "He speaks truth. It is the wish of your spirits that no war's to be fought. It'll save lives if your people keep peace."

Augustine told her what Eli said, and there was something akin to a plea in his voice. When the priest finished he gave Eli a shrug. "I told her the truth as best I could, Mr. McBee. You must understand that a concept like that is hard for them to believe. It is our good fortune that they believe Mr. Booker is the medicine man foretold in their oral tradition handed down from one generation to another."

Eli smiled when he looked at the girl again. "I hope you'll come to our camp at the river soon. We can talk. Maybe you can teach me some words in your language an' I'll teach you a few in English."

It was left to Augustine to repeat Eli's offer in words she fully understood.

"Maybeso come," she replied. She looked at the other women and when she did, Eli noticed that another young girl was watching Seth through her eyelashes. She was thin but shapely and a bit taller than the rest. Seth had noticed the looks she was giving him, and he pretended to ignore them.

Senatey spoke to the other girls, and they turned away for the center of the village. Eli watched her a moment, then put the jerky inside his shirt and led the way across a stretch of barren ground to a stand of trees.

When they reached the forest he spoke to Seth. "That one tall gal sure did appear to take a fancy to you. She liked to have stared holes plumb through you a while ago."

"Don't need no woman, Cap'n. Don't hardly get them kind of urges no more."

"You ain't that old yet," Eli joked, walking to a dim trail they had followed to reach the village last night. "When it gets cold you might be wantin' some company."

Seth chuckled. "You sure as hell was tryin' hard to get that pretty one to show up mighty quick. Damned if you didn't come close to makin' a fool outa yourself, all that talk about teachin' her English."

"She's a beauty. A man don't get too many second chances to have a beautiful lady around. I don't see nothin' wrong with askin' her to come for a visit."

"Mostly, a woman's a pain in the ass," Seth said. "They get in moods. Afore you know it they's got a grip on you an' you'll be chained to her like you was a runaway dog."

"I'll take my chances if it comes," Eli promised, thinking of how pretty Senatey's face was. "To tell the truth I figure I could get used to bein' chained to a girl like her."

"Nearly same as bein' in jail," Seth muttered, following Eli down a winding path hidden in forest shadows. As they had the day before, clouds came drifting from the south, and farther west they blocked out the sun entirely. "Looks like it could rain," Seth added, changing the subject when he could get no agreement from Eli on the subject of women.

Plodding along at the rear, Augustine still carried the small bundle of knives and beads, forgotten by all three of them during the council talks. "Above all else," he said, "it seems we may have averted a terrible war. You are to be commended for your showmanship, Mr. Booker. It appears to have worked."

Seth's voice had an edge to it when he spoke. "You's forgot about them Osages, Father. We ain't done nothin' to stop 'em from wantin' to fight. If they come back to this part of the country, all hell's gonna break loose an' we'll be square in the middle of it."

It was true, Eli thought. If Osage war parties returned to Kiowa lands, the killing would resume, leaving the Kiowas caught between a smallpox epidemic and bands of enemies who delighted in chopping off the heads of their victims.

"Maybe the Osages will stay put if this weather turns bad," he said. "Won't be long 'till there'll be snow on the ground."

Seth seemed to be contemplating something. "I sure as hell hope bad weather keeps things quiet. Main thing we gotta do is trap a bunch of beaver this winter. If we let them Kiowas draw us into a fight that ain't ours, we won't have nothin' to show for comin' all this way."

"Brother Bolivar and I will pray for peace," Augustine said a moment later.

Seth wagged his head. "It ain't that I got no belief in all that prayin' you're gonna do, Father, but when it comes to these wild Injuns I ain't all that sure the Almighty gives a damn what happens to 'em."

"I believe He does," the priest replied softly. "They are as much a part of the human race as we are and God loves all His children."

"Maybe," Seth muttered. By the tone of his voice Eli was sure he didn't quite believe it.

Chapter
Twenty-Seven

Clouds shrouded the moon. They had been walking since early morning, and as they crossed dense forests and vast, empty meadows, fatigue ended all but the most fundamental conversation. Eli led the way with Seth following at his heels. Augustine fell farther behind as their journey lengthened.

"I must rest," Augustine said as they walked through an oak thicket, then paused beside a fallen tree, gently sitting down on the moist, moss-covered wood. "My feet are too sore to continue for a moment. I'm sorry, my friends."

Eli gave their surroundings a closer look. "Good place as any to rest a spell, I reckon."

Seth paid particular attention to their backtrail. "I got this feelin' somebody's followin' us, Cap'n, but when I look back there ain't nobody there. Mostly, when I get this feelin', there's a reason for it, but I'll be damned if I can spot anybody back yonder."

"Maybe it's only your imagination," Eli said.

Seth wasn't having any of it. "Can't recall the last time I was wrong when the feelin' come over me. Only, this time I can't see nothin' but trees an' shadows. Ain't no moon or stars on account of all the clouds."

While Seth was talking Eli heard a noise to the
north . . . the sounds of horses moving at a slow gait.
He held up his hand for silence and cocked an ear,
holding his breath.

"Horses," he whispered. "Lots of 'em. Movin' over
yonder a ways. Can you hear it?"

Seth whirled, crouching down. "I hear it," he replied as he raised his rifle.

Augustine jumped off the rotted tree trunk, turning
his head so he could listen.

North of the thicket they heard the swish of unshod
hooves moving through tall grass. Eli attempted to
count the number of hoofbeats, how many horses were
traveling through night-darkened woods.

"Can't see a damn thing," Seth mumbled under his
breath with his rifle held against his shoulder.

"Sounds like a bunch," Eli said softly, easing his
Whitney's hammer to a firing position above the percussion cap. "No way to know until we see 'em."

They listened to the drum of hooves crossing soft
ground for a few minutes more. Once, Eli was sure he
saw shadows moving in the forest darkness half a mile
away, only the outlines of riders heading eastward.

"Maybe it's that other band of Kiowas. That chief
named Sees Far was supposed to show up," Seth recalled. "He never did make it to that council fire."

Eli continued to watch the trees. "Or Osages. Can't
tell from here . . ."

Augustine peered into black shadows blanketing
the forest floor. Thickening clouds in a night sky made it
almost impossible to see anything.

"I hear them now," he said.

"They's comin' from the direction of the river,"
Seth warned as he turned an ear to the west. "Sure as
hell hope they didn't find White Mountain's village.
Seemed like every one of 'em who could ride a horse
came with us. If they ran across that village with nobody
but womenfolk in it, they's liable to have cut off a few

more heads an' left 'em for the chief to find when he got back."

Eli considered what Seth said. "White Mountain's scouts found a bunch of hoofprints the night we was headed over to Lone Wolf's camp. That was why we stopped last night, until they was sure who made those tracks."

Augustine offered his opinion on the subject. "Word of the smallpox epidemic may have reached the Nah-taih. It would be a good time for them to launch a raid. They would have no way of knowing they were exposing themselves to smallpox."

Eli heard more horses trotting quietly through the woods. He wondered about Augustine's worries, that an Osage raiding party might strike White Mountain's village at a time when the Kiowas were unable to defend themselves.

"Whether we like it or not, we're involved in this war. We took a side with White Mountain's people when we helped him in that fight an' I reckon that's reason enough for the Osages to come back."

The soft whisper of ponies' hooves grew quieter, moving farther away. Seth lowered the muzzle of his rifle and let out a sigh.

"If we aim to hunt beaver on White Mountain's land this winter, I reckon it's only fair we took his side. Only thing is, we's fixin' to get ourselves caught up in a war we got no stake in."

The priest pointed due north. "We have no proof that what we heard is a Nah-taih war party. Until we know otherwise, let us assume the horses we heard belonged to Sees Far and men from his tribe. This is, after all, Ki-wa territory. I think it would be unusual for the Nah-taih to come back after what your guns did to them."

"Sure don't seem logical," Seth said, "why so many Injuns are ridin' around at night."

"I only hope Brother Bolivar is well," Augustine said, as the last sounds of hoofbeats faded into the night. "While I do agree it is unusual for so many Indians to be moving on a night like this, it may only be Sees Far and his tribesman heading for the council."

"I'd hate like hell to bet on it," Seth remarked.

"So would I," Eli added quietly, returning the hammer on his Whitney to his resting place. "Somethin' about this don't add up an' I don't figure a man can make a livin' gamblin' on what an Indian will do, regardless."

"We'll know, come daybreak," Seth said. "When we get to the river we'll find out if them Osages was out on a raid tonight. I got a funny feelin' in my belly that we ain't gonna like what we see when we get back to our canoe."

As the night silence deepened, Eli began to relax. "We got no reason to worry yet."

Even as the words left his mouth, a small voice inside his head told him something was wrong.

Dawn came gray and cold to the forest. After stopping for rest several times during the night at Augustine's request, they could see the Washita River valley in the distance as a mist rose above stands of red oak and elm and tiny meadows between thicker wooded places.

Eli's legs ached from walking so many miles. Augustine had begun to limp, complaining that one of his sandals rubbed blisters on his heel.

Seth marched forward undeterred by the distance, always with an eye on their surroundings.

"This is the emptiest country I ever saw, Cap'n," Seth said as they crossed a wooded hilltop. "Hardly a deer or a squirrel in these here trees. It's like everythin' moved off someplace real sudden."

Near the river, miles distant, Eli thought he could see a few columns of smoke rising. "Looks like fires are burnin' in White Mountain's village."

"Maybe," Seth said, "or it could be a sign of trouble. If Osages raided last night they could have burned everythin' to the ground."

"You've got a worryin' nature," Eli said. "Looks like campfires to me."

Seth's broad face pinched in a scowl. "I 'spose we'll know in an hour or so. Let's keep walkin'."

Crossing the ridge, they started down a long, twisting trail to the bottom of a snakelike ravine. Eli rested his Whitney on his shoulder. His legs felt heavy, like lead weights, and after a night without sleep his eyes batted continually as they made their way to the floor of the gulley.

But as they climbed out of the ravine his nostrils flared as he caught the scent of smoke on a westerly wind. Again, he had a vague sense something was wrong.

The scene they discovered when they came near the river was one of total destruction. Rows of blackened tent poles stood where tents had been before they went with White Mountain to Lone Wolf's village. The horse herd belonging to White Mountain's people was no longer grazing beside the river, and by all indications, the Kiowa camp had been sacked and burned to the ground.

"I felt it in my bones," Seth said when they came to a line of trees near the remains of the village. "They got attacked by Osages while we was gone."

Eli stood at the edge of the forest for a moment surveying what was left of the village. "This means war. White Mountain is gonna retaliate now, don't matter what you claim the spirits want."

"Unbelievable," Augustine said, his voice thickened by what he saw beside the river.

"It's time you started believin' the truth about these here Injuns, Father," Seth said. "Don't matter how much you want to believe you can make Christians out of 'em, this here's all the proof you need that fightin' is all they know. They been killin' each other since long before you got here an' a few words from a Bible ain't gonna change a damn thing."

Eli squinted in the sun's midday glare. "It ain't gonna be pretty, what we find down there. There'll be a bunch of heads in clay pots, if I'm right. Now there won't be no stoppin' White Mountain or all the other tribes from startin' a war against the Osages. It's liable to mean they ain't gonna listen to you no more, either, Seth. There ain't enough gunpowder in all creation to convince 'em otherwise."

"Maybe it's time we moved on further west," Seth suggested. "I sure as hell don't think we oughta be here when they start to even the score. Trappin' beaver will be nigh onto impossible if the two bunches start fightin' around here. We could get killed tryin' to run traplines."

"Maybe you're right," Eli said, sighing, watching towering columns of smoke from ruined lodges rise in still air. "A man's got no chance to survive this without bein' caught, one way, or the other. Both sides could be against us now."

"I pray Brother Bolivar escaped with his life," Augustine said.

Eli looked north, toward the camp where quarantined Kiowas had been moved. "We'd better see if any of them sick Indians had any better luck. From here, it looks like the main village was completely destroyed."

"Findin' a few sick ones ain't gonna make no difference," Seth said. "When Chief White Mountain finds out what happened here, he'll call all them other chiefs together an' this won't be no safe place for us to be. I say we get our gear packed an' clear out of here afore the killin' starts. Father Augustine said Comanches was worse'n Kiowas when it came to dealin' with their enemies, but I don't see how things can get no worse than what's fixin' to happen on this river. There'll be blood all over the place an' if we's got any sense, we'll make damn sure ain't none of it ours."

Eli let his gaze wander across the fire-blackened skeletons of tent poles near the water. "One thing's for damn sure. I don't figure White Mountain will wait for a spring thaw to get his revenge for what happened."

"All seems lost," Augustine said, peering into mist and smoke arising from what was left of the Kiowa village. "Now it would be foolish for Brother Bolivar and me to go upriver in the spring to continue our work on the mission. With an Indian war commencing between the Ki-was and the Nah-taih, this region is not safe for anyone."

"That includes a couple of fur trappers," Seth said with conviction. "The price of beaver pelts in New Orleans ain't nowhere near high enough to be worth dyin' for. We got ourselves in a hornet's nest here an' I say we get our asses out afore it's too late. . . ."

Chapter
Twenty-Eight

The scent of smoke came stronger to them before they were within half a mile of the village. And with the smoke Eli detected another smell, the suggestion of burned skin and singed hair mingling with scorched wood. It appeared from a distance the village was deserted, and he wondered if all the women and children had been attacked by an Osage raiding party.

"We should expect the worst," Augustine said, limping on his blistered foot, and from fatigue, aided the last few miles by a walking stick he found in the forest.

Seth's expression left little doubt he agreed. He swept the trees around them with cautious glances and kept his rifle ready. "Looks like they burned the place down," he said, his deep voice muted somewhat by the destruction he could see from afar. Lazy wisps of dark smoke curled from burned-out frameworks of tents, caught by the winds, drawn eastward on breaths of moving air.

When they came closer to the village Eli could make out the grisly signature of an Osage attack. Spread across the smoldering remains of White Mountain's camp, tall stakes had been driven in the ground. Atop each wooden stake was a human head. Most were burned beyond recognition, charred bones afixed to sticks of fire-darkened oak without flesh or hair. Grinning skulls with empty eye sockets, blackened by fire, had been turned to the east as a greeting for Kiowas returning home from Lone Wolf's council.

"Damn," Seth said under his breath when he got a better look at the severed heads. He stopped to examine a skull on the east side of the village. Bits of black, twisted flesh clung to the jawbone. "A son of a bitch who'd do this to another human bein' has got to be plumb out of his mind . . . crazy."

Augustine began to pray near one of the skulls, fingering a rosary hanging from his neck. Eli saw tears in the priest's eyes and running down his cheeks.

"Crazy, or downright mean," he agreed, when Seth gave him a questioning glance. "This ain't ordinary fightin', not war like we understand."

Seth wrinkled his nose. "Stinks worse'n hell, Cap'n. I say we get the hell outa here afore them Kiowas come back." He aimed a look toward the river. "Our canoe's gone. Can't see it from here."

"We can walk," Eli said, unable to take his gaze from one of the smaller skulls. "This one was just a kid. Why the hell did they cut off a kid's head like that?"

Seth made a face. "Why the hell do these here wild people do anythin'? Don't none of it make no sense. When them Kiowas cut open those dead mens' bellies it didn't make a lick of sense to me, tossin' their guts all over the place. These Injuns ain't the same as regular folks."

Augustine's soft prayers were the only sound for a moment, until a sap knot crackled in a nearby fire where the remains of a tent smoldered below charred lodgepoles.

"Maybe you were right, Seth," Eli said quietly, surveying what was left of the village. "Maybe we oughta take our chances with Comanches farther west. If we stay, our skulls could be hangin' on one of these stakes before spring. Ain't no amount of beaver skins worth dyin' for."

"Let's head upriver," Seth said. "Trouble is, looks like we lost our canoe."

"We can build a raft. . . ."

Augustine ended his praying suddenly. "Brother Bolivar! We must hurry back to camp to see if the Nahtaih found him! I only hope he's still alive."

Eli gave the burned-out remains of the village a final look. "No reason to stay here," he said. "They're all dead, the women an' children Chief White Mountain left behind."

Seth shouldered his rifle and started for the river, long strides carrying him to the water's edge before Eli got there.

"They sunk it," Seth said, pointing to the outline of their canoe resting on the river bottom. "All they done was punch some holes in it, looks like. If we got enough buffalo skins back at camp, maybe we can fix it. With a jug of pitch we might be able to patch it up."

Eli's attention was upstream. "I wonder if they killed the Kiowas we quarantined," he asked aloud. "Can't see no smoke from here. We'll come back for the canoe later. Tomorrow, if Father Bolivar is all right."

Augustine stumbled to the riverbank, leaning on his walking stick. His voice was full of resignation when he said, "Perhaps God did not mean for us to succeed here after all. Since I first entered the priesthood I truly believed God's purpose was for all men to know His grace. But what I have seen here tests my faith. How can men reason with a race of people who cut off the heads of women and children?"

"They ain't people," Seth said. "I figure that's where you been wrong all along. They's same as wild animals. You can't make a Christian or even no civilized man outa somebody who can cut off a little kid's head so's he can decorate a stick with it." Seth's expression hardened. "Sometimes there ain't but one cure for what ails a man who thinks he's meaner'n everybody else.

You kill the son of a bitch anyway you can, an' go about your business. Some folks don't deserve to live, Father. My mama called 'em a blight on this earth, them mean types. I killed my share on the Mississipp' over the years an' my conscience don't bother me a goddamn bit. When some no-good bastard ain't got no respect for another man's life, you's doin' folks a favor if you kill him. I took a few lives back when I poled the river. Maybe I saved a few whilst I was at it."

Eli thought about the pirates and robbers he and Seth had tangled with on the deck of a flatboat. "Seth's right," he said, turning upstream. "Some men got a killin' comin' to 'em. After what we seen here, I'd say that includes Osages, same as river pirates."

"God teaches that all of mankind is worthy of redemption," Augustine said. He shook his head when he looked back at the Kiowa village. "I confess I find it hard to believe that the people who did this will be admitted to God's kingdom. Like Brother Bolivar, I have discovered my faith in God's word has been tested by these Indians and what they are capable of doing to each other."

"Just so's they don't do it to us," Seth muttered after a second examination of the canoe submerged in shallow water near the bank. "I say we take our chances with them Comanches, or damn near anybody else. I got a feelin' this ain't no place for us to try an' make a livin' in the fur trade. I never was one to tuck tail an' run from trouble, but this war between Kiowas an' Osages ain't none of our affair. Hell, let 'em kill each other if that's what they's bent on doin'."

Eli started walking north along the river's edge. Augustine and Seth caught up with him a moment later.

They made their way beside the Washita, passing slowly among canebrakes and thickets of leafless trees. Bulrushes swayed back and forth in changing winds sweeping down from the northwest. As it had the day before, the sky darkened with clouds, and when the wind shifted, Eli thought he smelled rain.

Eli's first glimpse of the clearing where the quarantined Indians camped slowed his footsteps. Where tents once stood in the meadow, no trace remained of any buffalo-hide lodges, nor was there any sign someone had been there when he looked across the opening in the forest. Then he saw the rows of bodies covered in furry brown buffalo skins.

"They pulled out," he said, peering around a tree. "Looks empty, like nobody was ever here."

"They left their corpses," Augustine observed as soon as he had a vantage point between oak trunks. "Where could they have gone?"

Seth edged past Eli until he stood close enough to see what the others saw. "No tents," he said in a hushed voice, "only the dead ones layin' over yonder like they was afore we left. Can't make no sense out of it, how they knew to clear out."

"Perhaps someone warned them," Augustine suggested. "Owl may have seen or heard something in time to warn the others of an attack."

"Let's have a closer look," Eli said, moving forward until he stood at the edge of the clearing.

A few blackened places showed where firepits had been, and in spots, there was evidence of the campsite.

"Don't appear there was no trouble here," Seth said. "Heads ain't stuck on no pointed tree limbs."

"There'll be tracks," Eli said. "We can follow 'em to see where they went."

"We must proceed at once to find Brother Bolivar," Augustine was quick to say. "As you already know, he would have no way to defend himself if they found him."

"I offered to show him how to use a gun," Seth reminded the priest.

Augustine waved the notion away. "A member of the Franciscan brotherhood does not take lives, Mr. Booker. We devote our lives to saving others from sin. Teaching Brother Bolivar how to shoot a gun goes against everything he learned at the monastery where he took his vows."

"It might keep him alive," Seth said. "This ain't no place to be tryin' to save folks from sin. In case you ain't noticed, these Injuns don' give a damn about what makes a man a sinner."

Before Augustine could say more, Eli walked into the meadow for a closer inspection, looking for any evidence there had been violence here before the Kiowas departed.

"No blood I can see," Eli said, looking at the grass and a few barren spots where lodges once stood. "It don't appear they did any fightin'."

Seth came into the clearing more cautiously with his rifle held to his shoulder, pacing back and forth across dried tufts of prairie grass. "Maybe not," he answered, swinging his head in both directions as though he sensed something was wrong.

It was Augustine who heard the sound first. He froze in his tracks and pointed across the meadow. "Someone groaned over there," he said. "I'm quite sure I heard a human voice and it sounded like a groan, as though someone is in pain."

Now Eli heard it too, a soft noise coming from a spot near the corpses. "Over yonder. Behind that line of trees. It's real soft, but I did hear somethin'."

"Be careful," Seth warned, watching the place where Eli was pointing. "I got that feelin' again, Cap'n, an' it ain't often I's wrong."

Again they heard a voice from the trees, a faint cry so weak it was difficult to determine where it originated.

Eli pulled the revolver from his belt. "I'll go see who or what it is. Keep me covered with your rifle."

Moving forward in a crouch, pistol in one hand and his rifle in the other, Eli advanced across the meadow on the balls of his feet. He did not hear the cry again, or any other sound beyond the whisper of his boots through dry grass.

When he reached the first slender oaks he hesitated, aiming his Paterson in front of him. "Who's there?" he asked, feeling sweat bead on his skin despite a cool wind.

No reply came from the forest.

"Who's there?" he asked again.

More silence greeted him, and now he wondered if they had imagined hearing a voice.

"I heard somethin'. I'd nearly swear I did. . . ."

Suddenly, off to his left he heard a stirring, the crackle of leaves from the forest floor. He swung the barrel of his gun in that direction and crouched down.

"Who is it?" he asked, trying to see clearly in dark shade and the absence of sunlight because of heavy clouds overhead.

A quiet moan came from the same spot.

"Who the hell's there?" he demanded, cocking his pistol.

The rustle of dry leaves. Again, he heard moaning.

Creeping forward, covering his progress with the gun, he advanced deeper into the woods.

"Answer me!" he cried, thinking how foolish he must sound if the moans came from an Indian who did not understand English. He inched closer, making as little noise as possible, hunkered down to make a smaller target of himself.

He almost jumped out of his skin when he heard Seth yell, "You see anybody, Cap'n?"

Eli would not risk an answer now, not being so close to whoever was making the sounds.

His palms grew sweaty on the pistol grips and on the stock of his rifle. It seemed his feet made enough noise to wake the dead no matter where he placed his boots.

"I'm comin' in, Eli!" Seth shouted. "Don't shoot at nothin' behind you, 'cause it's gonna be me!"

A few yards more and he could make out the dim shape of a bare-chested man lying near the base of a tree. He appeared to be crawling, attempting to get behind the oak's thick trunk before Eli could get any closer.

An Indian, Eli thought, perhaps a survivor of the slaughter at White Mountain's village. He could be seriously wounded, or dying. Augustine would be needed to translate what the Indian said.

Or could it be an Osage?

He continued forward until he stood only a few feet from the body of a slender Indian boy. When the boy heard his footsteps, he turned his face toward Eli.

A gaping hole in the Indian's side dribbled blood down his abdomen and legs. But it was the boy's face that drew Eli's attention.

"Owl," he whispered, rushing toward him as he lowered the hammer on his revolver and tucked it into the waistband of his pants.

Chapter
Twenty-Nine

"*Tuh-yah. Tuh-yah,*" Owl whispered, his face twisted with pain. Eli knelt beside the boy, quickly examining the nature of his wound. A knife or a spear had torn into his right side just below his ribcage, exposing his internal organs. A sticky smear marked his passage across piles of fallen leaves where he bled on his way toward the tree.

"I don't know what you're sayin' to me," Eli said. He heard footsteps behind him. "Over here, Seth! This boy is hurt real bad!"

The thumping of Seth's boots beat faster. Seconds later, a shadow blocked out dim light from a cloudy sky above the pile of leaves where Owl lay.

"Damn," Seth sighed, bending down to inspect the deep gash in Owl's skin. "It's bad, Cap'n. Real bad. He'll be lucky if he lives, cut wide open like that."

"*Tuh-yah,*" the boy moaned again without opening his eyes.

"What is he sayin'?" Seth asked.

"Got no idea. Go get Father Augustine. Maybe he's tellin' us what happened back at the village."

Seth trotted off toward the clearing while Eli pushed Owl gently onto his back. When Owl felt Eli's touch his eyes batted open. He stared up at Eli a moment.

"Nah-taih," he said, struggling for air. "Nah-taih come."

"I know," Eli told him. "We found what they did to the kids an' women. Where are the others? What happened to the tents an' everybody who had the sickness?"

For a time Owl did not seem to understand, frowning. "Run away," he replied after a moment. "Go far. See Nah-taih come in sun sleep. Hear Nah-taih, hear fight. Mo-pe say run away. I go fight Nah-taih."

Eli recalled that Mo-pe was the Kiowa word for Owl. "You heard 'em comin' last night. You saw 'em an' told the others to run away an' hide."

Owl nodded once, barely a noticeable movement of his head.

Back in the clearing Eli could hear Seth yelling for Augustine to hurry. "Ain't much we can do for you," he said softly, when Owl's gaze remained fixed on Eli's face. "I can sew you up an' the rest'll be up to you. Too bad about what happened to the rest of your people. You shouldn't have gone back to help fight them Osages, weak as you were from smallpox. There's just so much any man can do. . . ."

Augustine and Seth came running through the forest. They could carry the boy upriver to camp and do the best they could for him, but odds were Owl would die from his belly wound.

Eil looked up at the empty branches swaying in strong winds above his head. Darker clouds blanketed the sky. The first big storm of early winter was on its way to Red River country.

"It's too late to head farther west," he told himself. "We ain't even got our canoe now." He thought about what was sure to happen when Chief White Mountain and the other Kiowa chiefs heard about what took place here. All hope for peace this winter was gone.

Part Three

Chapter
Thirty

Wind-driven sleet rattled against the sides of their lean-to in a monotonous, icy chorus serving as a reminder of the temperature. Sleet lay in thick layers over the ground leading down to the river, deepening on the slanted sod roof of the shelter. Mud chinked into cracks in the walls prevented most of the wind from whistling through on three sides. The lean-to opened to the south, offering more windbreak than escape from the elements. The tarp once covering packs in their canoe during the trip westward served as a crude flap. But the square of canvas over the front bulged and popped with every gust no matter how securely they tried to tie it down.

The lean-to was crowded with five men huddled inside it, and at night when they slept, bodies lay so close together arms and legs were often touching. Heaps of buffalo skins provided most of the warmth, since building even the smallest fire inside only filled the tiny building with smoke, giving off scant heat. A firepit had been dug near the entrance, which they used for cooking and to stay moderately warm when sheets of rain or sleet did not force them inside. But as the storm lasted a fifth day there seemed no end to it and no

escape from bitterly cold winds blasting through the
Washita Valley day and night.

Owl rested on a pile of buffalo robes, his thin face
reddened by fever. His wound was festering, yet to everyone's surprise he was alive, struggling to survive a
mortal wound and smallpox despite his frail condition.
The others were careful not to touch any of his open
pox sores. He remained asleep for hours at a time and
only awakened long enough to take spoonfuls of turkey
soup Seth made after a successful hunt in woods west of
the river. Seth reported a number of fat turkey hens
roosting in a draw close to camp, and after the storm
broke, he and Eli meant to hunt there again. The draw,
Seth related, fed into a creek where a dam provided
deep water for at least a dozen big beaver domes, a fur
trapper's paradise, he had said.

But it was Owl's story of the Osage attack on the
village that kept them uneasy, watchful during the days
and nights since they carried him to the lean-to. In a
voice so weak, it was all but impossible to hear, he told
Augustine how hundreds of Osage warriors surprised
White Mountain's village in the hours before dawn.
With a savagery Owl found difficult to describe the
Osage attack began. Women and children and men too
old to attend the council were butchered in their tents.
Screams filled the night, and soon giant fires blazed
from one end of the village to the other. The pony herd
was driven off before Owl and seven warriors from the
quarantined campsite arrived with bows and arrows and
spears. But it was too late to save anyone in the main
village, and only the predawn darkness allowed Owl to
escape with his life following an encounter with an
Osage spear.

Brother Bolivar described what he had seen and
heard that night. Towering fingers of orange flame lit up
an inky sky, and even from a distance he could hear the
screams of wounded and dying children. He hid in the
forest when the band of Kiowas with smallpox retreated
northwest following the river, not sure whether they

were friend or foe in the dark. He was still hiding in the trees when Seth and Eli and Augustine brought Owl to camp and crossed the river with him lying on a piece of rotted tree trunk, wading across with their rifles and pistols and gunpowder held high above the water.

That first evening after the attack the storm blew in, and now, for five days and nights they sat in their lean-to, listening to bits of ice drum recently sodded roof and walls, rattling when it struck ground or against trees surrounding their camp.

Bolivar's donkey stood behind the overturned cart with its tail to the wind, shivering under a coating of sleet clinging to its hide. Each day it seemed the temperature dropped a little more, and only this morning, Eli found a thin sheet of ice atop their drinking-water bucket.

Seth went outside to make coffee shortly after dawn while Augustine and Bolivar added water to last night's soup for Owl. Piling wood on their fire, Seth rubbed his hands together and cast a wary look downstream.

"I figured we'd be hearin' from White Mountain by now," he said, shivering in his moth-eaten blue mackinaw. He wore a black seaman's cap and an extra pair of woolen pants over his long johns today. "Even with this storm it ain't like them Kiowas to take things lyin' down. Maybe they's off trailin' them Osages back to wherever they come from." He glanced up at the sky. "Sure as hell ain't no fit weather to do no fightin' in."

Bolivar placed the kettle of soup at the base of the flames and gazed north. "I've been wondering what happened to the sick members of White Mountain's tribe," he said. "They couldn't be far, not in their condition."

Seth grunted. "A scared man can travel mighty far, Father. They saw an' heard what happened to them others. No tellin' how far they went afore they stopped."

"Those who are seriously ill will suffer greatly in this ice and wind," Bolivar said, stirring soup with a tin spoon. A blast of cold air sent pieces of sleet down his collar and he hunkered lower, closer to the fire.

Eli buttoned the top button on his greatcoat when more bits of ice struck his neck and face. "It's damn sure miserable. I hope it don't last much longer on account of we wasn't ready for cold weather yet. We need firewood an' more mud in the cracks in those walls."

"I did the best I could," Bolivar told him quietly. "I do confess to knowing little about the construction of sod homes of this kind."

"You did just fine," Eli reassured him, wheeling north when he caught a glimpse of something moving in the distance in spite of limited visibility in an icy downpour. He squinted to see what it was as pellets of ice struck his face and eyelids.

Beside the river, passing among scattered trees laden with accumulated sleet, a party of Indians rode slowly to the south. They wound their way along the Washita's bank following openings in barren oaks wide enough to allow their ice-dusted ponies room to travel. The Indians wore dark brown buffalo robes encrusted with what looked like snow.

"Seth! Fetch our rifles! We got visitors!"

Seth scrambled into the lean-to while Augustine and Bolivar shielded their eyes from falling ice.

"Ki-was," Augustine announced after a moment's inspection. "There shouldn't be any reason to worry. . . ."

Seth emerged from the canvas tarp with both rifles. "I got it in me to worry every damn time I see an Injun," he said as he handed Eli his Whitney. Then he looked upriver. "Ain't all that many of 'em, Cap'n . . . maybe twenty or so."

Eli wasn't counting. "Depends on which bunch they are, I reckon, whether to worry."

Bolivar peered around a corner of the lean-to. "We should run into the forest and hide quickly," he said.

"They's already seen our fire," Seth remarked, checking the load in his rifle, then the firing cap.

"Whoever they are, they're comin' mighty slow," Eli observed when he took his rifle. "They're ridin' out in the open too, so I don't figure it's us they want."

Augustine added, "They seem peaceful. It may be a hunting party sent out by the ones with smallpox who escaped that night Owl told us about. I beg you, gentlemen, please don't shoot at them until we know who they are . . . let us try to keep this peace."

"Wasn't plannin' on shootin' 'em yet," Seth said, with ice pelting the brim of his hat.

They stood around the fire while the Indians rode closer to camp. Several minutes passed.

"They'll have to cross the river if they aim to give us any trouble," Eli said. "Gives us more time to reload."

Augustine, with a buffalo robe given to them by Chief White Mountain wrapped around him, began to shiver. "Several appear to be women," he said in a shaky voice. "Riding to the rear leading five or six loaded packhorses."

Eli studied riders at the back, the last two who led ponies bearing packs. "I reckon a couple are women," he agreed, and as he did he recalled what Lone Wolf said about sending women and a few horses. "After what happened to White Mountain's people I never figured Lone Wolf would send us women. I judged they'd be too busy fightin' a war with Osages."

The Indians were close now, almost abreast of their camp on the far side of the Washita. An Indian riding at the front gave them the sign for peace before he swung his pony down to the river's edge.

"They's comin' across," Seth said under his breath. "It don't look like they's lookin' for a fight with us."

"They're peaceful," Eli said, lowering his Whitney. He was staring at one of the women riding at the rear. Even with sleet falling so heavily and a hood made of buffalo skin obscuring most of her face he was sure who she was. "That's the girl from Lone Wolf, the one named Senatey."

Seth gave him a glance. "There's two of 'em, Cap'n. Tell me we ain't gonna keep 'em. Hell, there ain't hardly room in that lean-to now with that wounded boy an' all. Promise me you ain't gonna let them women stay. They's only gonna get in our way."

Eli didn't answer him. The Indians rode their ponies into near-freezing river water and started across. He paid closest attention to Senatey when her pony struggled through river-bottom mud until it was belly-deep in water.

"It's her, all right," he said when he could see her face underneath the hood of her robe.

Seth let the muzzle of his rifle tip downward. "I got this feelin' we's gonna have us some female company this winter. But you remember, I said it was a big mistake."

The first warrior rode out of the river, aiming his dark bay pony toward the fire. Several more shivering ponies trotted out on the bank, shaking water from their coats as soon as they made dry land. Eli counted ten warriors and two women leading several packhorses, the men and women all clad in buffalo robes. The leader rode up to Eli, but when he saw Augustine he spoke to him as though he knew only the priest would understand.

"Nie tab-be che-id-ah-ha."

When the Kiowa spoke his teeth were chattering. He began to talk slowly, pointing east and then south. He needed several minutes to finish what he wanted to say.

Augustine told the others what the Indian said. "They are from Lone Wolf's band, bringing offerings to the two of you, to ask for your help fighting the Nah-taih. Lone Wolf sends two of his finest young women and enough food to last you through the winter. These warriors will erect a Ki-wa lodge for you, for they brought enough skins already sewn together and all you will need is the lodgepoles, which they will cut for you. Their war against the Nah-taih is not going well. Chief

Red Eagle's band was all but wiped out by a Nah-taih raid. Ten Bears is saying it is bad medicine to listen to your words of peace until springtime and he has called for a united war. As we already knew, White Mountain's village was completely destroyed. All the women and children were killed. Lone Wolf asks that you come quickly and use your thundersticks, as well as all your magic, to help them before more women and children have their heads cut off and their villages destroyed. In exchange, he offers the women and food and a lodge, and the right to trap furs in Ki-wa territory for as many winters as you wish."

"He wants us to fight," Eli said, turning to Seth. "It's not just magic they want from us now."

Seth's face gave no clue to what he was thinking. He held his rifle at his side. "I thought we come here so's we didn't have to fight for what we wanted like in the old days," he said.

Eli thought about what it would mean, to become a part of an Indian war where they could easily lose their lives. But for the past five days he'd been haunted by the memory of the skulls of so many children they found at White Mountain's village. "We did set out to live peaceful," he said. "Those stories we heard from Mose an' Frenchy about the Red River was the best beaver country in the world sounded mighty good. Maybe too good. I ain't gonna tell you what to do, Seth. You an' me are partners. But late at night these past few days I been thinkin' about all those skulls, the kids an' defenseless women who got their heads chopped off by that bunch of redskins called the Nah-taih. I never was one to go off half-cocked lookin' for no fight that wasn't mine. Only, this time, I believe I'll throw in with these here Kiowas an' use a gun to even things up a bit. You can stay an' run our traps if you take a mind to. Won't make no difference to me. But I aim to lend these Indians a hand for a spell. Shoot a few Osages if I get the chance. You can come, or you can stay. Won't make no difference to me."

Seth's cheeks hardened a bit. He stood there a moment as if he were undecided, then turned to Eli. "We rode the Mississipp' together a bunch of years," he said, his voice like the ice falling on his hat and coat. "I reckon I'll go along, Cap'n."

Chapter
Thirty-One

.

Augustine sounded utterly disheartened while he told the Kiowas what Seth and Eli said. As Eli listened to the priest's explanation he watched Senatey from the corner of his eye. She appeared to be watching him too, and that alone gave him hope she might view their forthcoming arrangement favorably. The thought of spending a winter with her seemed a pleasant prospect, so long as she did it willingly, not simply because she'd been ordered to by Chief Lone Wolf. He wondered if the differences in ages and background might prevent them from becoming as close as he hoped they could. After all, she was an Indian, from a culture so unlike his there was little they would have in common. Yet she was a beautiful woman, appealing to something buried so deep inside him that he could not define it. When it came to pretty women he seldom ever understood his attraction to them, nor did he care. It was merely that it was there, a feeling that would not allow him inner peace until he knew the woman intimately, or knew he had no chance to know her in that way.

The Kiowas listened to Augustine's translation. Sleet fell on their robes, their ponies, the ground

around them. Bolivar remained half hidden behind a
corner of the lean-to, poised like he was ready to run
into the woods if trouble started with the Indians. Eli
shivered uncontrollably as a gust of wind swirled between tree trunks to the north. One pony stamped a
hoof and then shook itself, when accumulated ice grew
too heavy on its croup and neck.

Seth edged closer to the fire, keeping an eye on the
Indians as he added wood to the flames. He said nothing more about Eli's decision right then, although Eli
could tell he wasn't happy about joining Lone Wolf's
band in a meaningless fight over territory and horses
and herds of buffalo.

Eli spoke to Seth quietly. "Look at it this way. They
said they'd give us trappin' rights here as long as we
wanted. This good beaver country could make us both
rich, really rich, an' I ain't forgot the notion of openin' a
tradin' post along the Red someplace later on, maybe in
a couple of years. We could run flatboats an' trade furs
for staples an' such like we talked about. We could wind
up bein' mighty rich men."

Seth gave him a doubtful look. "That ain't the real
reason we's gettin' caught up in this war, Cap'n. It's that
gal who's got your eye. She's got you so moonstruck
you's willin' to risk your scalp over her. Got nothin' to
do with openin' a tradin' post or gettin' rich sellin' furs."

There was a ring of truth to what Seth said.
"Maybe she's part of it. Hell, I been lonely these last
few years. Since I lost Marybeth, bein' gone up the Mississip' all that time, I've been lonesome for a woman, I
reckon. First time I set eyes on this pretty Kiowa girl I
just couldn't help myself. Could be I'm gettin' old, but
when a man takes a fancy to a woman's looks he oughta
try his luck, seems to me."

"You hardly know who she is," Seth argued, "other
than she's a wild Injun. She don't know much more'n
four words of English, so's you can't even talk to her
'bout different things, if you felt like it."

He looked at Senatey's pretty face again. "I'll teach

her, Seth. Whatever it takes, I'm gonna do it if I can, if she wants me."

Augustine fell silent as the leader of the Kiowa party spoke again, ending the conversation between Eli and Seth about women.

"He asks if you will go with them now," Augustine said. "He says the Nah-taih are moving toward Ten Bears' village and unless you come quickly, it may be too late. He told me the Nah-taih are very strong and the Ki-was are small in number. They brought gentle ponies, the ones carrying packs, hoping you will agree to ride with them, since a pony can cover more ground. Chief White Mountain and Chief Lone Wolf are bringing warriors to help defend Ten Bears' village, but they are not enough." Augustine paused to take a breath, and when he exhaled, curls of frost came from his mouth. "It is quite clear any hopes for peace this winter have been shattered. I don't suppose anyone can say it is the fault of the Ki-was, not after what happened to White Mountain's tribe, losing all their women and children. It would seem war is inevitable between them. And I'm afraid there is one more bit of bad news, my friends. Scouts from Ten Bears' village report that some of the Nah-taih now have guns. Only a few, according to a scout. However, one of them, a long thunderstick, belongs to the most feared Nah-taih chief of all, a man they call Iron Shirt. He wears an ancient breastplate from a suit of Spanish armor and the Nah-taih believe it makes him invincible. Flint arrows will not pierce it. Now, it would appear, he also has a rifle."

As Augustine was speaking, several Kiowas dismounted and went back to the pack animals. Thin horsehair ropes were untied, freeing bundles of buffalo skins aboard the pack ponies. More warriors swung down to help with unloading while Senatey and the other Indian girl remained seated on their horses, motionless, watching Seth and Eli with no trace of emotion on their faces.

"Tell the women we've got a sick Kiowa boy inside," Eli said when Augustine glanced his way, ignoring the warning that some Osages now had guns. "They can help you attend to him while we're gone an' put clean bandages on his wound, only make sure they don't touch one of his pox sores. Soon as this storm lets up they can help you gather firewood. Appears we'll have an Indian tent to live in the rest of the winter, so there'll be more room for all of us."

Augustine spoke to Senatey. She obediently slid off the withers of her pony and motioned to the tall woman behind her.

"Find out what the second woman's name is," Eli added as he watched her dismount. He recognized her, the tall girl who spoke to them at the village.

"She is called Wea," Augustine replied.

When the girl heard her name she turned her back on them to help unload the packhorses.

Eli looked at Seth. "I reckon I can ride one of them ponies without a saddle. Truth is, I never was much of a horseman. The weather's bad an' these ain't the best conditions we ever had for travelin', but if you're agreeable, let's get this finished, one way or the other."

Seth rounded his shoulders, looking up at the sky. "I'll fetch our gunpowder an' bullet molds, Cap'n. You find me the gentlest one of them ponies to ride." He hesitated before going into the lean-to. "Wea, she's a right pretty gal herself. If we get out of this scrape alive, maybe it won't be all that bad to have a woman like her this winter. The priest is right about one thing—it sure as hell ain't good news them Injuns has got guns." He ducked inside the shelter after a sideways glance at the girl.

Lone Wolf's warriors began unrolling pieces of buffalo hide on ice-covered ground. The women carried bundles of deerskin containing dried meat toward the lean-to. When Senatey came to Eli she stopped and tilted her head back so he could see the details of her face underneath the hood of her robe.

"I wait for you," she stammered, lips quivering in the cold.

He nodded and attempted a grin. "No tellin' how long we'll be gone, or if we'll make it back at all," he said. "But when we do, I can teach you some English words an' you can teach me some of your words, so we can understand each other better."

"I hear you, *Am-a-wau*," she said, lowering her eyelashes a bit before she went past him to the lean-to carrying her bundles of food.

He was quite certain she smiled at him before she went in, and the memory of it comforted him as he and Seth carried their guns and ammunition pouches and bullet molds in two calibers and a leather bag containing bars of raw lead to a pair of shivering ponies.

Augustine brought them buffalo robes, and when Eli tried one on, he found it warm and comfortable, the head of the buffalo cut so it formed a hood with strips of hide for his wrists and ankles to keep it wrapped around him in the wind.

Augustine and Bolivar bade them farewell as they gripped the sides of the little horses with their knees for a crossing over the Washita. Eli rode a gray mare with high withers, its ears laid back when entering shallow water near the riverbank. It was Seth's misfortune to be aboard a recalcitrant buckskin pony that refused to enter shallows without prodding.

They crossed without incident and came out on the other side to be greeted by a blast of freezing cold wind blowing down the river's course. When Eli turned back for a last look at their campsite he saw Senatey standing near the water, watching him. Three Kiowa warriors were felling trees for lodgepoles nearby. A fourth warrior had begun digging a firepit where the tent would be erected.

Eli waved to the girl as they struck a trot eastward in the company of six of Lone Wolf's men. They were headed into a war not of their own making, a fight with a neighboring tribe Seth and Eli had no quarrel with.

He wondered if they would survive it so he could return and have the chance to get to know Senatey. She was, in many ways, perfection when it came to womanhood, yet he was forced to consider whether or not she was worth dying for.

Chapter
Thirty-Two

Falling snow obliterated all but the most prominent features on mountain slopes northeast of the Kiowa village. Seth allowed as how he could not see more than a few hundred yards in front of him. Eli was forced to agree, albeit reluctantly. With driving snow blinding him he couldn't be sure if a shape in the curtain of white before them was a tree, a rock, or a man on a horse who sat still, waiting for the moment to attack. The whisper of snowflakes brushing against tree limbs and the softer plop of flakes falling to the ground were deceiving, noises that could be the quiet crunching of feet, or ponies' hooves advancing toward them. Sleet had turned to snow during the night, making riding a pony easier while traveling through softer drifts rather than across several inches of ice.

"Can't see a goddamn thing," Seth said under his breath. "I ain't sure what's out there. Could be nothin', or it could be an Injun creepin' up on us. This sure as hell ain't decent weather for a man to hit anythin' with a rifle, Eli. It's 'bout the same as shootin' blind."

Eli shuddered in the cold, trying to pierce a moving white veil dancing before his eyes when snow swirled on gusts of wind across the mountains. His powder charges and balls and bits of wadding lay in front of him on a piece of cloth in a hollowed-out spot in deep snow below a tree.

"We'll be able to see 'em when they get close," he said.

"That's what's worryin' me," Seth replied. "They's liable to be too goddamn close. We ain't gonna have time to reload but once or twice afore they'll be on top of us. Lady Luck sure as hell ain't showin' us no favors. . . ."

"They can't see us either," Eli said, sighting down along his rifle barrel, guessing at range. "We got five shots in our pistols if they come at us in a rush."

Kiowa warriors on snow-covered ponies hid behind trees on both sides of a knoll where Seth and Eli waited for the Nah-taih. Bows and arrows and flint-tipped lances seemed like poor weapons, compared to rifles and revolvers. Scouts reported a large force of Nah-taih warriors moving southwest through what had become a blizzard since they arrived at Ten Bears' camp near a creek the Kiowas called Wetumka. The Osage war party was expected soon, although without Augustine to translate what was said, Eli could only guess the enemy was close when several bands of Kiowas directed them to this mountain range by means of hand signs and hurriedly spoken words neither he nor Seth understood.

Off in the distance snow fell at an ever increasing rate on wooded valleys and steep hillsides.

"We'll have some advantage," Seth remarked, sounding like he wanted to believe it more than he actually did. "They's got to come at us across open spaces. Gives us more time to load an' be sure of a target."

Eli remembered the fight to save White Mountain's village and how their efforts had failed when another Osage attack came during the council. "All we can do is shoot fast as we can an' hope it turns 'em back before they overrun us."

Seth shook his head. "I sure hope you figure them two gals is worth it, Cap'n."

He'd been thinking about Senatey since they arrived a day earlier. "A man's gotta have somethin', or somebody he cares about. Those women may be a couple of Indians, but they sure as hell beat nothin', which is what we had before. I got tired of bein' lonely. . . ." He ended his ruminations abruptly when he saw movement through the snow on a mountainside. "Look yonder!" he cried. "Between those two hills!"

Seth peered above a snowbank in front of him. "I see it, a big bunch of riders. Looks like they's headed this way."

Eli watched the snakelike progress of dark figures crossing a blanket of snow. And now he could hear soft voices from Kiowas waiting in the forest above and below their position. "It's them all right," he said. Warriors from Ten Bears' village and Lone Wolf's band, along with White Mountain's tribesmen, had seen them too.

It was difficult to judge distance in heavy snowfall, and for a time it was all but impossible to guess how far away the Osage party was. Threading between snow-clad trees and brush, they came down the side of a mountain at a snail's pace, picking their way through deepening snowdrifts where winds swept the sides of open slopes. Now and then, when blasts of wind blew heavier snow over the low mountain range, Eli lost sight of them.

Seth raised his rifle. "Nothin' much to shoot at yet," he said. "They's gonna have to be a hell of a lot closer for us to have any chance knockin' 'em off them ponies."

"Hard to see how many's carryin' rifles," Eli said, as his belly began to roll in anticipation of an exchange of gunfire.

Seth seemed unmoved. "Takes a good marksman to hit anythin' from the back of a horse. Bad enough tryin' to shoot from the deck of a movin' flatboat in calm water. We's got nearly all the advantages, trees to hide behind, nothin' movin' between our legs to throw off our aim. Let the sons of bitches come at us with rifles if they take the notion, even that mean bastard wearin' the iron plate who claims he's damn near invincible. If he gets close enough I'll blow a fifty-six-caliber hole through his head an' when his skull springs a leak, let's see how long it takes him to die."

Eli noticed a familiar change come over Seth's face while he talked, a hardening of his cheeks, lowered eyelids, a subtle difference in his voice when he knew he was about to enter a fight. Now Eli watched the Indians riding toward them through shifting snows. He knew there was no better man to having siding with him in any kind of fight than Seth Booker, whether it was hand-to-hand, knives, or guns.

"They's damn near in range, them at the front," Seth said. "If it wasn't for all this goddamn snow I b'lieve I could pick one off right about now. . . ."

Eli wasn't so sure, guessing the distance between them and the first six riders wrapped in snowy buffalo robes who appeared to be scouts or an advance guard for the main party. "Better'n four hundred yards," he whispered. Farther back, lines of Osage warriors seemed to stretch for a mile or more into foothills between mountains, and he figured there were at least four or five hundred in all. Ten Bears and the other Kiowa chiefs could only gather slightly more than two hundred able-bodied men to defend the village. Eli didn't like the odds at all, and if a sizable number of Osages had rifles and knew how to use them, the fight wouldn't last long.

"I'd wait 'til I was sure, Seth," he said, tucking his robe under his chin. He and Seth both looked like Indians themselves dressed in buffalo robes dusted with snow. Seth's face was as dark as the curly brown fur covering the hood of his robe, and due to his size he could have been mistaken for a live buffalo rather than a man, Eli thought.

Abruptly the six scouts halted their ponies, pointing to the trees where Seth and Eli and the Kiowas were hidden. The Osages sensed or heard something ahead and now they hesitated, talking among themselves.

"I'm gonna shoot that fat one," Seth said quietly, moving his rifle muzzle slightly, cocking the hammer. "May as well let the bastards know we ain't gonna let 'em get no closer without sheddin' some blood."

It would be a difficult shot under the best of conditions, and yet Seth seemed sure he could make it. Eli held his breath, watching the heaviest-bodied Indian.

The roar of Seth's Whitney blasted from the trees. A whine followed the initial explosion when a rifle ball sped through the air, ending suddenly as the Osage was ripped off the back of his pony as though he'd been struck by lightning. He flew backward, arms and legs flapping at the same time his pinto pony lunged to one side and galloped off. The Indian landed on his back in the snow, still kicking furiously while his five companions wheeled their mounts and raced away toward the main group behind them.

Seth began reloading hurriedly.

"Nice shot," Eli said, keeping his eyes glued to the Osages nearest the front. "They'll be comin' now," he added with a note of resignation softening his voice.

Snow flew from the ponies' heels until the five scouts got to a group of warriors leading the party. He could see them pointing and gesturing toward the tree where Seth was hiding before they pulled their mounts to a bounding halt. For a few moments a conference was held. Eli could hear Kiowas stirring in the trees around him, preparing for battle.

When a break in the snowfall occurred, he saw Indians with rifles moving to the front where scouts were talking to some of the others. "I see four who've got long guns," he told Seth. "I reckon we're fixin' to find out if they know how to shoot 'em."

Seth nodded. "I reckon pretty quick Chief Lone Wolf an' all the others are gonna know a gun ain't magic. Leastways, we ain't the only ones who got 'em an' they'll know it."

"It was just a matter of time anyway," Eli said. "Won't be too many years 'til every Indian in these parts owns a rifle. We couldn't keep 'em no secret for long. There's always somebody who'll make a fast buck sellin' guns to whoever wants 'em, even a bunch of wild Indians. Same goes for all the beaver we seen. It won't be long 'til this country's plumb full of fur trappers like us."

Seth was watching the Indians, peering out from under his hood. "They's up to somethin' now, Cap'n. Here comes them four who's got rifles, along with a few more. The rest seem to be spreadin' out to charge us."

Osage warriors began fanning out to form lines in front of the trees, still keeping their distance. But while the battle lines were forming, eight or nine Indians rode slowly toward the snowy knob where Seth and Eli waited.

"Maybe they aim to talk first," Eli suggested.

Seth was quick to disagree. "They don't seem in no talkin' mood to me," he said, saying no more when the Indians rode up to the spot where Seth downed the first Osage.

They appeared to be examining the dying warrior, although not one dropped off his pony to offer any aid. For a time they sat their ponies surrounded by swirling snowflakes, until one of them holding a rifle turned his head toward the knob.

"Here they come," Eli said, lifting his Whitney until the butt plate rested against his shoulder, its brass patchbox long in need of a polishing. He gripped the cold black walnut stock with half-frozen fingers. Peering through the rear notch sight he moved the brass-blade front sight to an Indian's chest while trying to calm tremors in his arms from icy winds.

"Hard to figure," Seth said when the lone Osage heeled his pony forward. "Just one's comin'."

The Indian sent his calico pony straight for the knob where Eli and Seth were hidden behind trees. He rode at a walk, almost defying them to take a shot at him.

"I can kill him from here," Seth said, keeping his voice so low it was all but lost on the wind.

At a distance of roughly two hundred yards the Osage stopped his pony to stare at their low hilltop, resting the butt of his rifle atop his thigh. Then, while they watched him through their gun sights trying to guess what he was up to, he opened the front of his buffalo robe and let it slide off his shoulders to his pony's rump, his broad, shaved head thrown back as though he dared anyone to challenge him.

"That'll be that chief they told us about," Eli said, "the one who calls himself Iron Shirt. He's wearin' an old breastplate of some kind, ain't he? Looks like it's rusted mighty bad, but you can tell it's made outa metal."

Instead of answering Eli's question, Seth pulled back the hammer on his Whitney.

"What the hell are you gonna do, Seth?" Eli asked. "Maybe he just aims to talk. Look at how many Osages there are out yonder . . . must be close to four hundred. If you kill him they're liable to come for us all at once. We don't stand a chance of fightin' so many of 'em off."

Seth stood frozen beside the tree trunk. When he spoke to Eli his voice was a rasp on hardened steel. "He's got a killin' comin' to him, Cap'n. He's the one ordered them women an' kids dead with their heads chopped off. I'm gonna kill him in front of everybody, so won't nobody believe that bullshit he's invincible wearin' armor. This was your idea we come help these Kiowas win this war. You ain't gonna talk me out of it. Yonder's one bald Injun son of a bitch who's a dead man."

Eli's protest died in his throat when the hammer fell on a percussion cap. Seth's Whitney kicked, belching smoke and flame accompanied by a roar. Seth was rocked back on his heels by a heavy powder charge, and Eli was certain the extra gunpowder was intentional.

The Osage chief's spotted pony whirled when it

heard the explosion. Chief Iron Shirt toppled off one side of his mount, landing in ankle-deep snow on his hands and knees without his rifle. His horse bounded off, trailing its jaw rein. Iron Shirt shook his head as some of his warriors turned their ponies sharply. Rather than charging toward Seth, they were watching their fallen chief sway drunkenly, trying to keep his balance.

Seth was ramming another charge and ball down his rifle's muzzle. The sound of the gunshot faded, and now an eerie silence prevailed while both Osages and Kiowas alike looked at Iron Shirt on his hands and knees. Eli noticed a bright red stain spreading across snow underneath the chief's belly.

"You shot him plumb through his armor," Eli said, in the same instant noticing an Osage bring a rifle up among the group who had ridden behind Iron Shirt. Without waiting to see if the Indian meant to use his gun, Eli drew a bead on the warrior's chest. "Get down!" he cried to Seth. Allowing for drop at this range, he aimed high and pulled the trigger.

His gun blasted, rocking in his hands, spitting forth a ball of lead and a puff of smoke. The roar hurt his ears and he was momentarily deafened by it.

He sleeved a tear from one eye caused by burning gunpowder in time to see the Osage slump over his pony's withers, letting his rifle fall to the ground. His horse snorted and lunged into a run, which sent the Indian off its rump in a ball, rolling in midair before he landed and slid to a stop.

Now it was Eli reloading as rapidly as he could while Seth fitted a firing cap to his Whitney.

"Ain't nobody comin'," Seth announced when no Indians made a move to rush the hilltop. "They's got old muskets, Cap'n, a Hawken or two that'll sure misfire in this wet weather. It ain't their guns I'm worryin' about . . . it's how damn many of 'em there is against us."

Rodding a load into place, Eli fumbled with a firing cap due to cold fingers. "Maybe they ain't gonna charge at all, after you put a hole in their chief. It looks like they can't believe his magic shirt don't work. . . ."

A gun popped in the distance, a musket held by an Osage on a nervous bay pony. Somewhere high above their heads, Eli heard a ball snap off a frozen oak twig.

"Their aim ain't none too good, either," Seth said, raising his rifle. "If I get lucky I might be able to drop the one who fired up here at us." He steadied his aim and triggered off a shot. The boom of a Whitney again echoed across the snow-veiled distance.

Seth's bad luck and poor visibility caused a chestnut pony carrying an Indian with a musket to drop suddenly, collapsing on its side, legs thrashing. "Damn!" Seth snapped angrily. "I sure as hell been killin' a bunch of horses lately."

Eli watched the wounded pony struggle, until his gaze came to rest on Iron Shirt. The chief rocked back on his haunches, pressing his hands over a hole in his armor breastplate where a stream of blood fell down on his legs, coloring a widening circle of snow around him. His hairless skull looked odd, out of place in a snowstorm. His deerskin leggings were dark red as blood leaked from his belly wound.

"The chief's gutshot," Eli said. "It'll take him a while to die."

They heard soft footfalls in the snow behind them, and when Eli turned around, he saw Lone Wolf creeping through the forest in their direction. He came over to Seth and pointed down to the spot where Iron Shirt was kneeling.

"*Suvate,*" he said, almost spitting out the word.

Seth shrugged and looked at Eli. "Got no idea what he just told me, Cap'n."

Eli's attention was on the scene taking place around Iron Shirt. Several warriors had ridden over and dismounted beside him while two attempted to help him to his feet. He doubled over when they lifted him, and his legs refused to work properly as they helped him toward his pony.

"I can't believe they're all sittin' there watchin', like they can't make war without their chief to lead 'em at us," he said to Seth.

"It do look like they's leavin'," Seth agreed as he too saw what was happening.

Men lifted Iron Shirt over his pony's back as gingerly as they could. The chief, with his head lowered, allowed his pony to be led away from the spot where he had fallen, turning back toward the hills and mountains from which they had come.

A few at a time the other Osages reined their ponies away to follow Chief Iron Shirt.

"They're damn sure leavin'," Eli whispered, like he had just witnessed something akin to a miracle.

"Suvate," Lone Wolf said again, and this time his voice was much softer.

Eli carried his rifle over to Seth, where they stood together for a while watching the Osage war party depart. Several hundred warriors armed with bows and spears were riding off without ever firing a shot when their leader was wounded.

"It was a gamble," Seth agreed quietly. "But like I told you, the bastard deserved killin'. Maybe, if there is a Great Spirit someplace, he's restin' a little easier now, knowin' we got a little dose of revenge for all them women an' kids. . . ."

Chapter
Thirty-Three

The Kiowa lodge erected beside their lean-to was covered with snow when they rode trail-weary ponies down to the river. Smoke curled in lazy columns from the tent flap and firepit, rising on soft winds blowing from the northwest. It was a peaceful scene, their campsite on the Washita, although it presented a rather odd combination of Indian dwelling and a white man's shelter made of mud and sticks, when viewed side by side.

Senatey and Wea were standing on the opposite bank, having heard the ponies approaching. Augustine and Bolivar were unloading a cart full of firewood behind the lean-to.

"We's gonna freeze our asses crossin' this river," Seth said as they guided their mounts into shallow water. "Can't remember the last time I was so near bein' froze solid."

They crossed the Washita and rode out on the west bank with fatigue tugging their eyelids. Eli dropped off his pony and gave the rein to Senatey.

She tilted her head, brushing a lock of dark hair away from her face while staring into Eli's eyes. "Is no

more fight?" she asked, concern pinching her brow
while tucking her buffalo robe under her chin.

"It's over," he told her. "At least for now. The
Nah-taih have gone. Come spring, no tellin' what will
happen. It could be war all over again between the
tribes. I don't reckon we'll know 'til springtime."

"You stay me?" she asked, with just a hint of a
smile behind her liquid brown eyes.

"We're stayin' for the winter. Got plenty of traps to
set, now that it's cold an' the animals have thick fur."
He looked over at Augustine. "I hope it was quiet
'round here while we was away. How's the boy Owl?"

"Alas, I fear he died from his injuries while you
were away, Mr. McBee. He was strong, but not strong
enough. We buried him in a shallow grave behind the
lean-to yesterday. I'm sorry to be the one to give you the
sad news."

Seth handed Wea the rein on his pony. He looked
at her and she smiled, although she wasn't able to keep
her eyes on him for long, tilting her face toward the
ground when his gaze lingered.

"We've been teaching the women some English,"
Bolivar said as he rounded a corner of the lean-to. "And
you'll be surprised at how comfortable the Indian tent
is. It's warm, and there is plenty of room. The women
have been baking acorn bread and all sorts of good
things to eat. Wea speaks a few words of English now,
and as you know, Senatey understands and speaks a
great deal more."

Eli looked down at Senatey. "You understand what
I'm sayin' to you?" he asked.

She too, aimed her glance downward. "Some
words. Some no. Take time."

It was Seth who noticed the canoe. "Look yonder,
Cap'n. They brung our boat up here, an' it looks like
somebody got the holes patched with buffalo skin."

Bolivar told Seth how it was accomplished. "Wea is
a good seamstress, Mr. Booker. She sewed on skin
patches with a bone needle and deer gut. Then she

found tree sap to seal the mends so that it does not leak. It floats, and only in a place or two does it leak a small amount of water. In the spring, when sap is warmer, I believe the leaks will seal themselves. Wea is also making me a suit of deerskin which will be warmer than a monk's habit this winter."

Augustine scolded Bolivar. "When our mission is built we shall wear our habits, Brother Bolivar. It is the way of the Order, in case you have forgotten." He turned to Eli. "I trust you will inform us about the war. We have prayed for your safety continually and prayed that hostilities between the Ki-was and Nah-taih will end."

"It's over, for now," Eli said. "An Osage chief named Iron Shirt tested his magic powers against Seth. He took a rifle ball in the belly for his trouble, an' bein' gutshot, I don't figure he'll last long. I wouldn't say things was peaceful between 'em, but we don't look for no more trouble right away. The Osages had a few guns, old muskets, an' they thought that made 'em powerful. We had to kill some . . . gave 'em shootin' lessons, I reckon. But they pulled back after that. My guess is, it'll be quiet 'til warm weather gets here an' then we'll be gone downriver to New Orleans with our pelts."

Augustine gave Senatey a quick glance. "The girl may not be so easy to leave behind, Mr. McBee. In the words of her people, she has eyes for you. And if you have a successful season with your traps, why not come back year after year?"

"Hadn't thought that far ahead," he replied, looking deeply into Senatey's eyes. "Now that you mention it, maybe it'll be harder than I think to leave her. But a half-wild Indian girl, even one as pretty as she is, wouldn't be happy in New Orleans. She wouldn't know what to do in a city like that, an' folks can be mighty cruel sometimes. Even if I dressed her up in a white woman's clothes, nobody'd treat her the same. This is where she belongs."

Augustine's expression became thoughtful. "Per-

haps this is also where you belong. This region along the
Red River will be settled by white men one day. It is
inevitable that whites will push these Indians off the
most fertile and productive lands in the West. Tribes
such as the Ki-was and Nah-taih and Comanches are
doomed to extinction as they exist today. Nomadic people are in direct conflict with an American's ideas about
ownership of land. It was our hope at the mission that
we could teach them farming and peaceful relations
with their neighbors, and of no less importance the
word of God, so they might exist side by side with men
of other races without making war over claims to a piece
of territory or a buffalo herd or horses. This tribal system is all they know. Fighting each other is a way of life.
If we could show them a better way to live, there is hope
for their future living among white men."

Bolivar brought Eli and Seth tin cups of weak coffee while Eli was thinking about what Augustine said.
Eli could feel the girl watching him. He warmed his
insides with a swallow of hot coffee, for the moment
ignoring his frozen feet and hands after so many hours
aboard the pony in bitterly cold weather. "Me an' Seth
been talkin' about openin' a tradin' post somewheres
along the Red, maybe at the best crossin' spot where
quicksand ain't so bad. But with this country crawlin'
with Indians who got it on their minds to fight all the
time, I 'spect it'll be a spell before all that many white
men try to settle along these rivers. There'll be a few
trappers like us who take the risks, but until things quiet
down a bit I reckon this land belongs to Kiowas an'
Osages. We got lucky this time, on account of most Indians ain't never seen a gun. We fooled 'em with their own
superstition. I ain't gonna count on it happenin' again.
Four or five of them Osage warriors had muskets. It
won't be long 'til these Indians are armed with guns.
When that happens, anybody who tries these rivers is
gonna face tough times gettin' what they want."

"Someone has to begin bringing about changes,"
Augustine said. "A Christian mission dedicated to

teaching them the will of God is a starting place. A trading post is another way to bring Indians and white men together. If all the tribes had a place to trade animal skins for things they need, a spirit of friendliness and cooperation has a chance to succeed. I do hope you and Mr. Booker will consider it."

"We's talked about it," Seth said, warming his huge hands on the steaming tin cup. "We can see how the trappin' goes between now an' spring."

Eli reached for Senatey's arm. "Tie the pony up for me an' let's go inside where it's warmer."

She understood, leading his pony around to the back of the lean-to, where a crude corral of cut poles held Bolivar's donkey. Wea led Seth's pony away as he and Seth approached the Kiowa tent to look inside.

Piles of furry buffalo skins lay around a firepit glowing with red coals and tiny spits of flame. It was warm inside and there was a cozy feeling about the lodge when Eli ducked through the tent flap.

They placed their rifles and pistols and ammunition near a tent wall and sat by the fire warming their hands. By the look on his face, Seth seemed amused.

"I reckon this is home," he said with a note of disbelief in his deep voice. "Never figured I'd spend no winter in some Injun tent."

"We've been through worse," Eli remembered. "Can't think of no reason why a damn flatboat was any better."

Seth nodded quiet agreement.

"We could open us a tradin' post," Eli continued, gazing up at the flap above the firepit permitting smoke to escape. "If we spread word 'round New Orleans about this good beaver country I'd stake everythin' we got there'd be trappers up here next winter. If we had supplies they needed an' enough cash money to buy their furs so we'd make a profit, wouldn't be no reason to go back down to New Orleans 'cept to sell the pelts an' buy more supplies. It wouldn't be no bad kind of life, really. Better'n what we knew on the Mississipp' all those years."

"If we can stay clear of them Injuns when they's got their minds made up to fight, we'd be safe enough," Seth said, taking a sip of coffee.

Eli recalled how close they'd come to being in a one-sided fight with Iron Shirt's Osages. "Damn near everythin' worth havin' is a gamble. I say it's worth a try."

Senatey and Wea came through the tent opening. For a moment they stood near the entrance watching both men as if they needed an invitation to come closer.

"Sit beside me," Eli told Senatey.

Seth beckoned for Wea to join them.

Senatey sat very close to Eli's shoulder. He reached for her hand and held it gently. He felt strangely content with her at his side. "Tomorrow we'll start puttin' out traps," he said. "You can show us where the best beaver ponds are an' we'll teach you an' Wea how to help us run lines."

Seth pulled off his buffalo robe. He took Wea's hand and it seemed so small by comparison.

The fire burned lower and neither man appeared to notice as they indulged themselves in dreams of the future. Eli decided he could be happy here with Senatey, perhaps happier than he'd ever been before. Like Seth, he'd grown tired of a lifetime on the river. Settling down was sounding more and more like a good idea and he wondered if it was because of the woman.

Later, Senatey rested her head against his shoulder.

Afterword

The Red River has served as a boundary since early European exploration, first as a dividing line between Spain and the United States, and later between Mexico and America, then the Republic of Texas and the United States, and lastly, a boundary between Oklahoma and Texas as states. It often separated Plains Indian tribes as a territorial marker.

This story is historical fiction, taking place in a region once ruled by six Kiowa bands in loose alliance with the vastly more numerous and powerful Comanches. These tribes reached the peak of their power in the nineteenth century, until their populations were decimated by disease and better weaponry. Anglo-Americans and Spaniards first arrived in significant number in the 1820s, and this was probably the first introduction of epidemic disease, including yellow fever, which also wiped out thousands of Indians with no natural resistance to new illnesses. Thus the Kiowas and many neighboring tribes were reduced to guerrilla warfare when their numbers were not large enough to overpower their enemies.

Early trading posts were built along the Red, and many of them were quickly burned to the ground by outraged Indians bent on driving white men from their ancestral lands. But as one old Comanche chief described it, "We are like islands surrounded by white men. There is no place left for us." Thousands of white settlers came, escorted and protected by the U.S. Army, and not long thereafter every Plains Indian in America became the object of an extermination policy.

There is no record of Catholic missionary activity of any permanent nature along the Washita River or in western sections of Red River country. However, a stone structure of Spanish type that had fallen to rubble was reported on the lower Washita by cowboys passing through during the trail drive era.

A major crossing point for cattle herds during the 1870s was Red River Station, originally built and operated not far from the Red's union with the Washita by a half-breed Negro with an Indian wife, and a Scotsman. It served as a jumping-off place for huge herds of longhorns headed for Kansas railheads because it marked the safest known crossing for horses and cows seeking to avoid deadly quicksand going up the Chisholm Trail.

The Red River continues to flow as it has for centuries, for the most part unchanged by time. It still has its treacherous spots for unwary swimmers, and in floodstage it can be one of the most powerful and damaging bodies of water on earth. Its history is as varied as its moods. Careless men who failed to respect it perished. Others, who understood a river's changing temperament, lived in harmony with it, and some made their fortunes along its shores.

About the Author

Frederic Bean is a native Texan who used to raise and train quarterhorses. He is also an experienced auctioneer. In addition to writing *The Pecos River* for the Bantam's Rivers West series, Bean is the author of *Hangman's Legacy, Hard Luck, Gunfight at Eagle Springs,* and *Eden.* His next novel, *Sidekicks,* will be published by Bantam in November 1998.

The exciting frontier series continues!

〜〜〜〜 RIVERS WEST

Native Americans, hunters and trappers, pioneer families—
all who braved the emerging American frontier drew their very
lives and fortunes from the great rivers. From the earliest days
of the settlement movement to the dawn of the twentieth century, here, in all their awesome splendor, are the RIVERS WEST.